EVE TRAVIS AMAZED HERSELF . . .

She'd proposed to Jeff Kilburn out of pity. He was on the rebound from a disastrous romance with a girl who'd thrown him over to marry a titled heir. Almost unbelievably, Jeff had accepted!

Then Eve found out why. All the time she was feeling sorry for Jeff, he'd been pitying *her*. Jeff had known all along that the fortune Eve was to inherit had been squandered without her knowledge.

Now, returning from her honeymoon, she learned that Jeff's ex-fiancée's husband had been killed. Now he was free to marry the woman he really loved. Free, that is, if Jeff hadn't married Eve . . .

Books by Emilie Loring

- FOR ALL YOUR LIFE
- WHAT THEN IS LOVE
- I TAKE THIS MAN
- MY DEAREST LOVE
- LOOK TO THE STARS
- BEHIND THE CLOUD
- THE SHADOW OF SUSPICION
- WITH THIS RING
- BEYOND THE SOUND OF GUNS
- HOW CAN THE HEART FORGET
- TO LOVE AND TO HONOR
- LOVE CAME LAUGHING BY
- I HEAR ADVENTURE CALLING
- THROW WIDE THE DOOR
- BECKONING TRAILS
- BRIGHT SKIES
- THERE IS ALWAYS LOVE
- STARS IN YOUR EYES
- KEEPERS OF THE FAITH
- WHERE BEAUTY DWELLS
- FOLLOW YOUR HEART
- RAINBOW AT DUSK
- WHEN HEARTS ARE LIGHT AGAIN
- TODAY IS YOURS
- ACROSS THE YEARS
- A CANDLE IN HER HEART
- WE RIDE THE GALE!

Published by Bantam Books, Inc.

EMILIE LORING

IT'S A GREAT WORLD!

This low-priced Bantam Book
has been completely reset in a type face
designed for easy reading, and was printed
from new plates. It contains the complete
text of the original hard-cover edition.
NOT ONE WORD HAS BEEN OMITTED.

IT'S A GREAT WORLD!

A Bantam Book / published by arrangement with
Little, Brown and Company

PRINTING HISTORY

William Penn edition published January 1946
Grosset & Dunlap edition published May 1948
Bantam edition published May 1967

Published simultaneously in the United States and Canada

Bantam Books are published by Bantam Books, Inc., a subsidiary of Grosset & Dunlap, Inc. Its trade-mark, consisting of the words "Bantam Books" and the portrayal of a bantam, is registered in the United States Patent Office and in other countries. Marca Registrada. Bantam Books, Inc., 271 Madison Avenue, New York, N.Y. 10016.

PRINTED IN THE UNITED STATES OF AMERICA

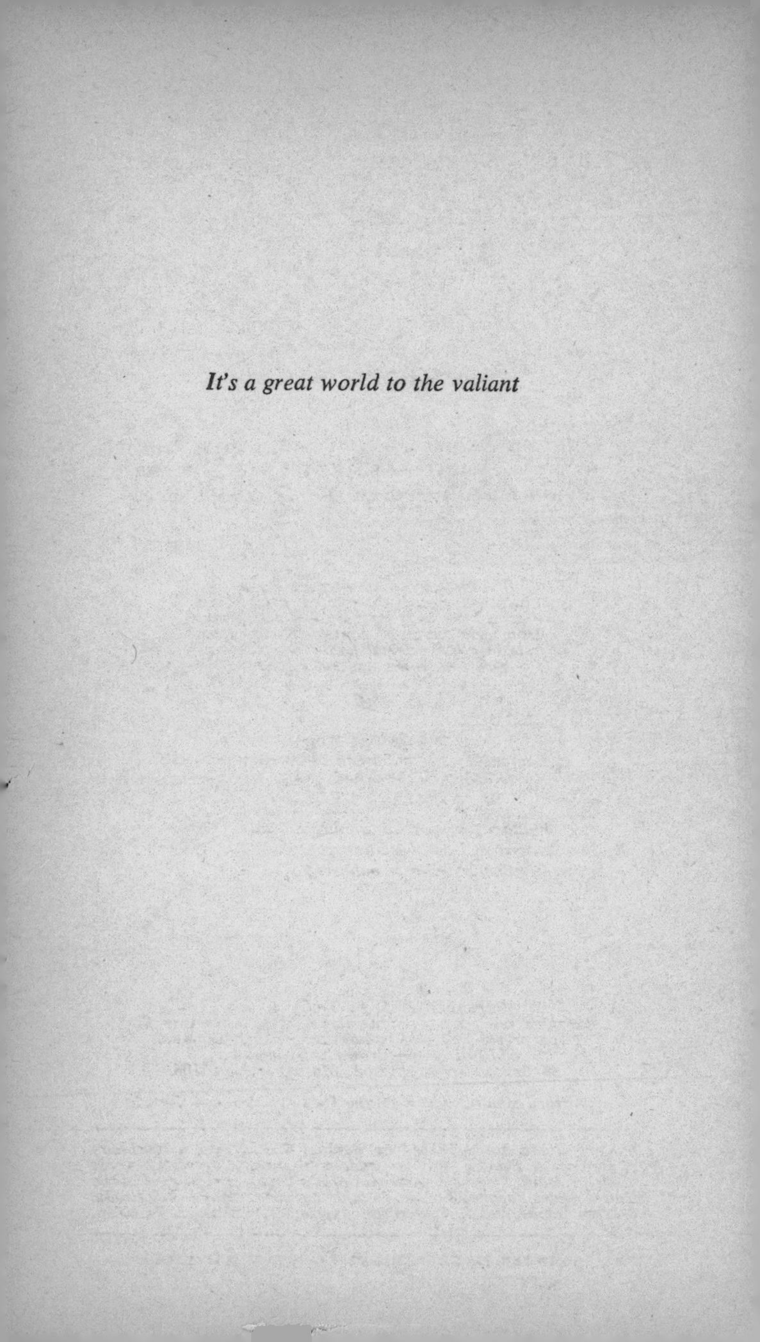

It's a great world to the valiant

AUTHOR'S NOTE

i

THE French window in the library shook from the impact of a frenzied fist. A white face pressed against the glass. Snack, the German shepherd dog, growled and bristled. Jefferson Kilburn dropped the automatic he held into a drawer of the flat desk. What had sent Eve to him in such a fever of impatience, he wondered, as he hurriedly unlatched the window.

A slim girl in a stiff damask-like satin frock of pale yellow brushed past him, a girl with dark hair curling from under a new-leaf green hat. The Boston terrier at her heels sniffed disdainfully at the shepherd and became absorbed in a study of the ceiling. There was terror in her eyes, her heart-shaped face was colorless save for the red of her lovely mouth. The room vibrated from her excitement. She flung the bridesmaid bouquet of mimosa to a chair and caught Kilburn's arm in both hands.

"Jeff! Jeff! You wouldn't—" Her voice broke in a strangled sob.

He flung an arm about her shoulders, kicked the long window shut and drew her toward a chair by the fire.

"Sit down, Eve, you're shaking. Get your breath and then tell me what has happened."

"I—I can't sit down, Jeff. I can't get my breath, until I'm sure—" she pressed her face against the gardenia in his coat lapel and shivered. "Until I'm sure you're here."

"Here! Where the dickens would I be? What's the matter? Look at me."

He raised her chin and held it until her tear-drenched eyes met his puzzled dark ones.

"Has all this wedding ballyhoo got on your nerves? Eve Travis, the most popular, the most stony-hearted of her set, with nerves! That, folks, is news. Or has the hospital to which you've been giving days and days as a clinic secretary turned you down? Here, let me wipe your eyes. That's better. I've known you, Kiddo, ever since you came into the world and I've never seen you cry before. You're too much of a fighter. There you are! Those internationally famous gold-tipped lashes are nice and dry."

Even as he teased and rallied the girl Kilburn was deeply

troubled by her emotional break-down. It was so unlike her. Had her uncle changed his mind and told her the bad news instead of leaving it for him to do? Scripture Travis had insisted that she would take it better from him. So like the old hypocrite to pass the buck. He tucked his handkerchief into the breast pocket of his morning coat and took a step toward the desk.

Eve gripped his arm with a force which made him wince.

"Jeff! Jeff! Don't! You wouldn't—"

He caught her by the shoulder and shook her gently.

"Snap out of it, Eve! Tell me quick what has made you like this or I'll lock you in and beat it over to your house and find out. Has that Ramsdell lad been troubling you again? Why did he rush on here for the wedding? Why didn't he stay in Washington where he belongs?"

A faintly contemptuous smile curved the girl's mouth.

"Don't be foolish! As if Seth Ramsdell could make me cry. It's you—Jeff."

The strained whisper twisted Kilburn's heart, but his voice registered only amused incredulity.

"What have I done now? Take off that dinky hat while you tell the Inside Story of your life."

He tossed the green hat to the desk and smoothed back a wave of her dark hair.

"There we are, all set for a conference—it's a conference year. You wouldn't prefer to sit down, would you, Kiddo? Being a perfect gentleman, I can't until you do and I'll remind you that for an old codger ten years your senior, I've had a hard day. Being best man at a wedding to say nothing of the aeons during which I presented guests to the bride and groom, have stiffened these antiquated legs."

She pressed her face against his shoulder again.

"Jeff, you're not old! You're so lean and dark and good-looking, and such a grand s-sport." The last word was a smothered sob.

Jefferson Kilburn frowned down upon her head. His nostrils went a little white.

"If it is Seth Ramsdell who has made you like this, I'll beat him up."

Eve caught his arms and held him as he took a step toward the window.

"It isn't Seth, Jeff! I told you, it's you."

"I? Perhaps you'd tell me also how I could make you cry when I've hardly spoken to you today. Have you eaten since breakfast? I'll bet you haven't with all the excitement at home. You're hungry, that's what's the matter with you.

Could you possibly release my arm while I ring for José to serve tea? No? All right, then come along."

She held tight to his hand as he pressed a bell beside the mantel. The sloe-eyed Spaniard who answered it smiled at the girl;

"Buenos días, señorita."

Kilburn gave his orders. As the door closed behind the butler, he drew Eve toward the divan at right angles with the fireplace.

"Sit down, and stop this confounded nonsense about something you think I have done."

"It isn't nonsense, Jeff Kilburn," the girl protested as she sat on the edge of the divan. He perched on the arm beside her.

"That brought the snap back into your voice. Something tells me that the normal Eve Travis is emerging from the fog and is that girl a temperamental party? I'll say she is. Look at the dogs. Squatting on their haunches regarding you as if they'd never seen you before. I don't wonder. You're a stranger to me. Don't talk. Wait until you've had your tea. This is the first time I ever wished you smoked." He pulled a pipe from his pocket. "Lucky it is filled. As you insist upon clutching my hand you might light it for me."

Two sharp little lines cut between his brows as he noted the unsteadiness of the rosy-nailed fingers which held the lighter. His eyes met Eve's above the flame. It was absurd to think for an instant that an act of his had changed a gay, boyish girl into this frightened young woman. He had loved her since she was a little tot, he had no sisters, she had made up for the lack. During his mother's life she had been like a daughter in the house.

Seated stiffly on the edge of the divan Eve still gripped his hand. The fire crackled sociably in the mellow dignified room; the flames sent pointed shadows flickering among the books like fingers pointing to a title. The tall clock in the corner tossed seconds into the ocean of the Past, as a fountain flings crystal drops into a pool. The dogs side by side on the hearth-rug, kept expectant eyes on the door; two long-ago Kilburns on the wall looked down upon their descendant with eyes shrewd, if painted. Through one of the long windows, the heir to their fortunes could see men on the Travis lawn taking down the marquee in which the wedding feast had been spread. Beyond them a great copper ball rested on the peak of a hill like a brilliant button on the top of a purple-green cap.

Not until the butler rolled the tea wagon in did Eve release Kilburn's hand. He was aware that she clutched his coat in place of it.

"That's all. We'll serve ourselves, José."

The man bowed in his best *caballero* manner and closed the door behind him. With a furtive glance at each other the dogs moved nearer the divan.

"I always think of a Spanish Grandee, when José enters a room," Eve observed in an almost normal tone. "He plays the guitar divinely. He played and sang at our Emergency Fund Concert while you were away. I wheedled him into doing it. He wouldn't allow his name to appear on the program and his eyes were masked. He stole the show. Perhaps he is the last of a royal Spanish family. Wouldn't it be romantic to find that he was heir—to a throne?"

"He's an heir, all right, if you believe him. Sometime I'll tell you about him," Kilburn promised in the hope of diverting her from whatever was troubling her.

"Will you really, Jeff? I love romance and his eyes are drenched in it." She shook her head at the dogs wistfully regarding her. "Don't come any nearer, young fellas. If you do, you'll get nothing. Remember that you're a visitor, funny-face."

The Boston regarded her steadily with large, round, dark eyes; Snack's, the shepherd's, expressed only bored indifference, though his lower jaw grew suspiciously moist.

Kilburn drew a sharp breath of relief and rose. Eve caught his sleeve.

"Where are you going?"

"It was my innocent intention to sit beside you. Of course, if you insist, I can perch here indefinitely, but—"

"Stop crabbing, Jeff, and sit here and have your tea. What's under that silver cover? Cinnamon toast, and José has brought some of his luscious lobster salad sandwiches, I could die eating them. You have the best eats here at Brick Ends. Better than at any house I ever visited—not excepting the Scandinavian—"

Deep dimples flashed as she smiled with lips a trifle tremulous and eyes in which a hint of terror still lurked.

"Are you starting for South America soon?" Her voice was strained.

"Drink your tea and eat something before you talk. I've lived years enough in the next place to you, Kiddo, to know that you go savage when you are hungry."

He watched her as she ate with increasing relish, sharing her toast and sandwiches impartially between the two dogs. Color had returned to her face, her hand was steady as she tossed the doily to the tray.

"There! The world does look different, not so drab. Go away, young fellas, no more eats for you. You'll lose your size-sixteen figures. That's a gorgeous sky, Jeff. Makes me think of a great turquoise matrix with all those streaks of silver gray clouds mixed with the blue. I love September. Great day for the bride and groom to start their wedding journey in a plane, though when I go off the deep end I intend to honeymoon on land. I adore the color and smell of the earth, don't you?"

"I do."

Kilburn pushed away the tea wagon, sent the dogs, who had followed close on his heels, from the room and returned to the divan. Eve was leaning forward, elbows on her knees, chin in her palms, frowning at her green slippers.

"Now, we'll hear all about it."

"You needn't pull your stand-up-and-surrender voice out of moth balls, Mister Kilburn. I want to tell you. I've had part of it on my mind ever since Moya went and got engaged to Sir Nigel Hyatt."

"Moya! What has she to do with your tears? I know that you two didn't hit it off but—"

"You go white even when you speak of her, don't you? Think I don't know that you've been off your head about her ever since she came to live with us six months ago? It was a mean break for you that Uncle Scripture imported his wife's niece. She being one of those 'who-is-that?' sort of persons who because of her swank and distinction sets strangers to wondering who she is. He thought that her cultured sophistication—'learn to be charming' stuff—would put a platinum finish on his hopelessly hoydenish niece, that's me, in case you don't know. No one wonders who I am, when I step from a train or a limousine."

"You have your points, Kiddo, but you needn't go autobiographical for my benefit. You'll be telling me next that for years after your father and mother died and left you—along with your fortune—in your Uncle Scrip's care—you were known as the million dollar baby. I know your family history from A to Z. I'm 'Jeff' to all your relatives. What I don't know is why you went completely haywire a few minutes ago."

Eve regarded him with wistful eyes.

"I wonder if I can make you understand? Sometimes you are dumb as an oyster, Jeff. As I said, I've known that you were desperately in love with Moya, that when Sir Nigel finally crashed through with a proposal—that boy knows the value of suspense—and she snapped him up, you acted as if your heart were breaking."

"Not quite so bad as that, Kiddo. It's a stout heart, takes a lot of breaking. You're letting that imagination of yours run away with you."

"Imagination! Didn't you at once decide you wanted a job in South America? Didn't you trek to Washington to get my Uncle, Senator Jack Holden, my mother's brother and the only near relative I have in the world beside Uncle Scrip—to send you there on some wild-goose chase or other? The Senator specializes in wild geese—mines, to you—I understand."

Should he tell her that the Senator had sent for him? That he had not sought the South American commission? Better not. He said instead:

"Suppose I did? Then what?"

"Now don't go wooden on me, Jeff, for I have a lot to say." She twisted the corner of a plump cushion—"I watched you all day, cat and mouse stuff—I'll hand it to you for putting on a great act. I'll bet that Hollywood-blonde maid-of-honor —she certainly has what it takes—thinks that she's your present heart-beat. If I didn't know that you were too sporting to hurt anyone or anything, I would think—"

"Stop thinking and talk. You watched me through the wedding. What next?"

"My word, but you've picked up the dictator complex, haven't you? It's a trend. Next I saw you coming out of Uncle Scrip's study. Your eyes burned like black coals with little red lights in them. Your skin was chalky. I tried to speak to you but your face was so terrible that my voice wouldn't come. You looked as if you were all set to shoot somebody. I thought—"

She shuddered and dropped her face into her hands. Kilburn laid his arm about her shoulders. Should he tell her what had driven the color from his face, what had been like thumbscrews twisting his heart? No. She was too excited and he did not know yet the cause of her tears. Instead he encouraged.

"Go on, Kiddo, get it off your mind."

"And then—and then, Jeff, I felt as if I would die if I couldn't help and I followed you. I didn't dare come into the house, but I tiptoed across the terrace and looked in the window. I saw you go to the desk and pull that ugly, stubby revolver from your pocket and then—I knew it was yourself you were going to—to—"

Her eyes, wide and tearless, now met his. With a smothered execration Kilburn pulled her to her feet. This time there was nothing gentle about the shake he administered.

"Have you gone crazy, Eve? Do you think I'm such a

darnfool that I would shoot myself—or anyone else for that matter—because a girl preferred another man to me? You read the papers, don't you? You know that there has been a wave of house-breaking, don't you? After Sir Nigel's family jewels arrived for Moya, your Uncle got fidgety and asked for a permit for himself and me to carry a revolver. He had received an anonymous note of warning that the jewels would be stolen on the day of the wedding. I consented to ease his mind though never have I been able to figure out just what good I and my trusty gun would be over here. Perhaps he intended to flash a lantern in the window as a signal; 'one if by land—and two if by sea.' "

Eve caught the lapels of his coat.

"Grand old sport. I might have known you wouldn't let a hard-boiled sophisticate like Moya spoil your life. But you still love her, don't you?"

"Little girls shouldn't ask questions."

"You might as well have said 'yes.' I'm not a little girl. You never will realize that I'm grown up, will you?" She slipped an arm within his. "Are you really going to South America?"

"I'm sailing day after tomorrow at midnight."

"It's a big country, isn't it?"

"Very big, South America."

"And frightfully lonesome?"

"I can imagine that the part to which I am going may be heart-twistingly lonely under certain conditions."

"I can't bear to think of you down there alone. Take me."

"Now you have gone completely haywire, Kiddo. Of course I can't take you."

"You could if we were married."

"Married!" His eyes brimmed with laughter. "Married!"

"Don't laugh at me! M-a-r-r-i-e-d. That's the way to spell it. You'll find the word in the dictionary. It's an old custom but it's still being done."

She wrinkled a finely modeled nose at him, but her mouth was tremulous and a pink stain crept to her forehead. He was not laughing now. He frowned at her incredulously. Not a trace remained of the terrified girl who had battered at the window, but she was still the child he had seen grow up, whom he had teased, comforted, dominated by turns. He had realized that she was young for her twenty years, but not young enough to make that proposition. Was she in earnest? If she were, could he make her understand that he had no intention of marrying—certainly not a child like her—without hurting her horribly?

Eve laughed, an unsteady laugh, but it helped.

"You look as stunned as if you had been struck by lightning, Jeff. I don't see anything so startling in my suggestion. You are going to a strange country with what you fondly believe is a broken heart. You'll be an easy mark for a designing woman, they say those ships fairly swarm with husband hunters. You wouldn't be lonely if I went along; and you wouldn't have to bring me a present as you always do when you come home from one of your engineering trips, nor say, 'Great Caesar, but you've grown, Kiddo.' "

"That doesn't get you anywhere, it only makes me realize how young you are."

"Listen, Jeff, don't pull any of that 'old man' stuff. You've brought me up in the way you think I should go. I'll never forget your eyes the evening you caught that tipsy lad dragging me off to his car—he's not likely to forget it, either. There is no one in the world I like as much as I like you. I adored your mother and father. I felt as if I belonged to them. Uncle Scrip is my guardian until I marry—I never could understand why mother and father picked him instead of Uncle Jock Holden—I can't have a cent of my fortune without his consent until then. Why do you look so startled? You know that I have money, oodles of it, even since the Great Crash. What good does it do me dribbling through Uncle Scrip's tight fingers? I've had a so-called companion —always a lady, always elderly—since mother died; I've been trailed by Secret Service men, for fear I would be kidnaped, until I'm desperate. Uncle Scrip wouldn't allow me to take that hospital job until I consented to having a plainclothes man drive me back and forth. I want my freedom. I want a chance to establish my own identity,—how do I know what I am really, what I would be if I were on my own? I want to go places alone the way other girls do. There's the Inside Story of my life you insisted upon hearing. Will you take me?"

Jefferson Kilburn frowned at her unseeingly. Eve thought she had money, "oodles of it." She didn't know that there were a few thousands only, didn't know that the story of the dwindling of her fortune, her Uncle Scrip had told him in his study after the wedding, had been the cause of the burning eyes and chalky face, which had terrified her. He had been appalled at the situation. Eve had been brought up in luxury. She had a beautiful voice, but it would take years before she could make money with it. She had been giving her services to the hospital as secretary but in these uncertain times when it came to a paying job, could she secure one?

Was her proposition the answer? How could he leave her behind for months with the possibility of her being dragged under by those two tragic D's, debt and discouragement? She might drift into an affair with some wild boy. He must be losing his mind to fear that for Eve who was so honest and straight and idealistic. Just the same if he took her with him, he would be sure she was safe. Of course, he was fond of her, but, he couldn't imagine being in love with her, not as a man should be with the woman he was to marry. What difference did that make so long as Moya was out of his life?

"Well, Jeff?" Her eager voice derailed his train of thought. "Why shouldn't we make a go of it? Think of the men and girls we know who were mad about each other, who trekked to Reno or points south, after a year or two of marriage. You know all my faults. I know yours—believe it or not, we both have plenty. I would be free, free to go places. Think of being chained to this suburb when the world is tingling with new ideas, with new discoveries; trying to conceive some of the inconceivable wonders of the universe; the mystery of the vast meteoric ring which eternally encircles the sun; a great plane to fly five hundred miles an hour through unresisting, thin stratosphere air. All this going on and I'm playing tennis and contract, and singing at dinky little concerts. I feel as if I were shut up in a cage. If you don't take me I'll run away. I'll go somewhere alone, or I'll marry the first man who asks me, get control of my fortune, give him a bonus, and have the marriage annulled. That's a thought!"

"Stop such cockeyed talk! What in the world has set you off on this tangent, Kiddo? You've seemed contented enough."

"I haven't been, I've been smoldering inside and that automatic in your hand set me on fire. Why not take me? You wouldn't have to go to that lonesome country alone and I'd watch out that no man-eating widow snitched you on the way."

"Suppose, Eve, you were to fall head over heels in love with an attractive youngster on this same perilous voyage? I've always thought that down deep in your heart you did care for Seth Ramsdell."

She shrugged. "I played around with Seth the winter I spent in Washington with Uncle Jock and Aunt Dorinda, while you were testing for oil wells in Paraguay, you may remember. He is Uncle Jock's right hand man. The Senator has a super-woman secretary to run his office now. I don't care for youngsters and I can't see myself head over heels in love. If I were married to you, Jeff, do you think I would do anything to smirch the name handed down to you by them?"

She nodded toward the portraits of the two shrewd-eyed men on the wall. Kilburn caught her hands tight in his.

"Look at me, Eve. Do you mean this to be a real marriage or am I to be shunted off as soon as you secure your money?"

Soft color stained her face:

"My goodness, I—I didn't think of it that way, but if—if you think it should be a real marriage, all right. Ever known me to be a cheat, Mister Kilburn?"

ii

RATHER terrifying to think how a few words may change for all time the patterns of two lives, Jefferson Kilburn thought as he looked down at the girl beside him in the maroon convertible roadster. His wife. It was unbelievable. Yesterday she had been little Eve Travis to him. Last evening they had talked matters out to this conclusion. There had been no suggestion of sentiment between them, he hadn't even kissed her when they parted, why should he when he hadn't kissed her for years? At midnight tomorrow they would sail together for South America. What would her uncle, Senator Jock Holden, say when he learned that his secret investigator was taking a wife along on a confidential mission? He answered his own question. Eve's presence ought to help lay suspicion as to the real purpose of his trip, which was to test a gold mine, an option on which Senator Holden had secured from a Secretary of one of the South American Embassies.

"A pig in a poke," he had written, "but I'll take a chance any time on a gold mine. Keep it under your hat until you have made your report. If I've been buncoed the boys on Capitol Hill will eat it up and laugh their heads off."

"I'm still here," Eve reminded.

Kilburn pushed the astounding news he had to tell the Senator tomorrow into the back of his mind.

"Think I'd forgotten? Not a chance. I like that costume you're wearing, particularly the close hat and the fur edging the swanky little cape. What is it?"

"Sable-dyed fox. I wore the white wool and Mother's pearls because they seemed bridey and as I'll never have another wedding—"

"I hope not. I intend to live to be a very old man, Kiddo."

"We'll have heaps of fun together, in South America, won't we, Jeff?"

"We will. I wonder if at first you will be homesick for cultivated, perfected New England. Eventually we'll land in a rough country."

"It is beautiful here. I love it."

His eyes followed hers to the smooth black road bordered with trees and shrubs which already had been touched with the light, cool breath of early autumn. In the west the clear blue of the sky was smeared with crimson clouds fringed with gold. The air was scented with spruce. A garden border was ablaze with scarlet zinnias, patched with purple and white and yellow gladioli, and gemmed with tall dahlias in pastel shades. Nearby a rock garden blushed with pink sedum and in the middle of an emerald velvet lawn a bronzed grackle glistened and pecked beneath the sparkling spray of a fountain.

Eve sat erect. At her suppressed exclamation, Kilburn looked at her quickly.

"What did that 'ooch!' mean? Not getting the jitters about breaking the news to your Uncle Scrip, are you? I'll do that."

"You are sure that the news of—of what we've done won't get to him before we do, aren't you, Jeff?"

"How could it? I only secured the special license last evening. Recently I have done a favor or two for the registrar and his clerk as well as for the justice of the peace who married us. They have sworn that they won't make the news of our marriage public until I give the word. I disapprove of the secrecy—you and I decide to marry, why not tell the world?—but because it seemed to mean so much to you, I gave in."

"But, it is for such a little while. Only until we see Uncle Scrip, and that will be in about five minutes now. I hate secrets, but I had a curious feeling that if what we were planning was known, some way might be found to stop it, and now that freedom to go and come as I please is in sight, I just can't live in Uncle Scrip's house another day, the old tightwad. Will he be furious with you, Jeff, because you didn't ask his consent? He really is my legal guardian."

"And a hot guardian he's been."

Kilburn shut his lips tight to keep back a few poison epithets which seethed when he thought of Scripture Travis. A guardian! What right had he to object to anything Eve might do? Not only had he lost the bulk of his ward's fortune, but out of the remainder, he had given his wife's niece, Moya, a generous dowry and a lavish wedding—not that Moya knew the source of the money. She would not have accepted if she had, he was sure of that.

Moya was lovely and he had been on the verge of asking her to marry him when Sir Nigel had made his entrance. "On the verge"—that didn't sound as if he had been much in love. Would he hesitate on the verge? No, if he knew himself, and he thought he did, he would plunge head-first when his time came. Plunge into love! That possibility was behind him. The girl beside him was his wife. He'd better get his mind adjusted to the new conditions. From this day on loyalty to her and her happiness were to be his absorbing interests. She had been part of his life since he was a small boy. Always her childish troubles had been his. She had a genius for companionship. She could be gay, tender, or sympathetic according to his mood. He had almost hated Moya when after her wedding, Scripture Travis had called him into his study and had asked him to break the news to Eve that she was practically penniless. It had taken all his self control to refrain from kicking the weeping old hypocrite through the window. He had agreed to tell Eve, if he were allowed to choose the time and place. Little he had thought then that the time and place would be on board a ship bound for South America.

"Better slow down, Jeff. Seventy per is a trifle speedy even for me. Were you rehearsing what you would say to Uncle Scrip?"

"Yes, or words to that effect."

"I wonder if he will stall about turning my property over to me."

"Our ship doesn't sail until midnight tomorrow. We'll motor to New York as soon as we've had a heart to heart with Scripture Travis and picked up your bags at the house. Your Uncle Jock is to be at the office of Barrett, Tarbell and Tarbell in the morning with final instructions for me. You know Barrett, my lawyer. We'll break the news of our marriage to him then and you will have legal advice as to the best way to close up matters with Scripture Travis,—ex-guardian—and what papers to sign for the transfer of your property."

She wouldn't know for a while that there would be but a few shreds of property, if any, to transfer. Would she blame him for not telling her the truth at once? What else could he have done than agree to her suggestion that he marry her? How otherwise could he be sure that she was safe and provided for?

Eve's voice interrupted his self-questioning.

"If Uncle Jock is to be in New York tomorrow, I wonder why he and Aunt Dorinda didn't come to Moya's wedding. Lucky I had bought my fall and winter wardrobe, Jeff. It would have given away the whole show had I asked Uncle Scrip for money for clothes. I sat up all night packing and spent every other moment poring over that colorful folder of the South American trip. Quote, Chan Chan the long lost capital of the Chimu Empire—enduring through the passing ages; Lima, where Inca kings once ruled in barbaric splendor; Valparaiso, muffled in cool greenery, surrounded by nineteen bluffs, unquote. I know it all by heart and oh boy, and oh boy, am I thrilled? I'm mad about travel. Perhaps sometimes we'll take that North Cape trip."

"Perhaps we will. Have you any money? I'll give you what cash you want. In spite of lean dividends and fat taxes I'm not quite on my uppers."

"I'll say you're not. You have a lot of money but if I hadn't more would I have dared propose to you? That's what I did, awful thought, the memory was what made me say 'ooch!' a while ago. Every time I think of it, I hear the icy chink of nervous chills in my veins and believe it or not, I've been in a constant state of chill during the last twenty-four hours. Then I say to myself, 'I'm trying merely to repair his broken heart, and incidentally get my fortune.' Was it only yesterday that I burst in on you with my mad proposal?"

"Not sorry that you have married me, are you?"

"N-not yet. Where was I when my conscience, or whatever it is that makes one terribly ashamed of oneself, jabbed? I know, we were talking of money."

"You were talking of money."

"All right, I was. If I was a million dollar baby when father and mother died, under Uncle Scrip's management there ought to be two millions or more now. You have so much money that every time you depart on an engineering safari our town fairly crackles with disapproval that you should go off on one of those dangerous trips when you might live in a bachelor apartment in New York or London or Paris winters and in lovely old Brick Ends summers. I wonder why myself sometimes."

"I beg to remind you, Mrs. Kilburn, that I'm no longer a bachelor. I'm a staid married man."

Eve's breath caught a little gasp. She put her hand to her throat and looked up at him.

"My w-word, Jeff, it sounds frightfully real when you say it that way."

"Say what?"

"That we are—are—"

"Married? 'M-a-r-r-i-e-d. You'll find the word in the dictionary. It's an old custom, but it's still being done.' "

"Don't joke, Jeff. I'm really horribly frightened. I feel as if I'd been under water for twenty-four hours, only coming up at intervals to say 'ooch' before I was submerged again. When I think of how I fairly bullied you into marrying me—" Hot color dyed her face.

He laid his hand over her bare hand on the third finger of which a narrow band of diamonds caught the late sunshine and sent back sparks of light.

"There is nothing to be frightened about, Eve. I'm the same Jeff to whom you have told your troubles all your life and I shan't turn suddenly into a stranger. Your wedding ring was my mother's. You have seen it on her hand. Next time that 'ooch' boils up, douse it with the remembrance of the grand time we'll have seeing South America—and from what you have saved me; loneliness and the possibility of being swallowed bait, hook and sinker by a man-eating widow."

"Your smile is one of the nicest things about you, Mister Kilburn, your teeth are so white below that small foreign looking mustache and your blue eyes turn so black, that I'll forgive you for making fun of my fears. Just the same, it was nine chances out of ten that a designing female would have landed you. Here we are! Look at Bingo! Wagging his stump of a tail off. There's nothing patchy about that Boston. He's white where he should be white and brindle where he should be brindle. Aren't his erect ears adorable? It will pull my heart up by the roots to leave him. Uncle Scrip's modern Colonial house with the woodvine looking as if red paint had been spilled over it, isn't in the same class with Brick Ends, Jeff, but the garden borders are glorious. I've never seen the second crop of delphiniums so tall nor the orange king calendulas so brilliant, nor the purple petunias and pink dahlias so enormous. That rusty helenium—"

"Stop and get your breath, Kiddo. Nothing to go panicky about. Here, grab my hand. Together we'll face the lion in his den, 'the Douglas in his hall.' Remember the hours we spent reading Sir Walter Scott?"

Hand in hand they approached the front door. At the steps Eve stopped, whispered;

"I have the queerest feeling. As if something had happened."

"Something has happened, hasn't it—"

"I didn't mean about us. I meant something tragic."

A maid threw open the door, a maid whose eyes were red from weeping, whose sharp chin shook uncontrollably. The fine organdie collar of her pale gray gown was awry. She wrung her hands.

"Oh, Miss Eve, thank the Saints you've come!"

"What is it, Annie? Has Uncle Scrip—"

"You're pinching my arm something terrible, Miss. It ain't your Uncle—"

"Come into the house, Eve."

Kilburn caught her hand and led her through the hall into the living room, crowded with rare Colonial pieces.

"Now, Annie, what has happened?" he demanded of the shivering maid who had followed them. "Where is Mr. Travis?"

"He's gone. He rushed off to her as soon as he got the message."

"Rushed to whom? What message?"

In the moment that Jefferson Kilburn asked the question and his hand tightened in hers, intuition flashed a wireless to Eve's mind. She thought she knew, as she so often did, what he was thinking and her heart turned to ice.

Annie sniffed.

"Oh, Mr. Kilburn. I supposed you knew when you and Miss Eve came in together. Mr. Travis tried to get you and left word with José for you to come to the city at once. Miss Moya, Lady Hyatt, she is now, I keep forgetting, and her husband were—"

"Were what? Stop blubbering and talk, woman!"

Eve glanced at Kilburn's colorless face, freed her hand and moved a step away. Annie gulped down a sob.

"I'm telling you as fast as I can, sir. Their plane crashed and—"

"Was Lady Hyatt hurt?"

His tormented voice turned the rest of Eve's body to ice.

"No sir. It was her husband who was killed—immediate—and they only married yesterday."

"My God!"

Kilburn crossed to the window and stood with his back to the room.

The low exclamation seemed to echo and re-echo through the stillness. What had he meant, Eve asked herself? Had the thought flashed through his mind as it had through hers that had he waited a measly little three hours more, he would have been free to marry Moya?

The maid wiped her eyes on her organdie apron and sniffed.

"I was saying to cook that Lady Hyatt would make a be-utiful widow, Miss."

"Did my uncle say when he would return?"

"No, Miss Eve. He said, not until he could bring Miss Moya, Lady Hyatt, with him. He sure thinks that the sun rises and sets in her shoes. He left this for you, Miss." Annie drew a note from her pocket.

Kilburn wheeled from the window and held out his hand. "Give it to me."

"Oh, no. I'll take it," Eve protested. "It's mine. That will be all, Annie. Tell the upstairs maids to make Miss—Lady Hyatt's room ready for her. She may come home tomorrow. I'll ring when I want tea."

Eve waited until the maid left the room before she slipped her finger under the flap of the envelope. Kilburn caught her wrist.

"Don't read that yet, Eve. I want to talk to you first."

"I'm here."

"You're not here. You've shut yourself in behind a wall of suspicion. Do you think I don't know you well enough to realize that?"

"Suppose I have. Then what?"

"Snap out of it. I can't say what I want to say through a stone wall."

"What is there to say? You said it all when Annie told you that Sir Nigel had been killed, not Moya. Aloud you said only 'My God!' but inside you said, 'She's free! I'm tied! Why, why didn't I wait? Why did I marry that kid—' "

Kilburn caught her shoulder in a grip that made her wince.

"Stop that fool talk, Eve. I thought nothing of the kind. I was horribly shocked that those two who had left this house so joyously only yesterday, should have crashed into tragedy."

"But you love Moya?"

"Did! Did! Did! Get that? I'm married to you, now. You're my wife."

"Oh, no I'm not. Do you think I'll live with a man who is in love with another woman whom he knows he can have? Moya always cared more for you than for Sir Nigel, his title tipped the scale in his favor, that, and the fact that his brother is a high potentate in an Embassy in Washington. Now, to quote Annie, she's a 'Be-utiful widow.' A man-eating widow, if you ask me."

"Eve, you're out of your mind."

"I was. I'm not any longer. I suppose this note from Uncle Scrip is to tell me that he will bring Moya here. That's all right with me. I shan't be here when they come."

"Of course you won't be here. You'll be on your way to

South America with me—Mrs. Kilburn. Don't read that letter until we're on ship board."

In answer she pulled the sheet from the envelope. As she read, her expression changed from surprise to incredulity, to anger. Her dark eyes burned with fury as she demanded;

"Why didn't you tell me? Uncle Scrip writes that you knew."

"Tell you what, Kiddo?"

"Don't call me that silly name! Don't you yet realize that I've grown up? That I'll never be young again? You knew that my money was gone yesterday when I—I asked you to marry me. I suppose you consented because you were sorry for me, thought I couldn't take care of myself—that makes you look guilty—you'll find that I can. I suppose this Colonial furniture and Mother's jewels are mine, or have those gone with the rest? You promised Uncle Scrip that you would break the news to me, didn't you?"

"I did. But it was agreed that I was to tell you when I thought it wise."

"Wise! Wise! Doubtless you thought it wise to let me brag about being a million dollar baby in your library the afternoon of Moya's wedding. Wise to let me ask you to marry me! Wise to marry me as you couldn't marry the girl you wanted. It burns me to a crisp when I think of it."

"That's enough, Eve. Remember that you are talking to the man you've married—irrevocably."

"Irrevocably! That's the joke of the week. That word was dropped from the marriage vocabulary years ago. From this minute you'll go your way and I'll go mine. Just as soon as I can manage it, you'll be free to marry Moya."

"And if I don't care to marry Moya?"

"Oh you will and I'll go on my own and—"

"You'll sail for South America with me tomorrow." He crushed her in his arms and kissed her eyes, her mouth, her throat, roughly, possessively. "You'll not go on your own—"

She twisted free and slapped his face.

"How do you dare touch me—like—like that? I will go on my own, Jeff Kilburn. Try and stop me."

He watched her as she charged up the stairs. Should he follow? He'd be hanged if he would. She could come to him. He shut the front door behind him with a resounding bang.

iii

JEFFERSON KILBURN frowned at the jagged panorama of the city's sky line visible from the open window of the office of Barrett, Tarbell and Tarbell. It was a blur of stone and smoke and patches of color where flags were flying, and windows glittered like burnished brass and far away a line of clothes blew in the wind. The sun had begun to slant. It gilded ripples on the turgid dark water of the harbor till it charted a golden course straight to the open sea. Ships looking like dots which were still a proportionate part of the design sent up white spirals of steam. Toward the west two towers, which seemed to belong to the air more than to the earth, added a thrilling touch of mystery. Near them a gold cross pointed the way to Heaven. From the canyon below which was a street rose the hum of traffic, the underground roar of a great city.

He impatiently pulled his hands from his coat pockets and thrust them back again. Was it only yesterday that he and Eve had been married? It seemed years. He had passed a sleepless night assailed in turn by regret, by a surge of protectiveness for her, and when he put his hand to his cheek where her slap still burned, by the blackest, most devastating fury he ever had known. He had sworn to himself that he didn't care if he never saw her again and then had telephoned her in the early morning. Annie, of the hatchet chin, had answered that she had left home in her car the evening before.

"I told Miss Eve as how she shouldn't go motoring off at night, she who's never allowed to go anywhere without a cop at her heels. With all the purse-snatchin' an' such goin' on, 'taint safe, but she just stared through me like I was a ghost an' ran out the door. She looked terrible white. I guess she was worried about Miss Moya, Lady Hyatt, an' was goin' to her though I'll say she never did seem to like her much. Hadn't you better look her up, Mr. Kilburn? She thinks an awful lot of what you say." Thus the voluble Annie.

He had not tried to find her. It might mean looking up Moya, and he had no intention of being drawn into that situation. She did not need him. Wasn't Scripture Travis with her? Should he meet Eve with them she would wilfully misunderstand his presence. He had made mistakes enough during the last twenty-four hours, he wouldn't add another. Kissing her had been the major blunder but her defiance had set what he had thought only brotherly love for her, ablaze.

He had come directly to his attorney's office on reaching the city, had made a new will, and except for a few legacies, had left everything to Eve. He had explained why to the astounded Barrett and had told him of the girl's loss of fortune. Then Senator Jock Holden had arrived and for an hour they had been conferring. His voice broke into Kilburn's train of thought.

"Come away from that window, Jeff, and give me your undivided attention. Evidently you've got something on your mind which isn't business, my business at least. We'll take that up later. Let's get busy."

He pulled off his black Stetson, built on the slightly, only slightly, modified lines of a ten-gallon sombrero. He brushed back a lock of tawny hair and slapped a folded paper down on the desk as Kilburn perched on a corner of it.

"Here's the data about the gold mine for an option on which I paid Señor Eduardo Enrique Alvarez, a Secretary to one of the South American Embassies, five thousand on his sale price of fifty. His father and a friend bought the lode outright before his country got wise and decided to sell concessions only. He tried not to show it, but he was pleased purple to get five thousand dollars—not *pesos*—for the option. Perhaps I've chucked the money away, —I bet I'll never see it again if the mine proves to be no good—but I played one of my hunches. The deed seemed straight enough. Alvarez had receipts for the taxes. He said that a syndicate was dickering for it. And now you come along with the yarn that your butler José claims that he owns the mine. How did he happen to tell you about it?"

"When he discovered two days ago that I was going to South America, in a surge of homesickness he poured out the story of a gold mine he had inherited from his father, that is, it is his unless he dies without heirs. In that case it goes to the son of the partner whom Don José Manuel Mendoza—my José's father, in case you care,—bought out. I put him through the third degree and found that the mine was located in the same zone as the one I was to investigate for you, that the name of his father's partner had been Alvarez."

"Fits like the missing piece of a picture puzzle, doesn't it? Too well. Could your man José have seen my letter to you and evolved this scheme?"

"No possible chance of that. I think he's honest. When he answered my ad for a butler he gave the Consul from his district as a reference, said in perfect Spanish, '*Es amigo mio y de mi padre,"* which translated means, 'He is a friend of mine and my father's.' The reference was first class and I engaged him."

"Hmp! Why is he in this country if he owns a gold mine?"

"Ran away. Affair with a woman, I suspect."

"It would be. Spanish, isn't he? Why didn't he look up Alvarez?"

"He says Alvarez thinks he is dead and that the mine now belongs to him, that he would put him out of the way if he found him. Which shows what he thinks of Señor Alvarez. He hates that *hombre* like poison. I gathered that both were after the same woman, a dancer, though he gave me no details."

"Will he sell the mine?"

"He says he would take two thousand dollars for it."

"Two thousand for the whole mine? I'll give him five now for it, Jeff. I'll play my hunch to the limit. If I sell it, I'll fix him up later. Get him on the phone. If he agrees have Barrett send him an agreement to sign. I'll leave my cheque for him. Look up José's claim while you're checking up on the mine. Take plenty of time. I know that you're an expensive expert, but the best is none too good for me. Nothing makes me so all-fired mad as to have a man try to put one over on me, and if that is what Alvarez has done—selling an option on a mine he's not sure he owns—I'll land him in jail. Keep all this under your hat. I'll be darned if I'll be pulled into a row between two fighting Spaniards. Has this man José told anyone else of his claim?"

"No. As I told you, he thinks that Alvarez might put him out of the way if he knew he were alive."

"When you phone put the fear of God into him about mentioning the mine until you return. I don't want anyone else to get a crack at it before I have a chance to close the deal with your José, if it is his."

"I'll do it, Senator."

"Put this data in your pocket. I gather from the report that only a rudimentary method, a cimbra, has been used as yet to work the lode. That is a flexible tree inserted in a hole, from the other end of which pends a stamp that moves up and down to crush the material."

"I've seen it work, Senator. It seems prehistoric. Have you seen samples of the quartz?"

"I've had one of the poorest assayed. Report on it was that it would yield $9.80 per ton. Alvarez claims that it will go as high as $17.50. The mines are located in a zone where placer mines have been exploited since the Conquest. They are at an elevation above sea level where the climate is mild and quite free from plague and mosquitoes; the workers to be hired are better than those found in most mining districts; good water supply; a railroad and plenty of timber to be had at a moderate cost, in fact, according to Señor Alvarez, everything is fine and dandy, but, here's the catch. He asked me to keep the fact that I had an option on the mine off the record for the present. Now I know why. I'll bet he doesn't believe that José is dead, and is afraid if he hears of the five thousand I've paid, he'll bob up. I never did like Alvarez. You can't have tricky thoughts without having them show in your face. I haven't lived forty-five years without being able to spot a crook when I see one if he is a Secretary of an Embassy which is the pet of the Administration."

"For the love of Pete, Senator, if you feel that way about the man why pay him five thousand dollars for an option? The mine may exist only on paper."

"That's why I'm sending you, that I may know what I'm up against. I told you I played a hunch. You are to decide if it was a hunch or a brainstorm. It may take months, now that José's claim has to be proved. No one is to know that you are going for me, understand? As much for your sake as for mine. I hope I'm not letting you in for trouble but Alvarez may not care to have an expert examine the mine—if there is a mine—it might be this for you, one dark night." His eyes twinkled as he drew a finger across his throat.

Kilburn laughed.

"Cheerful thought. I'm glad I made a new will this morning." He stood up and thrust his hands into his pockets. "I have left my property to your niece, Eve Travis. We were married yesterday."

"Married! You and that child!"

"I'm only ten years her senior, not quite in my dotage and you may take it from me she's not the child you think her." He put his hand to his cheek.

"Sit down! Stop pacing the floor. That's better." Jock Holden frowned at Kilburn as he returned to the corner of the desk.

"Give me the whole story, Jeff. Why the mad haste?"

"Scripture Travis told me the day that Moya became Lady Hyatt that most of Eve's fortune was gone."

"Gone! Gone where?"

"I don't wonder the shock turns your face crimson. Gone where most of the lost fortunes have gone during these last years, I suppose. When I thought of Eve who had been brought up in luxury having to join the vast army of job-hunters—"

"Job-hunter! Why should she hunt a job? She has me, hasn't she? Do you think I would permit her to work? Don't you know that her Aunt Dorinda and I almost went down on our knees to that scalawag guardian of hers begging that we might have her? We've got our boy, but we'll never have a daughter now. Would Scripture Travis let her go? Not he, the old hypocrite, and you married her to save her from work. Matrimony approached from an economic rather than an emotional angle. What a marriage!"

"Sit down, Senator! I deserve all you say to me. I never once thought of you. If I had—"

"You wouldn't have married her?"

"I didn't say that, sir."

"No, you didn't say it—but you looked it. Do you know, Jeff, you haven't the air of a radiantly happy bridegroom. Trouble so soon?"

Glad of an opportunity to free his mind, Kilburn told of the marriage, of the news that had greeted Eve and himself when they returned to the house of Scripture Travis, of the unfriendly parting. Slumped in a chair, his big head bowed, Jock Holden listened without comment until Kilburn concluded;

"That's where the matter rests at present."

"Stop snipping at the blotter with those vicious shears! The sound sets my teeth on edge. And you let her go?"

"I did, Senator. The climax was so unexpected—"

"Unexpected! Do you mean to tell me that in your thirty years you haven't learned more about women than that? Unexpected! My eye!"

"But I've played round with Eve since she was a baby and while she has been a firebrand with others she's never shown that side to me. When she finished telling me what she thought of me, my mind felt as if a wrecking crew had made a thorough job of it."

"Hm! It's a pity you didn't pick her up, bundle her into your car and teach her to behave. She's like her mother, who was a little fury at times, but, how we adored her. Even after all these years the memory of my sister brings a lump to my throat."

Jock Holden blinked heavy lids as if to clear away a mist which was obstructing his vision, glared at something beyond Kilburn's shoulder and demanded;

"How long has this romance between you and Eve been going on, Jeff? How long have you been in love with her?"

"That's the joke of the week, Uncle Jock, he hasn't been in love with me at all."

"Eve!"

At her first word Kilburn sprang to his feet and faced the girl standing back to the door.

Annie was right, she was "terrible white." Even the reflection from her rose-color suit didn't conceal that. Her dark eyes looked enormous with the shadows under them. Had she had a sleepless night as well as he?

Jock Holden held out his large, well cared for hand.

"Come here, child, and tell you uncle all about it."

He slipped an arm about her waist as she came close.

"We'll dispose of Scripture Travis first—and we won't say it with flowers. The old hypocrite has lost your fortune, Jeff tells me. I hadn't supposed that money could dribble through his tight fingers. I'll set my lawyers on his trail and try to salvage something from the wreck. It's an ill wind that blows nobody good. The fact that your fortune is gone is bound to get around and kidnaping will be out so far as you are concerned. Meanwhile don't worry. I'll make you an allowance that will buy all the pretties you want."

"You'll do nothing of the kind, Senator," Kilburn contradicted hotly. "I have provided an allowance for her. Barrett will deposit monthly to her account; all he needs is her signature, Eve Kilburn. You seem to have forgotten that she is my wife."

"I'm not your wife!"

Jock Holden looked up at his white faced niece before he glared at Kilburn from beneath bushy, overhanging brows.

"If that is true what sort of a yarn have you been handing me, Jeff?"

"Eve! Answer him! Tell the truth."

Kilburn's voice was low but absolutely authoritative. Had the girl's eyes been steel blades they would have slashed him to ribbons.

"Dictator! We did go through a sort of—of ceremony, Uncle Jock."

Senator Holden rose and loomed over her.

"A sort of—of ceremony!" He mimicked her voice to an inflection. "Eve, you haven't picked up the bug of that rotten short-term marriage stuff, have you?"

"She has not!" Kilburn snapped. "What sort of a rounder do you think I am to ask such a question, Senator? I told you here in this room not half an hour ago, that I procured a special license, that we were married, that we drove directly to Eve's home and there learned of the—of—of what had happened to—to Moya and Sir Nigel."

"Which news turned Jeff a shade whiter than he is now," interpolated Eve bitterly.

"Is that all there was to this lunatic marriage, Jeff?"

"That's all, there isn't any more, Senator. The lady changed her mind—as ladies will."

"You modern young people get my goat. The matrimonial junk piles are heaped with the results of trial and error marriages. Your voice sounds as if you hated the girl you've married, Jeff, and yet it couldn't have been all pity for her because she had lost her fortune, you must have loved her some to have asked her to marry you."

"Did he tell you that he asked me because he was sorry for me?" Eve demanded. "It's not true. He didn't ask me to marry him, Uncle Jock, that's the catch in the story. I asked him. I'll be honest. I didn't ask him. I practically forced him into the ceremony."

Holden dropped heavily into a chair. His face flushed darkly.

"Forced him! What do you mean, forced him?"

Eve patted his shoulder.

"I always think of the M-G-M lion when you growl, Uncle Jock, your hair is just the color of his shaggy head. I mean that after Moya became Lady Hyatt, I decided that I was fed up with Uncle Scrip and his tight-lipped, tight-fisted methods, that I was through living in his house, that I wanted to handle my own money; you know I can't have it until I'm married, that I wanted to be free, free, free! Evidently I was free and didn't know it. As I look back, I realize that there hasn't been a plain-clothes man on my trail for a week. I knew that Jeff was slated for South America, that he was broken-hearted because he loved Moya and she had married Sir Nigel. I figured that if I went with him he wouldn't be lonely and I would have my fortune. I proposed that he take me and—"

"You proposed that he take you! Gone Zuñi, have you, Eve? A Zuñi woman selects her own husband, when she gets tired of him all she has to do is place his shoes outside the door. Being a perfect gentleman he goes. So you proposed that Jeff marry you? How old are you?"

"Don't roar, Uncle Jock. I'm older than I was twenty-four hours ago, a whole lot older, believe it or not. It isn't my fault, is it, that the Hyatt plane crashed, that Moya is free and that everything is changed?"

"Changed only because you welshed," Kilburn accused.

"I didn't welsh! I didn't, Uncle Jock. If you had seen Jeff's face, heard his voice when Annie told him that Moya was unhurt—" She choked back a sob— "You wouldn't go to South America with him or anywhere else."

"I doubt if I would have been invited." The Senator stroked his chin contemplatively. "If you two parted forever last night, perhaps you will tell me why you are here this morning, Eve. Anti-climax, I call it."

"I came because I forgot this." She dropped a ring to the desk. It spun like the glittering skirt of a premiere danseuse and stopped.

Senator Holden regarded it from under bushy brows.

"So that's it. A wedding ring. If you're not going with your husband—"

"I'm not going with him and he isn't my husband. No one knows of that silly ceremony, and you may be sure that I won't broadcast the fact. If Jeff does—"

"Jeff won't, Miss—Travis. When that news goes on the air you'll do the announcing."

Senator Jock Holden put his big hands into sagging pockets of his coat and scowled at his niece.

"Well, for a man and girl who've been friends for years, you've made a mess of things. What are you going to do next, Eve?"

"I'll answer that question, Senator. She is sailing for South America with me to-night and she will announce our marraige. I'm no Zuñi. If you think I'm such a poor boob as to let her get away with—putting my shoes outside the door—"

"Hold your horses, Jeff. I don't want Eve to go with you."

"What right have you to butt in between—"

"Man and wife you were about to say, weren't you? There seems to be a difference of opinion about that. Well, it's this way. You are going on a secret mission, aren't you?"

Holden glanced at the open transom, crossed to the door and closed it. Back at the desk he explained;

"Voices carry. You are supposed to be an ordinary tourist, Jeff. You are of importance enough socially and professionally to have the news of your sudden marriage headlined. It would focus attention on you. I don't want that. Sail alone tonight. Finish up your job, then when you get back, you and Eve can—"

"I'll finish up that silly marriage business before—he gets back."

"You'll do nothing of the kind, Eve. Understand?" Holden brought his fist down on the desk with a force that set the pens jiggling. "You'll do nothing that will call attention to Jefferson Kilburn. You will be a sport and help. You've messed things up good and plenty now. You'll come to Boxwood with me. It's time that your Aunt Dorinda and Court and I had our share of you."

"I would adore visiting you at Boxwood, Uncle Jock—but—but—if Uncle Scrip doesn't know that I'm mar—"

"Oh, then you acknowledge that you are married, Mrs.—"

"That will do for that, Jeff. For the present, Eve is Miss Travis. I'd like to see your guardian stop you from coming with me to Washington, Eve. He won't. Go home and pack up—"

"I'm packed, thank you, and my luggage is in New York. I was just in time to prevent it from being routed to South America. Part—part of it is in the outer office, Uncle Jock. I—I—brought Bingo. You see, I couldn't bear the thought of leaving that Boston in the cold storage atmosphere of Uncle Scrip's house, so I went back for him this morning. Snack looked so forlorn that I brought him too. Jeff was leaving him with José and that Spaniard doesn't like him. I told you, you shouldn't leave him behind, Jeff."

Her voice and manner were more friendly than they had been since the moment Annie had hurled the news-bomb which had blown their comradeship—and incidentally their marriage—to atoms. Color had returned to her face. Kilburn's pulses quickened. She couldn't speak to him like that if she hated him. There was something to be said for the Senator's plan to go without her. She would miss him. Hadn't he been her confidant all her life? He would push the investigation and when he came back—

"Well," Jock Holden picked up his hat and pulled out his watch. "My plane is waiting. If you're coming with me, Eve—"

"I am, that is if it's a take-me-take-my-dogs invitation, Uncle Jock. I suppose they can be shipped by train." She paused on her way to the door. "Good-bye, Jeff, happy landings."

Kilburn folded his arms across his chest and leaned against the desk. His steady eyes met hers. His lips twisted in a smile, half bitter, half amused.

"So you are a cheat, after all."

Color surged to her hair and receded leaving her face startlingly white. She took a step toward him.

"I'm not a cheat, Jeff Kilburn. I am not! To prove it, I'll go with you to-night."

Kilburn laughed. It was a poor thing of its kind, but it served to bring the blood back to Eve's face. He said lightly;

"That's noble of you, but, to be quite honest, I don't want you."

iv

THE crimson afterglow of a winter sunset had turned the river to a stream of fire, had drenched shrubs, tree trunks and leafless branches with molten gold. It touched Eve's face with delicate rose-color light as singing softly under her breath, she approached Boxwood with Bingo, the Boston, and Snack, the shepherd, pacing slowly beside her.

The place was perfect, she thought as she thought every time she saw the stone house on a rise of ground, with its lofty white pillared porticos. Its series of vine-covered diminishing ells—their roofs pale yellow gold now—made her think of a kite with a long tail propped up against a cloudless sky fast darkening from blue to purple. Perhaps that wasn't a respectful simile to apply to one of the oldest and most historic manors of the countryside. No wonder her uncle loved it. It had been in a tragic state of disrepair when Jock Holden had bought it the first year of his senatorship. He had spent a small fortune restoring it to its old-time splendor.

Lawns were lavender and pink, vines were rusty amber in the sunset light. No touch of green anywhere. Nothing surprising in that. Hadn't Congress convened yesterday? January. A brand new year. Eve stopped singing as she thought of it. What had it up its sleeve for her? Financial independence? That seemed farther off than ever. For the last two months she had been looking for a position, but she was not expert enough to secure one. Employers were too busy to teach a novice. After the second time she was told that, she enrolled in a Secretarial School. She might be forced to ask her uncle to help her secure a job. She hated to do it. She wanted to find her own way out of the maze in which the loss of her fortune and her crazy marriage had landed her.

Her marriage! Crazy was the word for it. Her face burned to a crisp whenever the memory of that scene in Jeff's library forced itself into her mind. She had prided herself on her common-sense. Where had it been on the afternoon she had asked him to marry her? Her whole being had been turbulent with emotion. Perhaps the two never traveled together, perhaps when emotion burst in at the door, common-sense slipped out of the window. That sounded like a quote from the Wisdom of Confucius.

Over three months had passed since she had boarded the plane for Washington with her uncle. Unbelievable the swiftness with which human relations could change. One day Jeff Kilburn had been her best friend, the next day he was her husband—of sorts—then he had gone and had not come back.

Three months plus. During that time she had come of age and the Court had removed her uncle Scrip as guardian and had appointed Senator Holden in his place. If the Court had known of her marriage the transfer would have been unnecessary. Scripture Travis had sold his home, stored Eve's furniture and had taken his widowed niece to visit her husband's family in England.

Eve wrinkled her nose disdainfully. Moya, Lady Hyatt, might be widowed but she was far from bereaved. Wherever she was, she would have the time of her life. No word had come from Jeff since she had left him in Barrett's office. The memory of the hurried ceremony had blurred into a haze. Sometimes weeks, filled with gayety and sports and friends would go by without a thought of it, then a notice from Barrett, Tarbell and Tarbell that a cheque had been deposited to her account would bring memory surging back, would bring back the face of the white-lipped, blazing-eyed stranger who had caught her in his arms and kissed her until her heart had stopped. Did Jeff think she would touch his money after that? She'd show him.

Such a notice had arrived this morning. That was why all day she had been haunted by his eyes as they had met hers, by the lash in his voice as he had announced;

"To be quite honest, I don't want you."

It had grown increasingly evident that he didn't. She might as well acknowledge it. At the last moment she had wanted to go with him terribly. She still missed him achingly when she had time to think of him. Something deep in her mind needed him, something which defied anger and separation. Her uncle had not mentioned him and she had been too proud to inquire. Once her Aunt Dorinda had asked;

"What has become of that nice neighbor of yours, Jeff Kilburn? We have seen him so often while you have been growing up that he seems like one of the family. Court adores him. The last time you visited us I gathered from your constant reference to him that he was the biggest interest in your life."

She had made an evasive answer and her aunt had not again mentioned him. Evidently Uncle Jock had not told his wife of that silly ceremony the day before Jeff had sailed. Darn that old bank notice, she couldn't get him out of her mind.

Impatiently she raised a whistle to her lips. In immediate

response to the shrill summons, a bent, grizzled negro snuffled around the corner of the house. He blinked great obsidian eyes at her.

"Lordy, Missy Eve, you don't need to blow your head off wid dat whistle. I seed you comin'. Did you think I was asleep? Git down, you sassy pups! Does you suppose Old Reub wants his nice clean cloes all daubed up by dirty paws?"

He picked up the yelping Bingo and put an arm about Snack's neck as the big dog planted heavy paws on his chest.

"You pretend to scold them but you know you adore Bingo and Snack, Reub," Eve accused. "If you didn't they wouldn't like you."

"Dat don't follow sure, Missy Eve. Dat don't follow sure. Don't dis place look like a country club Sunday afternoons wid so many cars parked here? All belongin' to strappin' young men who jes' swarm 'cause dey are lovin' you an' are you lovin' dem?"

He chuckled and rolled his eyes till the pupils looked like black marbles bobbing in pans of milk.

"Jes' take dat young Ramsdell, de Sen'tor's right hand, he is. I've seed him comin' out dat door lookin' like he's comin' from his Mammy's funeral—yes'm I have. He'd step into his auto I'd brought roun' and he'd say;

" 'Nasty night, Reub', when all de time de stars would be a twinklin' an' a shinin' like the sky was all buttoned up wid brass buttons. An' den dere's dat Spanish gent'man, haven't seed him roun' fer long time. No, siree, lovin' don't alwus beget lovin'."

Eve laughed, though at the mention of Seth Ramsdell a guilty color warmed her face. She was conscious-free in regard to Alvarez at least, she told herself.

"Something tells me you are right, Reub, but just the same, I mustn't stand here talking to you. Aunt Dorinda probably is pouring tea this minute. I should be helping her. Any callers, yet?"

"Only de Colonel, Missy Eve, an' you jest couldn't think of Colonel Courtleigh, Retired, as a caller in dis house, he comes near to livin' here."

"I'm glad he has come. I adore him."

"You say dat, cause he 'bout sixty years old."

"What difference do years make, Reub? So long as one keeps on seeing the romance in life one is never old."

From the top of the steps she waved to the dogs who were regarding her with mournful eyes.

" Bye, young fellas. Stop looking at me like that or I shall burst into tears. We had a grand hike, didn't we? Down! Down, funny-face! That didn't mean that I had invited you to come in with me. Can't you see that inscription above the door? 'Leave dogs behind all ye who enter here'? Call them, Reub. You know that Mrs. Holden won't allow them in the house."

The negro chuckled.

"Yo jest jokin' about a 'scription ober dat do', I reckon, but I ketches what yo' mean. You oughter put de word 'boys' in too. You cayn't tell me not'in' 'bout dat lady an' her housekeepin', Missy Eve. Habn't I lived wid her an' de Sen'tor goin' on ten years? Don't she run dis place like a clock runs? Don't black Cato, de butler have to step lively, an doesn't dose two sassy yellow girls have to be at de foot of de back stairs ready to go up as de clock strikes nine? An' don't Massa Sen'tor ketch de debil if he ain't up so's his bed kin be made on de tick ob de clock? An' young Massa Court, he doan have no fun 'tall, cause he cayn't have no other boys to play wid him, dey might mess up de house.

"Come on, you rascallion dogs. Kin you mastificate two 'normous juicy bones? I don't think so much of dis classy canine caterer dat drives up in a cart all shinin' wid paint an' d'livers a stingy little dinner for you. No sirree."

"Don't feed them, Reub," Eve called, as talking to the dogs he shuffled toward the stables.

Of course he would feed them she thought as she entered the house. No wonder they adored the old man. There was something in what Reub had said about love not always begetting love. If Seth Ramsdell were to be believed it was a question if he could go on living without her and while she liked him she could go on living happily forever if she never saw him again.

Happily. Was she happy? She stopped before a mirror in the spacious hall as she asked herself the question. She tucked a lock of hair under her brown beret, unfastened the huge silver buttons of her green jacket. Smart effect. She had bought the costume because Jeff liked her in brown and green. The memory brought with it the expression of his mouth when he had accused;

"So you are a cheat, after all."

She must stop thinking of Jeff Kilburn, she must get a job which would fill her mind so full that there would be no room for him. Uncle Jock and Aunt Dorinda had been wonderful to her but she wanted to be on her own, she wanted an apartment to furnish with the Colonial pieces which had belonged to her parents, a place, no matter how small, which was all hers. She was no longer the grown-up million dollar baby, she was a girl with only a scrap of income, a voice—of sorts—a few trunks bulging with smart clothes and—a husband in the wilds of South America who didn't want her. Fortunately that last couldn't interfere with her life as the few persons who knew of the marriage had been sworn to secrecy.

She forced her attention to the reflection in the mirror. The glass gave back a portion of the fine old handrail on the curved stairway, the white paneling of the wall, the tall clock, the portrait of a Colonial officer in blue and buff. It was perfect but cold and lifeless. A brilliant cardigan flung on the stiff couch, a soft hat on the table, a bag of golf sticks in the corner would have made the place come alive but—they would have upset Aunt Dorinda for hours.

Eve's brows crinkled. Reub had said that the Senator would get "de debil" if he overslept. Was that the reason Uncle Jock was staying at his Club more and more? Since she had come to live with them she had realized that there was something tragically wrong between her aunt and uncle. He hadn't been at home for a week. Aunt Dorinda was a marvelous housekeeper. Was she falling down when it came to home making? There were women like that. What use slaving to make a house perfect if one couldn't keep the family coming home to it?

"So-o-o-o!"

The prolonged yell accompanied the progress of a boy down the handrail of the stairway, a boy whose face was as thickly powdered with freckles as an August night with stars. He landed on his feet in the middle of the floor, shook back a lock of sandy hair, grinned like a young demon and demanded;

"Wasn't that slick, Eve? You may be a wow at sports but I'll bet you couldn't do that."

"I'll bet I could, Court, if I had on knickers like yours. I've been mad to try it ever since I came to Boxwood. Some day when I come in from tennis in shorts I will."

"You'll try it? I done you wrong, gal, I done you wrong. You're not kidding?"

"I am not. When I get the chance watch me, just watch me. Meanwhile you'd better brush you hair and come in for tea."

"I've been in, Eve. Lookee!"

He pulled his hand from his pocket. In the palm glittered two bright silver half dollars.

"A little chicken-feed, the Colonel called it when he tucked the money into my hand. I ask you, what's the good of money when I haven't any boy friends to spend it on? I'm nearly thirteen, as tall as most fellas fifteen, and I don't know how to play baseball. If mother only wouldn't be so afraid to let me have fun."

The wistfulness of his voice and big blue eyes brought a lump to Eve's throat. No one knew better than she what it meant to be kept in a strait-jacket of restraint. She started to put her arm about his shoulders, remembered in time that he hated anything which savored of petting, so tucked the ends of his tie under the collar of his blue jacket.

"Cheerio, Court. Some day you'll be going away to school and then you will have heaps of boy friends."

"Believe it? Honest? I want to be an army officer like the Colonel. Do you think I'll ever go to West Point, Eve?" His eyes were like blue stars.

"I do. I must go in for tea now but I'll be up to read to you after you have had your supper. We've left Lancelot in a tight spot. We must get him out. Okay, my valiant Knight?"

"S'all right by me, fair dame. I'll say you're a honey, Eve."

He wasn't allowed to have playmates, where did the boy pick up his slang? Probably from the men at the stables, Eve decided as she watched him take the stairs two at a time. At the bend he looked down and with thumbs in his ears waggled his fingers. She threw him a kiss in response, laughed and entered the library.

V

A TALL man of rare distinction, with smooth silvery hair and a clear-cut profile which might have been designed for a coin, rose as Eve entered the library. He put down his cup with haste and an air of relief that set the girl's lip twitching with laughter. One couldn't imagine Colonel Carter Courtleigh, Retired, really liking tea. A frosty glass of fragrant mint julep a-tinkle with ice seemed as inseparable from him as the monocle dangling from its black ribbon. But, Mrs. Holden, behind the tea-table, was a total abstainer and her guests, while they remained her guests—became total abstainers from the force of her convictions.

The Colonel bent deferentially over the hand Eve extended;

"You are lovelier than ever, Miss Eve. Our soft Southern air has brought delicious color to your cheeks and brilliance to your eyes. Not much like your harsh New England, is it?"

"I'll have to break a lance in defense of New England, Colonel, I adore it. I grew up there."

"Yes, yes. I remember. Your mother was a Southern belle

but she didn't live long after she went to that stern and rock-bound coast. Miss Eve grows to look like her mother, doesn't she, Dorinda? Of course, she'll never be the beauty Mrs. Travis was, she was incomparable. She—"

"Come and get your tea, Eve," Mrs. Holden interrupted in a voice slightly husky. "And don't allow your feelings to be hurt by the Colonel's comparisons. He always makes the same comment—to the girl—when he meets the daughter of one of his old loves."

"Tear-gas has nothing on you, Dorinda, for deflating the pride and cocksureness of a man," Colonel Carter Courtleigh protested.

The firelight threw little dancing shadows on the pine paneled wall with its lovely soft patina as, seated in a slipper chair, Eve drank her tea. The Colonel was right, she admitted, Aunt Dorinda had a deflating effect upon almost everyone she met.

She appraised the woman presiding at the tea-table. Her satiny dark hair was twisted in a knot at the nape of her neck; her prim black gown would have been scorned as old-ladyish by a modern older woman of eighty. There was no reason for her to look so antiquated. She had a brilliant mind and a fund of information about politics and policies, national and international, which few of the men who came to her house could equal. She wasn't forty and she had an allowance fit for a queen, probably much bigger than most queens had today. Her skin was soft and young, her blue eyes were brilliant as sapphires, her teeth were perfect, it was her tightened mouth and her Victoria ensemble which detracted from the charm of her face.

"Stop staring at me, Eve, as if I were the pig-faced lady and smile at the Colonel," Mrs. Holden commanded. "Inflate his ego, which he accuses me of deflating by my tear-gas methods. Tell Eve what you have just told me, Carter. Perhaps she will suggest a solution of the problem. Jock will listen to her when he wouldn't to me."

The Colonel took up his position on the hearth rug back to the fire. He looked slightly Daniel Websterish as he thrust one hand beneath the front of his morning coat and wholly West Pointish as he stood sturdy and straight and strong.

Eve thought irrelevantly;

"The army and the law. He took the army first. When I have sons, I'll have them begin military training early. Not that they may become soldiers, but that at sixty odd, they may still carry their shoulders back and their stomachs in and look as if they could face defeat and death unafraid."

"She isn't listening to me, Dorinda."

"I'm sorry, Colonel," Eve apologized. "You will forgive me, won't you, when I confess that I was admiring you so hard that I didn't hear what you were saying? I was wishing that Court might have military training,"—that was carrying war into the enemy's country, she thought, as she glanced at Mrs. Holden from under her lashes— "and that the boys I know carried themselves as you do. Lucky for me they don't, I suppose, or I should be breaking my heart over them. I call that almost as subtle as one of your compliments, Colonel Carter Courtleigh."

The Colonel set the monocle at the end of the black ribbon spinning with one hand and stroked his chin with the other. His expression bordered on the fatuous.

"When your dimples flash like that, Miss Eve, I have a mad impulse to reach for the moon and hand it to you on a jeweled platter, provided that you want the moon."

"Meanwhile you might tell Eve why you came here this afternoon," Mrs. Holden suggested crisply.

"The impelling reason was the same as always, you and your stimulating tea, Dorinda."

Eve was quite sure that the lid of one of his eyes dropped slightly at the word tea. She disciplined a laugh as the Colonel proceeded ponderously.

"Do you think it fitting, Dorinda, to tell a young girl what is, after all, largely cloakroom gossip?"

"Nonsense!" Mrs. Holden's protest was a cross between a laugh and a sob. "The modern girl doesn't go through the world with eyes bandaged and ears stuffed with absorbent cotton to shut out ugly sights and sounds, Carter. If the truth were known, I haven't a doubt that Eve knows more about the deviltry going on than I know. Tell her, she may think of a way to help. Jock adores her. So do I. She is our child now."

The softening of Dorinda Holden's voice, the tenderness of her eyes as she smiled at Eve tightened the girl's throat. She was guiltily aware of the many times she had wondered how her uncle could keep on living with such a cold woman. Now she knew. When her eyes and mouth smiled like that she was adorable.

The Colonel testily voiced Eve's thought.

"Don't take life so hard, Dorinda. When in doubt, laugh. If you would smile more often and not dress like a relic of the turn of the century, there wouldn't be any problem. I don't know where you picked up such a queer twist, dammed if I know."

"Suppose you leave my 'twists' out of it, Carter, and get back to the 'problem.' The room is likely to be flooded at any moment with Eve's followers and before they come I want her to hear what you came to tell me."

"All right, all right, Dorinda." The Colonel frowned at Eve. "It's about the Skinner female. Skinner by name and Skinny by nature."

"Vera Skinner!" she exclaimed incredulously. "Uncle Jock's office secretary? What has happened to her? He hasn't lost her has he? That would upset him. I understand that her efficiency and generalship make the heads of the Department appear like apprentices, but, roughly speaking, she is my idea of something alive which might have crawled out of a fallen meteor. They are finding things like that, you know."

The Colonel shook his head.

"A beautiful girl should not permit her tongue to sharpen, Miss Eve. Leave that to the disappointed, disillusioned women."

"Why shouldn't she say what she thinks, Carter?" Mrs. Holden sprang to Eve's defense. "She is right about the woman's idea of her own importance. Miss Skinner apparently thinks that she is the hub about which all governmental activities revolve. Recently I have discovered that she is the author of that anonymous magazine article which set forth the importance of a super-secretary in the life and success of her employer; of how into her sympathetic ears he pours the details of his trials, and tribulations, business and domestic. My fingers itch to reply with the wife's side of the story; of how she listens to that same employer for hours and hours —if the minutes were laid end to end—growling about this wonder-woman's mixing of papers, long lunch hours, interminable 'phone conversations with friends, lack of manners, and general bossiness. She—"

"Now, now Dorinda stop and get your breath. Your cheeks are burning like red stop lights, and your eyes are blue flames. Cool off, my dear, while I talk to Miss Eve."

Colonel Carter Courtleigh turned to the girl who had been gazing at her aunt in fascinated unbelief. She was magnificent when she flared like that and very beautiful. It was with difficulty that Eve fixed her attention on the man standing before the fire.

"It's this way, Miss Eve. Jock's friends and constituents are getting pretty sick of being dictated to by Vera Skinner —Skinny to them—as to when they can and more often when they can't see the Senator. We've all protested to him about her officiousness but he comes back with the reply that while she may have her faults she is invaluable. None is so blind as he who will not see. But yesterday, she went too far. She snapped at a Head with a capital H. You would know she'd do it, she's a brick-top. The fact that she didn't know to whom she was speaking and that she was all sugar when she discovered her mistake, didn't help. Jock was called to the carpet. He was made to understand that either Miss Skinner leaves his office or he will be forced to hop off the political band wagon."

"That mustn't happen! A Senator told me yesterday that he was the most personally independent chairman that his committee had had in years, with fewer strings tied to him." Eve was on her feet. "We must do something to help, Aunt Dorinda."

"You must, Eve. I have done and said all I can. Jock won't listen. He accuses me of jealousy."

"Jealousy! You jealous of that red headed, green-eyed woman, with her thin angular face, that sloppy dresser! Why, she isn't even pretty."

The Colonel chuckled.

"Talk about man's inhumanity to man. You haven't left the woman her clothes even, Miss Eve. I won't say that she's *une femme fatale,* like Cleopatra, or Helen with the face that launched a thousand ships, but Miss Skinner has what it takes to make men fall for her. She flatters their ego, makes them think they are world-beaters. I may be a traitor to my sex, but mighty few [illegible]n resist that. Jock's a mule. It would be like him to kick over the traces because he was being dictated to, refuse to let the woman go and take the consequences and the consequences will spread and spread in widening circles as water ripples from a stone flung into it. No one can tell how far the circles will go nor what objects they may touch and change."

"That's a terrifying suggestion. If one thought of that each time one made a move, one would be afraid to make a decision."

"The Stop, Look, Listen habit would save a lot of trouble, Miss Eve. Put on your thinking cap and give us an idea how to meet"—He paused as two young men came into the room. "Too late. Enter the advance of the storm troops."

"Cheerio, Colonel," Eve encouraged. "I have a double-track mind. I can think of Uncle Jock even when I am talking to others."

"Gaunt, gangling Seth Ramsdell always makes me think of young bashful Abe Lincoln," confided Colonel Courtleigh, as he watched a tall man cross the room. "A heavy rather than a romantic lead, if one were casting him in a play. Nice manners. He has gone to speak to your Aunt before coming to you. Who's the thin-waisted man with a misplaced eyebrow, waxed to needle-points, on his upper lip, olive skin, black hair and the wary eyes of a bandit who came in with him?"

"Señor Eduardo Enrique Alvarez, he is a Secretary of one of the South American Embassies, he hasn't been here for weeks. 'Lo, Seth, did you and Señor Alvarez drive down together?" Eve asked with a wicked disregard of the war for her favor which had raged between the two before Alvarez went away. She clasped her hands behind her as they simultaneously extended theirs.

"I have breathed the rarefied political air of Washington long enough to have learned not to play favorites. Just the same, I am glad to see you both. Colonel, may I present Señor Alvarez."

"Servidor de v. caballero."

The older man bowed in his best military manner, in response to the South American's suave acknowledgment of the introduction. As Alvarez spoke to Eve the Colonel adjusted his monocle and said cordially;

"Always glad to see you, Ramsdell. My assistant tells me that you obtained some of the most spectacular names on Capitol Hill as sponsors for that Red Cross Benefit I'm working on. He says that you're 'the berries.' That is his term, not mine, but I presume you know what it means."

The eyes of Seth Ramsdell which had followed Eve and Alvarez as they crossed to the tea-table, came back to the Colonel. His face flushed to the edge of his thinning hair.

"It means a whale of a lot when you say it, sir."

"I am glad of that. You won't be a Senator's right-hand always, Ramsdell. A man can't get anywhere these days unless he is willing to peel off his coat and dig in, and you peel and you dig. What's the name of the chap who has dragged Miss Eve to the tea-table? I didn't quite get it, though I understood his assurance that he was my servant. His eyes are black and yellow like a tiger's. More Indian blood than Spanish, if I know my South American, and I do. In swagger he's a cross between a bull fighter and a Mexican bandit."

"That is Señor Eduardo Enrique Alvarez."

"The way that name rolled off your tongue gave away what you think of him. You must learn to be more diplomatic, Ramsdell, if you are set on making the grade in Washington. A little hokum is a helpful thing. Having delivered which bit of advice, I'll admit that I don't like him either."

The Colonel adjusted his monocle and looked at Eve sitting against the background of ferns and palms and orchids of a great bay window. Alvarez was paying ardent attention to what she was saying.

"Don't waste any more time with me, Ramsdell. Go take

Miss Eve away from her musical comedy admirer. You can do it, can't you?"

Ramsdell's laugh brought youth and color to his grave face.

"I'll make a big try at it, Colonel. If I fail I'll come back and get you to show me. I bet you could do it and how. And that isn't hokum, either."

Across the room Eve was saying to the man beside her;

"I was dumb with surprise when I saw you come in, Señor Alvarez. I thought you had left us forever for the wilds of South America."

A shadow swept across his face. "Almost as if he had dropped over it an ugly devil mask," Eve thought, and was promptly ashamed of herself.

"I have been on business for the Embassy. You do not think I would leave you forever, señorita? It would be impossible." He spoke with a slight foreign accent which had its charm.

Eve smiled at the tall youth who was looking down at her with his heart in his eyes.

"Seth, get your tea and bring it over here. Señor Alvarez is telling me about his trip." As Ramsdell turned away she reminded;

"Tell me more, señor. Once I almost sailed for South America."

"I should not speak of business to a charming señorita. I am too fast becoming Americanized. I should tell you instead of the beautiful woman, your cousin, who was the toast of the ship on the return voyage."

"My cousin! I have no cousin coming from South America."

"No? Then I was misinformed. Lady Hyatt told me that you were her cousin when I spoke of knowing Senator Holden."

"Moya! Moya coming from South America? I thought she was in England."

"I am sorry, señorita. You go quite pale. I have said something I should not have said? We will forget it. You will accept the Embassy invitation to the Pan American Ball, will you not? Say yes, that I may dance with the most beautiful girl in the world!" He pressed ardent lips on the back of Eve's hand.

"Home is the sailor, home from the sea," boomed a voice in the doorway.

"It's Uncle Jock!" Eve sprang to her feet with the glad little cry of welcome. She started forward, stopped. Her mind went into a merry-go-round. Beside the Senator, regarding her with steady eyes, stood Jeff Kilburn.

vi

"HAD Jeff seen Señor Alvarez kiss my hand?" Eve wondered in the breathless instant she watched him cross the room to speak to her aunt. What if he had, she demanded of herself furiously. Her hand was her own, wasn't it?

Jefferson Kilburn turned away from the tea-table and approached her.

"It seems ages since I've seen you. Great Caesar, but I believe you've grown, Kiddo."

His voice, his smile, the old familiar greeting, the clasp of his hand, which never yet had failed to set Eve's heart glowing, loosed a flood of emotion. She tried to speak. Her voice wouldn't come. She bit her lips hard to steady them. He spoke quickly to the glowering man beside her.

"Greetings, señor. Curious how we are constantly running into each other. Alvarez and I came back from B.A. on the same ship," he explained to Eve.

"You made queek time getting here, Señor Kilburn. When we docked at New York, you and Lady Hyatt were bound for New England. I would be sad to think she did not go when she so much wished it."

His voice was soft, suave, yet Eve felt that the air had become subtly charged with distrust and hatred. Something had tightened, something intangible, but something violent.

"That's nice of you Alvarez, but there's no occasion for grief. We made it all right, and here I am. There are such things as planes you know."

The realization that Jeff had not only been on the ship with Moya but had taken her to New England touched Eve like a breath from the Arctic. It turned her to ice. She said, not because she cared, but because she had been dummy long enough;

"I thought Moya was in England, Jeff."

"She was, but she got restless and picked up the Cruise bug. Alvarez and I happened to take the same ship on its way back from South America. She came to Washington today by train—she won't step into a plane, small wonder. She has come to visit the present Lord Hyatt, who is connected with a Legation. Here's the Senator."

Eve slipped her hand under Holden's arm.

"It's wonderful to have you back, Uncle Jock. We have missed you frightfully."

"Who's we?"

"Aunt Dorinda, Court and I, to say nothing of the dogs. I hope you are planning to stay, there is so much I want to talk over with you. I've been trying for a job. I didn't want to ask you to help me find one, but I may have to. I'm tired of having nothing to do."

"Permit me, señorita, to offer you one." Alvarez was eager. "We need a secretary who can speak and write perfect English at the Embassy—"

"And attend to correspondence in regard to gold mines?" Holden inquired. He laid one of his large hands on the shoulder of Kilburn who had taken an impetuous step.

Alvarez twisted a waxed end of his small black mustache. There was a flash of white even teeth between his red lips.

"But Senator Holden, the Embassy is not interested in gold mines. Perhaps Señor Kilburn is, yes? I have been told that he is what you call here—a consulting engineer. He has been in South America? Maybe he went to look at a gold mine?"

Kilburn shook his head. "You've got me wrong, Alvarez, my speciality is oil."

"He's been looking up prospects for me in case I switch from gold to oil. Telephone for an appointment in the morning, Alvarez. I've heard of something which may interest your Embassy. Until then, good-bye."

Jock Holden made a dismissing gesture toward the broad door which opened into the hall. For the fragment of a second Alvarez hesitated. Then he pressed his lips to Eve's hand, bowed to the two men watching him and strolled nonchalantly from the room. Eve protested;

"Why did you do that, Uncle Jock? You fairly turned Señor Eduardo Enrique Alvarez out of the house. You practically handed him his hat."

"He had hung round long enough. Here comes Seth Ramsdell looking more like the lean and hungry Cassius than ever. Some day that boy is going to eat you, Eve. Personally conduct him to the stables and show him my new Thoroughbred, or anywhere so you get him out of this room. I want to talk to your aunt and she is posted at the tea-table to stay as long as one guest remains. Don't look at Jeff with that why-don't-you-go-too-expression. He is staying here tonight."

"Here—at Boxwood?"

"Why not? He is my expert adviser—on oil wells. Steer the Colonel into my study, Jeff, probably he's dying of thirst. I'll join you there in a few minutes. Well, Ramsdell, how goes the battle?"

Seth Ramsdell looked at Eve and grinned boyishly. Her eyes were on the two men who were leaving the room.

"Which battle, Mr. Senator?"

"At the moment I was referring to the names of the career boys you are getting for the Red Cross Benefit."

"Oh that! The Colonel told me a few moments ago that my list was the berries."

"That ought to set you up. Try for that new Senator who has taken office on a platform pledge to end poverty in his state. He was elected by the old-time, house-to-house-kissing-baby method. He should be easy meat. Eve wants to show you the new Thoroughbred. Run along, children."

Seth Ramsdell followed the girl to the terrace. The sound of their footsteps on the flagging thinned into silence. Jock Holden crossed the room.

"Come away from the tea-table, Dorinda. I feel as if you were barricaded behind that mass of silver and china. That's better," he approved as his wife seated herself in a corner of the broad couch. Hands in his coat pockets he stood back to the fire and announced;

"I have rented the Washington house of a defeated Senator for the rest of the winter. May buy it if I like it. He'll never be sent back. It is large and completely furnished. Made me think of a movie-set, you know the sort, conservatory with birds and goldfish, tapestries, suits of armor on the grand stairway, the last contribute to an atmosphere of mystery, but we'll get used to it. We move in tomorrow."

"We?"

"You didn't misunderstand me. I said 'we.' You and Court and Eve and I."

"But I detest being in the rush and whirl of Washington, Jock. It is no longer a charming Southern city, it is afloat with tea and cocktails; it hustles and surges and seethes with office hunters, code protesters and adjusters, to say nothing of the thousands of tourists who flock there by air, cars and railroads. It is so peaceful here at Boxwood, besides the city is bad for our boy."

Holden shrugged;

"Peace! Who wants peaceful living? There will be plenty of time for that later. We'll keep this place open and come here week-ends. For reasons you wouldn't understand I must be in the rush and whirl. I intend to stage a hospitality act which will make the town and points east and west sit up and take notice. Fine food has a marked effect on the law of increasing ballot-box returns. I mean to have every move of mine news from now on. You may stay here, I won't force you to go with me, but if you do I shall live in the town house and Eve will be my hostess. Of course, the busybodies will immediately set tongues to clacking and broadcast the news that you and I are no longer happy together, but—"

"Are we, Jock?" Dorinda Holden's clear blue eyes met her husband's grayish green ones.

"We would be if you weren't such a confounded stiff-neck."

"And just what is your idea of a stiff-neck, Jock?"

"Just what you are, if you ask me. You won't have wine served in the house because you don't approve of it. Who are you to decide what another person shall drink? You dress like a woman of 1890; you have a dust complex and an order complex. I'm taut every instant I'm in this house for fear I may leave a coat or a hat somewhere and bring that rigid look to your jaw—"

Dorinda Holden held up her hand.

"That will be enough for the present. I—I had forgotten that you admired me so tremendously."

"There you go, being sarcastic. That's another trait of yours I hate."

"Another! I shall have to keep tabs on my fingers. Let's get back to the town house proposition. Is—Miss Skinner one of your reasons I wouldn't understand, for staying in the city?"

"What do you mean by that?"

"You really should cure yourself of roaring, Jock, it won't jibe with that hospitality act you are planning. The Colonel has told me of your office secretary's latest *faux pas."*

"Infernal old gossip! What did he tell you?"

"That it had come to a choice between dismissal of her, or the loss of your political head. That last, if it happens, will put you in the headlines, but after that you will rate only an unimportant news note on an inside page, if you get that."

"All right, suppose I lose my political head? I will still have my money with which to get a lot out of life, won't I? No one is going to get away with threatening me."

"You don't like it, do you? And yet that was what you were doing to me a few moments ago."

"I threaten you! Don't be silly."

"Didn't you say that if I would not go to the town house you would put Eve at the head of it? Do you think a wife wouldn't consider that an insult? You have turned the spotlight on my faults and failings, Jock. I will pull yours out into the limelight. Your blind spot is that you never try to see the other person's side. You hate advice, yet you don't hesitate to advise your friends, even acquaintances, on any subject whatever; how they should spend their money; where they should live; the friends they should make; I even heard you holding forth to young Curtis when he told you that a baby was coming, that it shouldn't have happened, that he couldn't afford to have a family yet."

"Well, he can't."

"How do you know? It is more probable that he can't afford not to have a family. Children make a man ambitious and Curtis is inclined to be lazy. In the lean early years of our marriage you would have snapped off the head of anyone who had presumed to tell you that you couldn't afford a child. If you would occasionally—just once in a while—stop and think if you would like what you are about to say or do, said or done to you, Jock, you would be a much bigger man than you are now. As a prescription for fair living nothing has as yet been suggested better than the Golden Rule offered by a Certain Man almost two thousand years ago."

"Your eyes are deep blue sapphires when you are angry, Dorinda. They are beautiful. Suppose we shelve the little game of truth we've been playing and get back to the question of the town house."

Dorinda Holden rose. She was almost as tall as her husband, her head with its smooth dark hair was regally set. Her lips widened in a smile which gave beauty and life to her austere face.

"You're a trader, Jock. I will make a trade with you. Promise to get rid of Miss Skinner as soon as you decently can and I'll have the wheels of the house you have hired running smoothly tomorrow night and be there, too."

"You are butting in on my business. I don't tell you how to run this place, do I?"

"I have known it to happen. It is next to impossible for you to keep your hands off another person's life."

"People are so stupid. I give them a shove in the right direction. I do it to help."

"What you think is the right direction, you mean, you are always so magnificently right. Try giving your own affairs a 'shove.' The Skinner situation has gone beyond business now. It has become a personal matter with you. The Colonel said this afternoon that if you refused to let the woman go the consequences would spread in widening circles, as water ripples from a stone flung into it. You are an expert at throwing stones that start ripples, Jock. Some day one of them will create a tidal wave which will wash over all of us. Don't turn on your gimlet-eyed expression. As I have repeatedly told you, I am not jealous of Vera Skinner. I can't bear to have your career—and you can have a career—ruined through sheer pig-headedness."

"Pig-headed! Do you think I haven't thought of getting rid of Skinner? I'll own up that this last break of hers made me see red. But, she has my business at her tongue's end—"

"When business gets as far as the end of a woman's tongue it is apt to drip off."

"What do you mean by that? What have you heard?"

"I have heard nothing, but Eve saw Señor Alvarez and

your office secretary together at a Supper Club the other evening."

"Those two together! Impossible! Skinner hates that oily *hombre* like poison!"

"Does she? Perhaps she is cultivating a taste for poison. Well, is it a bargain? I am really an excellent housekeeper, and there would be no gossip if I went along. And, mighty as you are—as you think you are—in the hearts of your constituents, you come from a district where the sanctity of the marriage tie is the foundation upon which the character of its Senator must be built, and if you can't hold your local group, you won't make your way in State and national fields, you may be sure of that."

"I won't be preached at."

"But how you adore preaching. I'm waiting. If I am to go with you, I should be about the business of starting the town house wheels now. Miss Skinner or your wife? Sounds like a campaign slogan, doesn't it?"

Jock Holden regarded her from beneath bushy brows.

"I don't understand what has come over you, Dorinda. You never have interfered in my business before."

"Miss Skinner or your wife?"

"You of course, but I realize that I am putting myself on the spot—"

"What do you mean by that, Jock, that someone might—"

"There, there, don't choke over it. It was my slangy way of expressing the fact that Skinner won't be what you would call pleased. I don't know who I can find to fill her place. She is a lady—"

"Train Eve."

"Eve! Eve is too young."

"No, she isn't. Haven't you noticed how she has grown up since she came to us? She has had some experience, and she has been attending a Secretarial School for the last two months. She thinks I don't know it. If you could see the letter the clinic head, under whom she worked at the hospital, wrote her when she left, you wouldn't hesitate to try her. You could trust her to be courteous and at the same time unyielding when it came to your interests. She hasn't said anything but I feel her restlessness. She has been taking voice lessons but only half-heartedly practising, and she is determined to have an apartment of her own as soon as possible. It would be the best thing in the world for her to have an absorbing interest."

"Restless, is she? Know why?"

"No. I thought at first that it was the result of her disillusion about her uncle; it must be something of a shock to learn suddenly that one's fortune has vanished into thin air;

—it had grown to three millions, I heard—then, I wondered if she missed Jefferson Kilburn. When she visited us before, his name was always on her lips, 'Jeff wants me to do this,' 'Jeff thinks,' etc."

"Doesn't she talk about him now?"

"I can't remember that voluntarily she has mentioned his name once during the months we have been together. Something must have happened between them."

"Hmp! Something has."

"What? Jock, you haven't been putting a finger in their affairs, have you?"

"There, Dorinda, there, of course I haven't. I felt that there was a rift in their friendship when I saw them together this afternoon. I thought it a pity. That's why I asked Jeff to stay with us. I—"

Eve entered the room and stopped.

"Oh, here you are, Eve. Talk about angels—"

"Were you talking about me, Uncle Jock?"

"What modesty! You have the gayest little laugh, honey. When I hear it this topsy-turvy world steadies. You said you wanted a job. Rather work for me or for Alvarez?"

Eve noticed for the first time lines as if etched with a pen point at the corners of his rather prominent eyes. Was he worried? She answered fervently;

"You, of course. But, you have the priceless Skinner."

"I'm thinking of letting her go."

"Hooray! Does the Colonel know?"

"So he has been talking to you too, has he? You will have to work under Vera Skinner for a week or two, Eve, while you learn the ropes."

"Oh, no, she won't Mr. Senator!" The red-headed woman in the doorway contradicted sharply. "I hand in my resignation to take effect this moment."

Jock Holden's eyes contracted.

"Why are you here, Miss Skinner?"

The woman shrugged, looked from him to his wife standing motionless with one white-knuckled hand gripping the mantel and back to him before she mocked;

" 'Miss Skinner!' Getting formal, aren't you, Mr. Senator, and perhaps a little deaf? I told you that I am resigning my position with you. Señor Alvarez has offered me a job at his Embassy and I'm taking it."

vii

ONLY the crackle of the fire, the tick of the clock and the faint hiss of steam escaping from the massive Georgian silver hot-water kettle, broke the silence in the library. Eve's glance stole from the slight red-haired woman in black with the insolently curved painted mouth, to her uncle who was regarding his office secretary from under heavy lids, then on to his wife standing near him. It stopped there. What thought had touched Dorinda Holden's lips with that Mona Lisa smile?

"What's back of this theatrical claptrap, Miss Skinner?" Something in Jock Holden's voice sent little chills creeping along Eve's veins.

"It isn't theatrical claptrap, Mr. Senator. I heard this morning from excellent authority that you had been ordered to put the skids under me. I've beaten you to it, that's all. Of course, if you are brave enough to tell the person who laid down the law to you that you are competent to manage your own business—"

"That will do."

The redness of Jock Holden's face frightened Eve. It looked as if the blood must burst through the skin. His eyes were mere points of light.

"If you have agreed already to take the job Alvarez has offered, by the way, he offered it to Miss Travis a few moments ago, why waste time coming here?"

The woman tilted her chin with the air of an impertinent red-headed woodpecker.

"Thought I'd give you a chance to show that you are big enough to do as you like. I don't have to work, no one knows better than you, that I am well fixed financially, Mr. Senator, but Alvarez has made me a grand offer. I am to have charge of his private business on the side. He considers that my experience in managing your affairs could be of great help to him."

"I get you. You'll sell information, will you? Go on. Be sure that you are selling the right thing. You see, I have known of your friendship with Alvarez for some time and have suspected treachery."

Amazement, incredulity, vindictiveness, followed each other with lightning rapidity in Vera Skinner's eyes. Her fingers fumbled at the clasp of the pearls about her neck. The softly glowing string swung from her extended hand.

"When I heard that I was losing my job with you, Mr. Senator, I knew that I must return these. That's why I wasted time coming here. They are too valuable to send by messenger."

Her eyes flashed to the woman in front of the fire. Jock Holden's usually ruddy face was curiously gray as he agreed harshly;

"All right with me if that's the way you feel about it. They were given to you, you may remember, as a reward for faithful service, and for no other reason. They might turn black if you wore them now."

He held out his hand. Vera Skinner's fingers tightened on the necklace before she dropped it into the outstretched palm. The gleaming end of it dripped from Holden's coat pocket as he suggested;

"You have made your grand gesture. You have returned them. You have stirred up trouble, that's why you did it, isn't it? You have handed in your resignation. A cheque for salary due you will be sent tomorrow. Nothing to keep you here, is there?"

"Of course there is, Jock," Dorinda Holden protested, "Miss Skinner should have a cup of tea before she returns to the city. Giving up a string of pearls, pearls as perfect as those, must be a heart twisting experience for a woman."

From behind the table with its steaming hot-water kettle she regarded her husband's office secretary with cool courtesy.

"Cream or lemon?"

"Neither, Mrs. Holden. I don't care for your tea, which, with your out-of-date clothes, is one of the jokes of Washington. Everyone knows that the Senator has to entertai[illegible] a Club because he can't do it properly at home; tha[illegible] are too high brow to carry on for him socially."

"That's enough from you." Holden interrupted furiously.

"I'm through with your wife, Mr. Senator. As for your niece, I suppose she tipped you off about Alvarez. I thought there would be trouble when I saw her at that Supper Club. She is to take my place! I heard the arrangement when I stood in the doorway. Pretty, but dumb, I'll say. When she has hopelessly messed up your affairs, don't call upon me to untangle them."

Jock Holden crossed to the broad doorway. He spoke to the grizzled-haired black butler in the hall.

"Have Miss Skinner's car brought round, Cato."

The woman waited for the fraction of a second before she left the room. Eve wondered as she looked at Jock Holden's savage face how she had dared hesitate that long. The tap, tap of heels on the tiled floor of the hall diminished, a distant door closed.

To break the tension Eve observed with unsteady gaiety;

"At least the efficient Skinner admitted that I am fairly goodlooking." She glanced from her uncle standing before the fire to his wife gripping the back of a big chair. "Seth will be here before I am dressed if I don't hurry. I promised to read to—"

"Stay where you are, Eve. I want to talk to Dorinda and I want you to hear what I have to say."

Jock Holden drew the pearls from his pocket and tossed them in his palm as if testing their weight.

"This is the necklace the jeweler sent you by mistake six months ago, Dorinda. You wouldn't listen to my explanation then and you never have been really my wife since, just an exceptionally good housekeeper. Now you know for whom I bought the pearls. Miss Skinner had done a difficult piece of work for me. I gave them to her as a mark of appreciation, and for no other reason, for no other reason. You may believe it or not. Either way makes no difference to me—now."

Why didn't his wife assure him that she did believe him, Eve wondered passionately. One couldn't listen to him and think he was lying. She watched her aunt, one hand at her throat as if it had tightened unbearably, as she said coolly;

"As it makes no difference to you, Jock, I needn't answer. Miss Skinner showed a nice sense of impartiality. She called you dumb, Eve, and declared that my teas and my out-of-date clothes are the joke of Washington. She inferred that socially, I am a dead weight on our Senator. For my share of her caustic appraisals I thank her. It slashed my mind wide open, and let in a flood of light. I'm looking at myself from the outside now. Her resignation settles the question of the town house. It will be open and ready for you tomorrow, Jock, I shall be there with the servants."

"A town house! Are you and Uncle Jock leaving Boxwood, Aunt Dorinda? Then I'll get a small apartment."

"Nonsense, of course you are coming with us, Eve, dear. Our Senator is embarking on a hospitality campaign. He needs you and me to charm his constituents and—can we do it?"

Her husband and Eve watched in speechless surprise as Dorinda Holden left the room. Had the Dallin bronze Indian on a pedestal in a corner given vent to a war-whoop and cast his spear, Eve could not have been more amazed than she was by the tone of her aunt's voice and the gamine quality of that "and can we do it?"

There was a curious expression in Jock Holden's eyes as they met Eve's. He held out his hand;

"Come here! I've had Dorinda on the carpet, now I have something to say to you, young woman."

Eve felt the color burn to her hair as she approached him. Was he about to speak of her mar—marriage? How the word stuck in her mind.

"Don't look at me as if you were scared to death. Dorinda says that the best thing I do is to give advice, advice that I would kick like a steer about if it were handed to me, that I am everlastingly trying to manage other people's lives. From now on I'm dumb. So don't be afraid that I'm going to lecture you about your treatment of Jeff Kilburn—though I will say in passing, that you should acknowledge that mar— There I go, handing out advice. Forget it. Do you still want to come into my office after the melodrama Skinner staged this afternoon?"

"More than ever. I am thrilled to have the chance—that is, if you believe I can make good, Uncle Jock."

"Don't question it. If you think in terms of defeat you will be defeated. Pin on your red badge of courage. It's a great world to the valiant. Hold your head high and believe in your star and in the man you love. If more women did that, men's shoulders would be straighter."

Was he thinking of his wife's distrust of him? Eve agreed gaily;

"From this moment I will believe in my star, Uncle Jock, and if, how, and when I make mistakes, I will visualize that illuminated quotation from T. Roosevelt in your study;

" 'Show me the man who never made a mistake and I'll show you the man who never accomplished anything.' "

"That's the spirit. I'll have you take over one of Ramsdell's jobs. He clips all news and editorial items that have a slant on me and pastes them up in loose-leaf note-books. I don't like to talk about myself, but take it from me, those note-books are getting bulky. You and I—good heavens, I had forgotten that you and the Colonel were waiting for me, Jeff."

"The Colonel is no longer waiting, Senator." Kilburn closed the door to the study and approached the fireplace. "He had an engagement at six."

The old clock in the corner caught its breath and wheezed the hour.

"Six o'clock!" Eve was aware that her voice showed a hint of panic. Jeff Kilburn was so tall and remote, and commanding—that was the only word that expressed him—that he sent a shiver along her nerves. "I ought to be dressing. Seth is coming back to take me to that gorgeous new Supper Club."

"You'll have to cut out these late parties if you take that private secretary job, Eve."

Kilburn held the light motionless above his pipe.

"What private secretary job? You haven't accepted Alvarez' offer, Eve? If you have, give it up. I won't permit it."

"That's the funniest thing I ever heard, Jeff Kilburn. Do you think you can disappear for over three months and come back and dictate to me the way you used—"

"That will be about all from you, young woman," Jock Holden slipped an arm about Eve as if to palliate the sternness of his voice. "She isn't going to the Embassy and Alvarez, Jeff, she is coming into my office."

"Yours! What has become of the incomparable Vera Skinner?"

"She is taking the position Alvarez offered Eve."

Kilburn's whistle was low and prolonged.

"All my rough reports on the gold mine went through her hands I presume, Senator?"

"They did. I had no reason to question her honesty—but she knows nothing about—well, you know. I told Alvarez to phone for an appointment in the morning. I will ask him a few questions about the son of his late father's late partner and watch him squirm."

Seated on the arm of the couch, Jefferson Kilburn removed his pipe to observe thoughtfully;

"I wouldn't do that, Senator."

"What do you mean, wouldn't do it? Are you giving me advice?"

Kilburn laughed.

"You must be psychic. That's just what I was doing. Alvarez must not suspect what you have up your sleeve. If he does, you'll never get that five thousand back nor the chance to show him up for what he is. Perhaps I am being too communicative before your new secretary? She has been stepping out with him, I understand?"

Eve's eyes and temper flared.

"Do you think I'm not to be trusted with a secret, Jeff Kilburn? Have I told a soul about our—"

She turned her face against Jock Holden's sleeve. He patted her shoulder.

"Of course you are to be trusted, honey, but, I warn you there are a lot of men in Washington—and women too, who don't care how they get information so long as they get it. And remember that every spot in the city may have the broadcasting properties of the talking stone in Statuary Hall in the Capitol—if there are ears to listen, understand?"

Eve nodded gravely.

"I do. Working for you means something more than just taking a job, Uncle Jock."

"Why antagonize Miss Skinner just now, Senator?" Kilburn protested. "I can see how she could misrepresent your interest in the mine, and stir Alvarez' Embassy into a seething hornets' nest. Can't you entice her to stay until we get the matter cleaned up?"

"Don't listen to Jeff, Uncle Jock. You and I have signed on the dotted line, already, haven't we?"

Kilburn watched her as she smiled radiantly at Jock Holden. Of course her uncle would let her do as she liked, equally of course he would be too occupied with large affairs to know what was happening to her personally. Well, that would be his own job. Eve was his. Was she lovelier than ever, or did her eyes seem deeper, her hair a bluer black because months had passed since he had seen her? She had changed. She had acquired poise. Her fingers had clung to his when he had shaken hands with her in this very room an hour or more ago. He hadn't been mistaken. Had she missed him? Absence had made him realize that the girl he had regarded as a child, was the girl who had kept him from finding a woman whom he loved enough to marry. Once he had been tremendously attracted to Moya, but on the ship coming from South America, her clinging-vine line had been boring. He had had a lot of it. Because of what he had heard of Alvarez he had blocked the man's pursuit of her at every opportunity. It was incredible that once he had thought her habit of cupping her chin in her hand and looking up with soulful eyes fascinating. Rather terrifying to think how completely a man's point of view could change in regard to a woman. It had taken all his self-control to keep from writing to Eve while he was away, but he had determined that she should think the situation out uninfluenced by any word of his.

"Looks to me as if your oil expert had gone to sleep, Uncle Jock." Eve's voice derailed his train of thought. "You and I had better tiptoe from the room that his nap may not be disturbed."

Kilburn dropped his pipe into his pocket.

"Perhaps I was dreaming, Kiddo, but I'm wide awake now. Let's go stepping somewhere in the bright lights tonight."

"No. No. I can't. I told you that I had a date with Seth Ramsdell."

"Why so panicky? It's all right with me. I might call Moya at her hotel and we'll make a foursome."

"Moya! Always Moya! Why is she like a Northwest Mounted? Answer. Because she always gets her man."

"Stop fighting, you two!" Jock Holden commanded. "Don't you know that I've got a lot on my mind? Think you are right about keeping Alvarez guessing, Jeff. Remember, Eve, you've never heard of a gold mine. I'll talk with him in the morning and sort of string him along."

Kilburn thrust his hands into his pockets. He fixed steady eyes on the man and girl standing before the fire. His voice was brittle as he suggested;

"And while you are talking with Señor Alvarez, Senator, tell him to keep his dirty mouth off my wife's hand. If you don't, I will and—you won't care for the way I do it."

viii

EVE murmured something and left the library. Kilburn followed her with his eyes. He was sure that she ran across the hall, he could hear the quick tap-tap of heels on the tiles. That word "wife" had been in the way of a small electric shock. As if he had divined his thought, Jock Holden inquired;

"How long will you let the situation between you and Eve remain as it is, Jeff? Love her, don't you? Even I, who Dorinda claims am dumb about such things, can see that."

"Yes, I love her, love her enough to let her have her fling at what she calls freedom."

"Eve's not the sort men make passes at, but they fall for her, fall for her hard. Think you'll like seeing them hanging round her?"

"Can't say that I'll like it but if it is part of her idea of freedom I will have to take it. I'll get into the stag-line myself, I'm not worried. She is too honest to let a man get in very deep."

"Uhuh? Perhaps not, but she is planning to go to Reno and have her marriage to you annulled."

"What!"

"You heard me the first time, Jeff."

"Is she in love with Ramsdell? I've suspected that she cared for him more than she realized."

"And she thinks you are in love with Moya, Lady Hyatt. Perhaps she's right. Where there is smoke, there is apt to be fire. I was tempted to tell her that you were off your head about the girl you married, then I had a hunch I'd better not."

Kilburn went white.

"Loud huzzahs for the hunch. Keep out of my life, Senator. I neither need nor want your help in managing it."

Holden chuckled.

"Just like that."

"You've got the idea."

"All right, Jeff, all right. Some day you may be yelling for help, and I'll keep my hands off. But I'll remind you now of the fact that if you don't watch out, you are in for a trimming."

Kilburn crossed to one of the long windows which opened on the terrace. The rings of the crimson damask hanging clicked sharply as he pushed it back. Outside all that was left of the afterglow was an amber light on the horizon which turned to apple green as it mounted and fused into the night sky.

So, Eve was planning to have her marriage annulled, was it because of Seth Ramsdell, he asked himself as he watched four dark shadows wing across the glow. The Senator prophesied that he was in for a trimming if he didn't watch out. It would have to be some trimming to make him give up the girl he'd married.

A vine brushed stiff fingers against the glass. Suddenly a star shone bright and clear. The color on the horizon turned to opal and silver. He drew the hanging and returned to the fire.

"Looks as if it might be a good duck season," he suggested and lighted his pipe.

Holden grinned.

"I gather that the subject we were discussing is closed. As they are saying of one of the rookie Congressmen, I am respected but not listened to. Sit down, Jeff, and give me the inside dope about Alvarez. There was something between the lines of your letters that I wasn't smart enough to get. One reason—there was another—I asked you to stay here tonight was that we might have a fireside chat—it is being done—offices have ears and, I am beginning to believe, tongues."

He selected a cigar from a humidor on a small table and sank into a deep chair. He stretched his legs toward the fire.

"This is restful. I can feel the knots in my mind untangling. You're on the air, Jeff. You warned me not to close the deal with Alvarez and is that South American all steamed up about the delay? I'll say he is."

Kilburn stood with one arm on the mantel and looked down at the big man in the chair.

"I judged so. He was on the ship coming up from B. A. He went down by air. From the day I arrived in the vicinity of the mine he claims, until I boarded the ship for home, I'm willing to swear I was shadowed, and that I was never more than a jump or two ahead of the shadow. Luckily I looked up José's claim before I went to the mine or I might never have secured the facts we want. Here are my notes. Keep them in your pocket. As you say, offices have eyes, ears and tongues."

Holden reached for the note-book.

"I'll look these over tonight. You have proved José's claim. What are we waiting for? Why can't we set off the bomb under Alvarez?"

"We are waiting for a certified copy of the will of Don José Manuel Mendoza, José's father. I found it in the records. You will find scraps of it in that book with a few other facts which I won't mention aloud. I was promised a copy when I returned to the city. I didn't return after I discovered that I was being shadowed. Didn't want Alvarez to suspect that I had been looking up records. An incipient revolution broke out and Americans were advised to leave the country. I had accomplished all that I could, so departed. It was alleged that the revolt was financed in the United States. It broke soon after the arrival of Alvarez. Merely a coincidence I presume."

"Of course. Tricky as he is, Alvarez wouldn't try to stage a revolt. Too risky. He was there on this mine business. He must know that I would look up his claim before I paid him fifty thousand bucks."

"He may know that, but he doesn't know that I found something else."

"What?"

"The record of his marriage."

"Married! That *hombre* married! He's been making love to Eve!"

"So I gathered. Now you know why I won't have him kissing her hand."

"Is the woman alive?"

"Very much so."

"Did you see her?"

"Yes. She's a dancer. Beautiful and sparkling like a Christmas tree with jewels. I asked a few discreet questions. First, had she a husband? 'No, no, señor!' I was assured that the jewels were real—that the woman permitted no lovers—that the town buzzed with conjecture as to where they came from."

"Alvarez, of course. That's why he is so keen for money. Probably already he has spent my five thousand on her, not on a musical comedy revolution. Well, I had kissed it goodbye. What's holding up the copy of the will?"

"I suppose that Alvarez has been pulling strings."

"What will you do if it doesn't come soon?"

"With your approval, Senator, we will ask for an appointment with the Charge d'Affaires of Alvarez' Embassy, and lay our cards on the table."

"Hmp! Do you think he would keep the situation secret?"

"I'll impress upon him the fact that if he doesn't the aforementioned situation will be tainted with death."

Surprise catapulted Holden to his feet.

"D—death! For whom?"

"For José and perhaps—for me." Kilburn drew his fingers across his throat. "You suggested that before I started for South America."

"Stop your grinning, Jeff! This is serious. I was only kidding that day in Barrett's office. Do you think I would have sent you had I believed harm would come to you? I couldn't care more for a younger brother than I care for you."

He walked across the room, came back.

"Jeff, not an hour ago Dorinda accused me of forever chucking stones that set consequences spreading in widening circles. It appears now that I've heaved a gold mine into pretty sinister water. The first ripple touched you and Eve, she wouldn't have made that lunatic proposal to you if you hadn't been about to sail for South America on my business. Looks now as if the circles would widen and crack down on José, but I don't see why Alvarez should drag you into the scrap."

"He suspects that I was investigating the gold mine, also he resented bitterly my interference in his devotion to Moya on the ship coming up from B. A. She came into quite a bunch of money when her husband died, and that black-haired boy loves money. He may suspect that José is alive. He wants that fifty thousand dollars for the mine and he wants it quick. Possibly he is planning to buy off the little dancer so that he can marry an American heiress. He is playing a dangerous game, but he has a subtle mind, a cool head and no scruples about getting what he wants. I heard things about him. Some disgusted me. I will admit that some scared me. Now that he has your late secretary for an ally we'd better watch our steps."

"In spite of the evidence here this afternoon I can't believe that Vera Skinner would doublecross me. You don't think she would, do you, Jeff?"

"How can I judge? I've never seen the woman. She might not under her own power, but she is stepping out with Alvarez now, isn't she? Whatever you do, keep that notebook under lock and key. Hey, Court! Come in! I've been wondering where you were."

The boy in the doorway made a rush at Kilburn and caught him around the waist. Jock Holden's voice interrupted the friendly tussle.

"That will do, Court. What d'you mean coming into the library in your pajamas."

"Pajamas! Gee, Pop, I've got a wrapper over them, haven't I? Cato told me that Jeff was here and I just beat it down to see him."

"I've been away for a week. You didn't beat it down to see me, did you?"

The boy shook his tousled head.

"Didn't think you'd give a hoot to see me, Pop." His voice and eyes were troubled. Kilburn laid his arm across his shoulders.

"All right, young fella. Run along up stairs. Your mother would have a fit if she knew you were here dressed like that."

"I'm going. You won't leave without seeing me again, will you, Jeff? I've been practicing that hold you taught me with one of the stable boys and say, can I lay him flat?"

"Court!"

"I'm going, Pop."

Kilburn walked to the door with him.

"Drop into my room in about half an hour, Court, and I'll find out if you're good, and how!"

"Gee, Jeff, you're a grand guy."

He shot out of the room. Kilburn watched him charge up the stairs.

"He's a great kid," he said and returned to the fire.

Jock Holden frowned.

"You think so. He's a great overgrown kid, too tall for his age. He irritates me. Perhaps it's because it makes me so mad to think I allow him to hang around at home when he ought to be at school."

"Why don't you send him to school?"

"His mother wants him here."

"But he is your son too. If you think he should go why not insist?"

"You're asking me! I don't insist for the same reason you are letting Eve persist in her fool idea of freedom. Get me?"

Kilburn laughed.

"I get you, Senator."

Holden linked his arm in his.

"Come on and I'll show you your room, Jeff. We'll finish our talk after dinner, for the first time in weeks I have a free evening, that is, if you haven't a date."

"Didn't you hear my girl turn me down? I think we should decide what we will say to that Charge d'Affaires, Senator."

An half hour later, as he was thinking of Eve and brushing his hair furiously before the mirror in the spacious chintz-hung bed-room, he answered a knock.

"Come in!"

Court tiptoed into the room and cautiously closed the door behind him.

"Almost ran into Mom in the hall. She would have thrown a fit if she had suspected what I have on."

He flung off a wrapper and stood clad in bright blue trunks only. Muscles rippled under the smooth skin of his beautiful body as he doubled up his fists and pranced forward.

Kilburn laughed and flung off his silk lounge coat.

Court grinned.

"Gee, Jeff, you look like one of those snappy magazine ads of men's underwear. Suppose I'll ever be as tall and straight as you are?"

"Taller and straighter, probably. Come along, stout fella! Let's tangle! Show me how good you are!"

At the end of five minutes of tussle and strain and hard breathing on the boy's part, Kilburn laid him flat on his back.

"There you are, m'lad. You shouldn't have let me get that grip on you. You should have done this. Watch!"

"Okay!"

Court scrambled to his feet. He perched on the back of the divan at the foot of the bed as Kilburn illustrated his point.

"See where you fell down, Court?"

"Sure. I see. Let's try it again."

"Not tonight. I'll be late for dinner if I don't get a move on."

"Mind if I stay here while you dress?"

"I like your company. How are the lessons going?"

"Nothing doing just now. Old Pete's on vacation."

"I take it that 'Old Pete' is the latest in tutors?"

"Okay. He's all right—but, he's so darned stiff, and—and old. If only I could go to school. Skinny says I should."

Kilburn stopped in the process of bowing his black tie.

"Who's Skinny? The stable boy you've taken on?"

"Skinny a stable boy! That's a scream. She's Pop's office secretary."

"Miss Skinner! When did she tell you you should go to school?"

"She didn't tell me, I heard her telling Pop. I guess he thinks a lot of what she says for he lets her take me places."

"What places?"

Court dug his feet into the divan, planted elbows on his

knees and rested his chin in his hands. His cheeks were red, his eyes were big and dark and earnest as he explained;

"You see, it's this way. I wouldn't have much fun if it weren't for Skinny. She taught me to drive a car. She takes me to ball-games and rodeos and movies. She sneaked in this pair of blue trunks for me. Mother's afraid things like that will make me rough, but Pop, even if he does think I'm kind of dumb and no count, would put up a fight to have me go and Skinny would take me and we'd eat peanuts and popcorn and buy stuff in bottles to suck through a straw. Usually I'd be sick as a horse when I got home but it was worth all I had to take."

"You like Miss Skinner?"

"Sure. She's swell. Don't you like her?"

"I've never met the lady," Kilburn slipped into his dinner jacket. "Zero hour, Court. You'd better toddle off to bed. I'm ready to go down."

"Okay, Jeff. I'll remember what you said about that clinch. It was a grand wrestle. Lucky I saw Eve gumshoeing down the stairs just before I knocked."

"Lucky! Why?"

Court nodded toward a door in the side wall.

"That's her room. If she'd heard us scuffling she would have busted in to know what was going on. Girls are like that, don't you think?"

Kilburn's eyes came back from the door.

"Think what? Yes, yes, I do. Good-night, Court. See you in the morning."

As he entered the library, Jock Holden, standing before the fire looked up.

"Room comfortable, find everything you wanted, Jeff?"

Kilburn's amused eyes met the twinkle in his.

"Everything, thank you. Nice room. So many doors. Something about it made me think of a movie I saw years ago."

"A movie?"

"Yes. It was called The Man Who Played God."

The laughter left his eyes.

"It's a risky business to play God, Senator. Don't try it."

ix

THE recently opened Supper Club was done in rose color with silver lacquer trim and gold fittings. It was dimly lit and throbby with music. In the circular room where dancing went on, the tables, placed around a slowly revolving platform on which were grouped the dusky-skinned musicians in cloth of silver mess jackets and cloth of gold trousers, were slabs of synthetic pink tourmaline, bordered with glittering green jewels, also synthetic. The silver frames of the chairs and benches were covered with dusty pink leather with here and there one of tourmaline green for accent. A recessed service bar was laden with chafing dishes, and salad bowls. Behind it presided a huge chef, black as ebony in contrast to his tall snowy cap. The lights in gold sconces around the room were pointed flames.

At one of the tables Eve shrugged off a honey-colored wrap which matched her deftly simple frock of soft, gleaming satin. In a mirror, she caught the reflection of her head, of the sleek swirl of her dark hair which ended in a delicate mass of short curls, of the sheen of pearls about her throat.

"Not too hard to look at," she thought. She colored as she met Seth Ramsdell's amused eyes.

"Like yourself a lot, don't you?" he teased.

"Sometimes and this is one of the times," Eve admitted brazenly. "I've never been here before. The decor makes me think of something concocted by a chef for a prize-pastry contest, left up to harden. The rose-color walls do a lot for the skin you love to touch, don't they? They bring a youthful tint even to older faces. What a glamorous pla[illegible] and isn't the ensemble divine?"

Harps throbbed, flutes sang, oboes brooded and through their rhythm the violin of the leader wove a thread of melody; notes like the rippling of water, notes limpid and soft as strung pearls, notes drawling sensuously, notes that broke into blood-quickening syncopation. The music submerged Eve in a high tide of emotion. One sentence recurred over and over in her mind like a refrain;

"Tell him to keep his dirty mouth off my wife's hand!"

The remembrance of Jeff's eyes as he had looked at her, shot her heart to her throat, dropped it in a tail-spin, and took her breath with it. They were the eyes of the stranger who had caught her in his arms and kissed her furiously that afternoon in Uncle Scrip's living room.

In an attempt to get her thoughts under control, she concentrated on the dancers as they swung past. Citizens from all parts of the country and of foreign countries were mixed together. People of different races, aims and backgrounds swayed and laughed and loved to the same swinging pace of the music.

Seth Ramsdell tapped her hand.

"You are supposed to pay some attention to your boy friend when he takes you out, you know."

Eve looked at his strong rugged face. He was unlike the other men in the room, he would be noticeable in any crowd. Tonight he had thrown off his usual gravity and seemed young and boyish. He was exceptionally distinguished in evening clothes. He hadn't Jeff's ease of manner in whatever situation he found himself, but few of the men she met had. Jeff was a cosmopolite.

"I'm sorry, Seth. I'm not much good as a companion when I come to a place like this. I get so absorbed watching people and wondering if under the social veneer they are saints or sinners or just ordinary well-meaning persons like myself who are gluttons for making mistakes."

"You! You make mistakes! Don't be foolish, you're perfect. What will you have to drink?"

"All sorts of fruit juices with heaps of ice and sparkle."

"Champagne will fill that order. Waiter—"

"No. No champagne. Just what I said, fruit juices with sparkling water."

With a disdainful sniff the waiter departed. Ramsdell laughed.

"He evidently thinks we are hicks from the prohibition belt, Eve. What's wrong with wine? You're not a total abstainer like Mrs. Holden, are you?"

"I am not. I started out tonight with the determination that I would be a sport, that I would drink what others drank, but, when I've decided to do what others do, I always crash against something like that."

She nodded toward a young woman in a backless silver frock at the next table. She had flung an arm about her escort's neck, and was gazing up at him with lack-lustre eyes and cooing at him through scarlet lips stretched in a silly grin. On the stage a man imitated in succession a flivver, a vacuum cleaner and an airplane. As Ramsdell's eyes came back to Eve she said;

"Just as I had decided to become the life of the party, my eyes lit on her. They would if there was anything like that within a mile to light on. Doesn't she look cheap even in that ravishing frock, which I happen to know is hot from a Paris opening? How do I know that I wouldn't make as silly a fool of myself as she is making? I won't take a chance, thank you."

"You, look like that! Don't be foolish. You couldn't. It isn't only that you are lovely, Eve. You have so much character."

"Have I, Seth? I wonder. If I have it must have been

inherited from mother and father for the women who looked after me never gave me the careful spiritual and moral training which would keep me up to the level my birthright demanded. I was guarded physically, I was trained in what they considered good manners—a little old-fashioned now, perhaps—for which I am unutterably grateful, but character, if I get what you mean, I have had to work out for myself—with—Jeff Kilburn's help. He has brought me up in the way I should go, believe it or not."

"It's always Jeff Kilburn with you," Ramsdell interrupted testily. "Whenever you speak of him I think of those lines from Paradise Lost about Adam and Eve;

> " 'For contemplation he and valor form'd,
> For softness she and sweet attractive grace,
> He for God only, she for God in him.'

"You think he is perfect, don't you? I wonder you haven't married him long before this."

"Mar—marry Jeff!" Eve realized her breathlessness and disciplined her voice. "As if Jeff ever would care for me that way! Who's being foolish now! We were talking about character, not marriage. Perhaps had my parents lived, I wouldn't have felt such responsibility about myself, but long ago Uncle Jock told me how mother and father planned for my coming while I was still playing with the angels, what high ideals they had for their child, and how they adored me the short time they had me. I have tried to be what they would want me to be. I couldn't let them down, could I?"

"Beautiful!"

Eve shook off the hand on hers. "Good heavens, Seth, how did we get so solemn? You'll never ask me on a party again. Forget my 'no mother to guide her' sob story. Let's dance."

As she danced Seth's words, "You have so much character," wound like a minor refrain through the silvery, electric fabric of the music. Character. Her "character" was a joke. Would a girl with character beg a man to marry her and then refuse to live up to the contract? She would if she found that he was in love with another woman, Eve triumphantly flung the answer to her accusing conscience.

When they were back at the table Ramsdell asked;

"Heard of the ark of a house Senator Holden has hired for the winter?"

"Yes. The news broke this afternoon. Aunt Dorinda will have her hands full running it. It will take a positively feudal array of servants. I wonder why he is taking it?"

"I've heard from a person who is too much in the know to be wrong, that he has been picked for the coming man, and our Senator knows that the man who makes the grade in this town is the man who moves the quickest."

"You admire Uncle Jock tremendously, don't you?" Eve asked to the accompaniment of the ensemble leader's sugary crooning.

"Admire him! I love him. Perhaps it is because we are so different. I'm cautious, always getting in out of the wet, if I can. He is one of the unstampedables, if you get what I mean. He might be deluged with telegrams to oppose a measure and if he didn't believe in opposing it, he wouldn't. He would be shrewd enough to remember the vast number of voters from whom he had not heard. He isn't afraid of losing his seat, that's the answer."

"Unstampedable! Reminds me of Fitz-James in The Lady the Lake;

" 'His back against a rock he bore
And firmly placed his foot before:—
"Come one, come all! this rock shall fly
From its firm base as soon as I:" '

"That might be Uncle Jock's theme song. Unstampedable. It's a great quality, isn't it?"

"It is, especially for a man in public life. We have come to accept corruption in high places as a matter of course, but, Senator Holden is straight, absolutely straight, and you may take it from me that his rise in influence is the nearest thing to a fairy story in Washington. He knows human nature. I've seen him put his divining rod down into the heart of an ugly opponent until he found a spring of sympathy. He received six thousand requests for copies of that last speech of his which fact gives you a rough idea of his popularity."

Eve twisted her glass and watched the bubbles rise in the hollow stem.

"I wish that he and Aunt Dorinda were happier together. I wouldn't say that if I didn't consider you one of the family, Seth."

"Thanks. I take that not only as a compliment, but as a prophecy. Now, don't get restless, that's all I'll say—for the present. To return to the Holdens. I have a hunch that misunderstanding between them will straighten out now that the temperamental Skinny is shaking the dust of our office from her feet. It's time. When a woman is in love with her boss, she'd better quit."

"Seth! You don't think that Uncle Jock—"

"Don't look so horrified. Didn't I tell you he was straight? He has made a success of his own affairs which can't be said of every man who has been sent here to help conduct the Nation's business. Vera Skinner had begun to think she was the whole works. I heard her snap at a crowned head and I knew what she had coming to her, but, I wish it hadn't come just now."

"Can she hurt Uncle Jock?"

"She can, by starting a whispering campaign—from absolutely nothing. I'd give a month's salary to find out what she has up her sleeve. She has been running round with that slick Alvarez. If I knew their game, I'll bet I could block it, if there is a game. There isn't anything she can know about the Senator's methods that I don't know, and as I've told you, they are straight. In spite of that whenever I think of her, I go pebbly with gooseflesh."

"I wonder if I can help?" Eve leaned toward him and said mysteriously;

"There is one thing you don't know, you repository of innumerable political secrets."

"Gosh, how your eyes sparkle when you're excited, Eve. Make me think of black diamonds. What don't I know?"

"You don't know who is to succeed the Skinner menace. I have her job!"

"You!"

"Your shocked incredulity is an insult, Mr. Ramsdell."

"Quit y[illegible] kidding, Eve. Is it true? Are you to take her place?"

"I am—unless Uncle Jock succumbs to pressure—her pressure and takes her back. Even persons as dominant as he have been known to yield."

"He won't. Not after this. See who's coming in! They team up well. The Colonel says that Alvarez' eyes are tiger eyes, black and yellow. How they shine! Must be his brain glowing. It has been discovered that brains glow."

Eve's eyes followed Ramsdell's. Vera Skinner, with Alvarez beside her, was dramatizing their entrance by pausing in the doorway. Her frock was a brilliant green above which her flaming hair looked like a huge exotic blossom. Heads turned. Women's eyes and men's eyes raked her from head to foot, before they began to whisper.

"The plot thickens," Ramsdell said and cocked a bushy eyebrow. "Let's dance."

When they returned to the table Alvarez was waiting. Seth's "slick" is the perfect word for him, Eve thought as she noted the gloss on his hair, on his evening clothes, on his shoes, even the petals of the gardenia in his lapel seemed to have an extra sheen. He smiled the caressing smile which suggested ardent devotion and promised nothing.

"At last, señorita! May I have the honor of a dance?"

Eve looked at Seth Ramsdell.

"Sure," he approved. "I'll ask Skinny to step with me."

They danced to the rhythm of drums, to ecstatically singing violins, to the windy, insolent snarl of horns, to shimmering, lilting, exuberant notes.

Alvarez bent his head until his lips touched her hair.

"You dance like a dream," he said softly.

Eve looked up at him. She thought:

"Your eyes are black and yellow. Tiger eyes. Do I dare play with a tiger? I'll have to if I want to find out what plan you and Miss Skinner have up your sleeve which may harm Uncle Jock."

Aloud she said;

"There are dreams and dreams, señor. I hope you mean that I dance like a good one?"

"As if there could be a doubt. If only I saw you more often, señorita! You seem so far away in that house in the country."

"Haven't you heard that we are moving to town tomorrow? Hasn't Skin—Miss Skinner told you? She is your secretary now, isn't she?"

"I wonder if I should have said that?" Eve asked herself as she saw his face darken.

"Not yet, not until I am sure that you won't take the position I offered you this afternoon."

"Sorry. I couldn't possibly take it. I'm engaged—"

Alvarez lost step.

"To Señor Kilburn?"

Eve's heart bailed out and dropped, a stunt which was becoming unpleasantly frequent. Could he know—of course not. It was maddening that she couldn't get Jeff out of her thoughts tonight. She said;

"Señor Kilburn has no use for a secretary. I am to take Miss Skinner's place in Senator Holden's office."

"So that is it. Why do I waste a moment talking of positions and what you Americans call jobs, when I have you in my arms, señorita?"

"But, I adore hearing about business and I suppose that some of the affairs of an Embassy come under that head. I hope you will tell me a lot about it. Anything to do with diplomacy fascinates me. Besides, whatever interests you interests me."

She smiled up into his eyes. It was the first smile of its

kind she ever had attempted. Its result was startling.

Alvarez caught her close. Laid his cheek against hers;

"Querida mîa," he whispered. "Do you know how you set me ablaze? Do you know how beautiful you are?"

Eve felt as she had when as a child she had lighted a firecracker and the whole bunch had gone off in her hand. She answered;

"I have my own small share of vanity. The music has stopped. I must—must go back to Seth," she insisted more in the manner of a frightened school-girl than the sophisticate her smile had indicated.

Alvarez crushed her hand in his.

"But I shall see you soon,—"

"Of course. Oh, Seth—" Ramsdell's rugged face seemed like a dependable rock in a tempestuous sea. "One more dance and then I must go. Good night, Señor Alvarez."

She extricated her hand before he could lift it to his lips. As she and Ramsdell glided into a dance she asked;

"You couldn't request the leader to strike into Yankee Doodle or the Star Spangled Banner, could you? Either would be a grand antidote to the love-making to which I've just been exposed. Fascination, Latin-style."

"Did that—"

"Help! Don't stop short in the middle of this crowded floor, Seth. See that couple glare at us. Being a perfect lady I won't repeat what the gentleman said under his breath. not so much under, though, that I couldn't hear it. Alvarez did nothing. I just don't care for his tropical manner, that's all."

"I'll bet you gave him some encouragement."

"Don't growl. Didn't you say that you would give a month's salary to find out what game Vera Skinner and Alvarez had up their sleeves? I merely fired the opening gun in my campaign to find out."

"If that's why you were casting soulful glances at Alvarez —I had my eye on you—you can cut it out. That's no reason for doing it, it's an excuse. I'll do my own sleuthing."

"Man's ingratitude to woman. My glances weren't soulful —one would think you were talking of Moya—and I shall continue to observe the Skinner influence on men and morals, thank you."

Conversation limped after that. It ceased altogether as they started for home in Ramsdell's lemon yellow speedster. Eve snuggled into her corner of the soft brown leather seat. If Seth wanted to glower, let him, she had tried only to help.

Gorgeous night! The horizon glowed pink from numberless incandescents. Delicate as fairy webs, mysterious as giant listening-posts, radio towers pierced the purple canopy of the heavens. Overhead blazed Orion, mighty hunter of the skies. Moonlight silvered fields and distant roofs. The stars seemed nearer and brighter than the lights which jeweled the river front and shadowy bridges.

"Look at the stars, Seth. See that brilliant new one which has traveled millions of light years to get here. Greetings, Nova Hercules! Try to feel cross with me when you look up at the heavens. It can't be done."

"I'm not cross with you, Eve. It gave me the jitters when I thought of you getting mixed up with that hot South American."

"Let's forget him. Give me points on my new job. I have a lot to learn about Uncle Jock's office and you are the man who knows all the answers."

She plied him with eager questions until they reached the white pillared manor house, gleaming like mother-of-pearl in the moonlight. The sonorous, majestic chime of a steeple bell stole across the silent fields as he slipped the key in the door. It struck again and lingeringly trailed away along the river.

Eve held out her hand.

"Thanks for a perfect party, Seth."

His fingers crushed hers.

"Beautiful! Marry me, Eve?"

"Don't spoil our marvelous evening, Seth. Please don't spoil it. I have told you a dozen times that now that I can go and come as I please, I won't give up my freedom for anyone. Good-night."

In the dimly lighted hall she leaned against the closed door and listened until she heard his car start. She drew a long breath of relief. That was that.

Only the tick of the old clock disturbed the quiet of the house. She might have been treading the sands of the desert so lightly she crossed to the foot of the curving stairway.

"Just a moment, Eve."

She turned. Jeff Kilburn stood in the library doorway. She could see the glimmer of red embers in the fireplace behind him.

Thump! Thump! Thump! The beat of her heart drowned out the tick of the clock. She put her hand to her throat to stop the throbbing.

"Goodness, Jeff. What's the idea jumping out at me in the dark? That's one of Court's kid tricks."

"Sorry I frightened you. I have something to tell you."

He was nearly at the foot of the stairs.

front-page lines necessary. Be a good girl and in June you and I will trek to Reno and have that lunatic marriage wiped off the books clean as a whistle. Till then forget it."

As if she could, now that Jeff had returned. If she could forget everything else, she couldn't wipe from her mind his face when he had heard of Moya's accident nor the fury of his kisses—fury was the only word which expressed the way he had caught her in his arms, even the memory of it set her pulses quick-stepping now, kisses meant for Moya. And she had struck him, struck him hard. She was horribly ashamed of herself for that. She should have remembered that he had thought for a moment that the woman he loved had been killed, that he wasn't responsible for what he did.

He had touched her life in so many ways, tenderly, gayly, authoritatively and with unfailing sympathy. Instead of being furiously hurt and angry with him that last day she should have talked the matter over with him calmly. Calmly? That word was a joke when even the thought of meeting him was like fingers tightening on her throat. If she had spent the same amount of gray matter on her new job that she had used avoiding Jeff Kilburn, Uncle Jock wouldn't still be mourning the loss of the super-efficient Skinner.

"Come in!"

Had she put off going down stairs so long that a maid was rapping to remind her that dinner was served? Instead of the maid she expected, Jefferson Kilburn entered and closed the door behind him.

"Why! Why, Jeff!"

He laughed. She adored his laugh.

"Glad you haven't forgotten my name, Kiddo. Corking room you have here. *Objets Modernes* and then some. Slightly motion-picturish but effective. Like it?"

"Love it," answered Eve fervently.

"Like your job?"

"Immensely. Am I working and am I working? What I did at the hospital was mere kindergarten. Now I am typing, bookkeeping, filing and taking dictation on a machine besides being a sort of watch-dog and interior undecorator. The exotic Miss Skinner had her office draped and furnished like a drawing room. Uncle Jock ordered me to restore it to a work-room. The Senators are wonderful to me. They call me Miss Secretary, which makes me feel terribly important, like a member of the Cabinet, almost. It is exciting to be working in the midst of the most thrilling city in the world. If there is anything in environmental stimulus a person will get it here. I'm not too expert in taking dictation so I have subscribed to a series of late afternoon lectures on literature. By the time I have taken those down and done the required reading, I ought to be able to enter a shorthand prize contest, besides knowing a lot about modern American writers."

Trivial inconsequences. She was aware that he stood waiting for her to finish before he brought up the matter which sooner or later—preferably later, if he asked her—must be threshed out between them. If only she could wake up and find that the marriage had been nothing but a nightmare.

"Sit down, Eve. I want to talk to you. Our situation calls for action and here I am."

In spite of his smile there was a tension in his voice which sent little nerve caterpillars crawling along Eve's veins.

"I'll take the shock standing, thanks. You believe in direct attack, don't you?"

She glanced at the clock, which for purposes of artistic unity had been sunk into the façade of a Chinese pagoda.

"Never mind the time. Your aunt gave me ten minutes. She knew that I wanted to talk with you. That is all I need. Still feel that our marriage was a mistake?"

His voice was disarmingly amused, so like that of the boy and man with whom she had grown up that Eve's nervousness vanished.

"I do, Jeff, of course I do, and it doesn't make it easier to bear to know that it was entirely my fault—you didn't have a chance to escape me, knowing as you did that my money was gone—and then—then I was so hateful to you. I have asked and asked Uncle Jock to sell a few of the securities I have left to finance a trip to Reno, but—"

"Is it as bad as that? Come here."

He caught her hand and drew her toward him.

"Who's the man?"

"What man? You don't think I want to marry someone else, do you? I'm not that foolish! It's you of whom I am thinking, not myself."

The fervor of her voice brought the color to Kilburn's face, the tense line of his jaw relaxed.

"That's mighty nice of you," he smoothed back a wave of her hair. "Because I feel so infernally guilty about that marriage ceremony, I'll let you set your own rate of exchange. I should have known better."

The relief to hear him say that, the incredible relief. Eve's world turned rose-color.

"Lot you had to say about it, Mister Kilburn. Didn't I fairly shanghai you into it and then when I reached home and—and—heard about Moya and my money—I—I just couldn't take it. I'm sorry, my point of view is different now,

I don't wonder you refused to take me to South America with you."

Kilburn's brows went up.

"I refused to take you?"

"Yes, weren't the last words you said to me in Barrett's office, 'To be quite honest, I don't want you'?"

"Sure I said that?"

"Am I sure! It clangs through my mind a dozen times a day. But that's past, it is the present I am thinking about. Uncle Jock has promised to take me to Reno in June and he begged me—"

"There's something wrong in that picture. I can't see Senator Holden begging."

"Commanded is better. Will it be an awful bore for you to wait until then to be free?"

Kilburn spread the rosy-tipped fingers he still held on his palm and regarded them thoughtfully.

"No. No. It seems a long way ahead but June will be okay. The North Cape trip will be about right in July. I suppose it will take till then to get the annulment through the mill."

"My word, has it gone so far that you have planned your honeymoon?"

"I wouldn't say 'planned,' but I happen to know that she loves to travel and of course, if I can, I want to make her happy."

"Darn! I've been mad to take that North Cape trip. Now you'll get there first. You can go right on with 'yo' courtin',' that's what Reub calls it, in your best high-pressure style and have the girl ready to say 'yes' when we get the decree."

"Swell! That is an idea! Shake!"

Kilburn gave the hand he held a friendly squeeze before he released it.

"Oh, just one thing more, Eve. Now that we have come to what the law would call 'an amicable settlement out of Court,' you will stop dodging me, won't you?"

"How did you know I was dodging you, Jeff?"

"When a girl has sudden and apparently compelling business elsewhere whenever a man enters a room, after a while he would begin to think himself an outlander, wouldn't he?"

Eve tucked her hand under his arm and sniffed at the gardenia in his coat lapel.

"I'm simply mad about you in evening clothes. I'll never dodge you again, Mister Kilburn."

He raised her chin until he could look into her clear, eager eyes.

"Promise?"

"Cut my throat and hope to die. Oh, it's grand to be friends, Jeff! I have missed you frightfully. I'm sorry that I—" Impulsively she pressed her lips to his cheek.

"Don't!"

He jerked back his head, color flamed to his hair. Eve felt her face burn in response. Her eyes blazed behind a mist of tears.

"You needn't be so touchy. I—I was only trying to tell you that I was sorry that—that I struck you that—" Her voice trailed off in a whisper.

He put his arm about her shoulders.

"Forget it, dar—Kiddo. Forget everything about that day. You and I are beginning over again from this minute, remember. Hear the chimes? Does that mean dinner?"

"Yes." Eve turned away and drew her fingers across wet lashes. "We must go down. It's a duck dinner. Our Senator and a pal week-ended on the edge of a low, marshy inlet and came home with a hunter's sack full of birds."

As they left the room Kilburn inquired;

"What people are coming tonight?"

"Two couples from the Senator's home district. I took the wives sight-seeing today. They were dears if slightly overrouged. What do you think they wanted to see most? First, the dresses worn by 'First Ladies' at the National Museum, next the Tomb of the Unknown Soldier and third, Whistler's Peacock Room at the Freer Gallery."

"What a curious combination. Other guests?"

"Yes, some of the Senators on Uncle Jock's committees, an odd man for me, a lovely lady for you and one for Colonel Courtleigh."

"Who is the odd man for you?"

"Señor Eduardo Enrique Alvarez. I wonder of what use that man can be to his Embassy. He is a Secretary but he is forever somewhere else. I don't know who the lovely ladies are because I came home late from a tea—Uncle Jock says that if I drop out socially he will discharge me—and haven't seen Aunt Dorinda. The two who had accepted regretted last evening. One had a cold. The other had been called out of town."

"What's the idea having Alvarez here?"

"Diplomacy, Mister, diplomacy. I suspect that he, or his government, has something Uncle Jock wants. Don't scowl. Bad enough to have that grim armor to pass without adding to the gloom."

She stopped on the broad landing to look up at the figure in the corner.

"Observe him! I've never been accused of being timid but

if you were not here, Jeff, I would race past and pelt down the stairs. This stout knight in the complete armor of chain mail dates back to 1195. Isn't that a vicious face under the leather hood? If they had planned to use the gentleman as a household pet, they might have painted a more agreeable expression on that wooden head. At the foot of the stairs we are now passing a complete plate armor. Notice the slits where the eyes should be in the armet, that's the head covering in case you don't know."

"I didn't until you told me. Where did you get the information?"

"I looked it up for Court. He and I are reading Howard Pyle's King Arthur and His Knights and the boy is living in the age of chivalry. He was tremendously interested and a little afraid of these figures—though he wouldn't acknowledge it—when we first moved in. I don't wonder. Now he is decidedly fratty with them. Addresses them as Sir Knight, his father as Sire and I heard him calling his tutor's attention to his mother as 'Yon dame.' I expect at any moment that Plate Armor may raise his visor and whisper hoarsely, 'Touch me not, Lady!' My word, I thought one of them stirred then!"

"Your imagination has been infected by the movies, Eve, it is wasted in the Senator's office. Here's where we make our grand entrance. You know whom you will draw for a dinner partner, now I'll learn my fate."

As he entered the Louis XVI salon, with its ceiling and mirrors and flower paneled walls which had been brought from France, a small woman in gauzy black left the colorful group near the fire and came forward swiftly. She held out two slim white hands, pouted her crimson lips, looked up with big, wistful violet eyes, beautiful eyes without depth, and exclaimed;

"Jeff! At last! It's divine to see you! When Mrs. Holden asked me this morning to fill in at dinner tonight she said that you would be here—but when you didn't come—I suspected that you had side stepped and gone somewhere else. You must be snowed-under by invitations."

Kilburn freed his hands from the clinging fingers.

"I have been made welcome to the city. Am I late, Moya?"

His eyes followed Eve in her glittering frock, rested on sleek, tight-lipped, slim-waisted Alvarez as he bent over her hand. Not until the South American had lingeringly released it did his attention return to the woman beside him. He caught up the conversational ball as if his eyes had not played truant.

"Hope we haven't delayed dinner. That is an unforgivable sin in this house and would put me in Mrs. Holden's black book. I would be sorry for that, I admire her tremendously. Here's someone else. She evidently realizes the dramatic value of a late entrance. What an interesting face under the mop of flaming hair. That slithery black gown gives her figure the alluring curves of a match, but, what beautiful arms, what long, slender hands. Know who she is?"

Moya twisted her rope of lustrous pearls and raised thin eyebrows which were too black to belong legitimately to the same family as her golden hair.

"Don't you know, Jeff Kilburn?"

"The scorn in your voice at my ignorance makes me humiliatingly aware that I should, but I don't. Is she a Pulitzer Prize winner, an escaped royalty, one of our foreign ministers, or governor of a state? That last is being done now. She looks capable of intrigue in the manner of Machiavelli. Machiavelli, said he, explaining to she, was a tricky Italian, you know. Mrs. Holden is signaling to me. That means that I am to take the late arrival in to dinner. Throw me a life-line, quick. Who is she?"

"No one of importance. Merely Senator Holden's late office secretary, Vera Skinner. Skinner! What's in a name? Something tells me that that has been said before. I wonder why she was invited. They say—" she shrugged. "Why should you take that person in when I am here?"

"Doubtless, Moya, the beautiful Lady Hyatt is being reserved for someone of importance."

Kilburn crossed the room in response to the compelling eyes of his hostess. As he reached her she turned to the woman beside her and said in her slightly husky voice;

"Miss Skinner, may I present Mr. Kilburn? Perhaps you do not need an introduction. You—"

"We've not met. I was on vacation when he came to Washington, and—as you may remember—I am no longer in Senator Holden's office. I know Mr. Kilburn only through letters. He writes a corking letter. Still investigating oil wells, Mr. Kilburn?"

The eyes that flashed up to his were green and amber. He had seen those shifting colors in the eyes of a cat. Sultry eyes. Suspicious eyes. What did the woman mean? She had seen his correspondence in regard to the gold mine, but she could know nothing of José's claim. He was aware that Alvarez beside Eve had stopped talking to listen. He could feel the South American's eagerness to hear. He laughed.

"Nice of you to be interested. Re: oil wells, as they would

write in a business letter, I'm all through with that sort of work."

"What work are you doing?" Miss Skinner inquired smoothly, too smoothly. He answered theatrically;

"I'm in diplomacy now."

"Diplomacy? Sort of a jack-of-all-trades, aren't you? And how long will you be on that job?"

For an instant his eyes lingered on Eve as she passed with Alvarez.

"Only death and taxes are certain, I may not get the matter settled until June, though I hope to put it across by cherry-blossom time." He offered his arm. "Shall we follow our hostess?"

xi

THE conservatory was so beautiful that the owner of the house should be forgiven for the armor on the stairs, Eve thought, as she listened to the drip of the fountain into the marble rimmed pool and the sleepy trill of a bird. She drew a long breath of air scented with the fragrance of moist warm earth and flowers. The dark green of towering palms, the vivid emerald of tropical ferns, the massed pink poinsettias, yellow roses, blue iris, and golden rain of mimosa, made a perfect background for the metallic shimmer of the women's gowns, and the sombre black and white of the evening clothes of the men.

The dinner had been a success. That the food would be perfect was a foregone conclusion in Dorinda Holden's house, but the greatest contributing factor had been the mood of the guests. Burdened with problems of their own and the Nation's, as many of them undoubtedly were, they had created an atmosphere of gaiety, as if their spirits were bound on a glorious adventure, giving no thought to material values. The out-of-town visitors had glowed with pride in their Senator and had straightened visibly and listened breathlessly at each casual mention of the White House. A number of the men had round, rosy faces and their expressions were nothing short of cherubic as they smoked and drank their coffee and—marvel of marvels in this house—sipped liqueurs. Wines had been served at dinner, fine wines, not a brand too many, not a glass too much.

What had brought about Dorinda Holden's change of viewpoint? Vera Skinner's slash at her teas and out-of-date clothes? If the ex-office-secretary's jibe had worked the miracle, she rated the Congressional Medal, Eve conceded.

The clinging silver lamé gown of the hostess was the last word in fashion, her dark hair had been dressed by an artist who realized the beauty of her perfect features; regal was the only word which adequately described her emeralds. She had smiled at her husband across the length of the table. Was it peace between them or only an armed neutrality?

"A penny for yout thoughts, Miss Eve," bargained Colonel Courtleigh as he sat down beside her on the green-cushioned marble bench.

"You don't go in for bidding in a big way, do you, Colonel? Any one of my thoughts is worth more than a penny, believe it or not. I was looking at Aunt Dorinda and wondering—"

"You needn't say it, I know. It knocked the breath out of me when I saw her beautiful shoulders bare, and when Cato appeared with sherry and *hors d'oeuvres*, I was on the verge of a nervous break-down. She has dropped years. She had begun to settle down, life was getting drab. The truth is that when you have stopped thrilling to romance, when you tell yourself that you are too old for sentiment in life or fiction, you have stopped growing spiritually. Look at Jock. He has put something across. What? He is twinkling like a whole row of electric lights. It isn't because of what he drank, he barely touched the wine, I watched him. I saw Dorinda smile at him at dinner, such a beautiful smile. I hope and pray that those two will patch up their differences and begin again. They are the dearest things in life to me."

He cleared his throat.

"Where were we when I burst into sentiment? You should have sidetracked me, Miss Eve."

"But I love your 'sentiment,' Colonel."

"Has anyone ever told you, my dear, that your manner to older people is the sweetest, the gayest, the most tender in the world? Your lovely soul seems always to be just behind your eyes. I don't wonder your Uncle Jock thinks you are perfect."

"You are exaggerating, Colonel, but who am I to protest when I am fairly lapping up your praise?"

Eve glanced at her uncle. His head was bent as he listened to the red-haired woman who was talking to him eagerly.

"Do you suppose Uncle Jock is what you call 'twinkling' because he is with—with her again?" she asked gravely.

The Colonel adjusted his monocle and stared gloomily at his host.

"I can't believe it of Jock. Why in thunder was his late office-secretary invited? What d'you mean having her at this party?"

"Why glare at me, Colonel? I didn't know she was coming. Perhaps Aunt Dorinda invited her to prove to the world that she is not jealous of Vera Skinner, that there is no truth in the whispers going the rounds that Uncle Jock likes her —too much. Perhaps she wanted her to see her in all her gorgeousness. There is no reason socially why she shouldn't be here. She is a lady, the daughter of a defunct Senator. I did not know that Lady Hyatt was to be a guest."

"Don't speak of those two in the same breath, child. Look at the beautiful little woman, lovely child, in her gauzy black against the mass of pink poinsettias, so unaware of the picture she is making. I don't wonder that Jeff Kilburn looks as if he longed to be that jeweled cigarette holder she is placing between her lips."

"Hok—" Eve swallowed the rest of the word. In polite society—and this was super-polite society tonight—one didn't say "Hokum" in response to an elderly man's remarks even if they did impress one as being saccharine. Moya, unaware of the picture she was making? That was the joke of the week. Chin cupped in hand she was looking up at the man beside her with worshipping eyes. Her line certainly mowed down the males in squads. Governments might rise and fall, the world might change in every other way, but the clinging-vine woman would continue through the ages to put it over the good-comrade girl. Jeff Kilburn needn't 'ook quite so bowled over even if she were his heartbeat and he were taking her to the North Cape in July.

At last he was tearing himself away. She watched him as he joined a group of Senators. One, built on Falstaffian lines, flung an arm about his shoulders and drew him into the circle. Then Alvarez joined them and they stopped talking and were absorbed in lighting fresh cigars.

"Agree with me, Miss Eve?"

"I"m sorry, Colonel, agree with you about what? I—I was admiring the beautiful Moya so hard that I didn't hear your question."

Colonel Courtleigh swung the monocle on its black ribbon.

"Hmp! Your face tells tales. It was not registering what I call admiration. I was observing that it looks to me from the benignancy of their expressions, as if Jock's Committee men would back him up tomorrow when he asks for money. He's a fire-eater when it comes to fighting for an appropriation, but even a fire-eater can't battle alone and he has some back-seaters on his committees. Nothing would so bewilder them as responsibility. After they are all set he will have to get public opinion back of him. By indifference, citizens can paralyze the arm of the law, by a whole-hearted interest in it, they can give it life and power. I don't mean a high and dangerous wave of hysteria. A steady sea of determination to restore law and order is what this country needs. Sorry. There I go again, discoursing."

"You are not discoursing. I love to have you talk to me as if I had brains. Besides, I'm in the army of workers now."

"Like it?"

"Love it, but it keeps me on my toes. Our office is the most exciting place. Every time the door opens one hears the faint, far chant of the approaching Choir of Trillions Invisible. As you may have suspected, your fire-eating Senator has a slave-driving complex. He is a quite different person from Uncle Jock at home. A psychiatrist would doubtless diagnose his as a 'split-personality.' Court is getting to be just like him."

"Now there's a boy! Tried to get here early to see him. How is my namesake?"

"This is King Arthur and His Knights week with him. It's a heavenly change from his sleuth complex. Before he left Boxwood he got hold of a skeleton key, and experimented with it on every door in the house. I am sorry to report that it worked. He is versatile in his accomplishments."

"Smart as a steel trap, isn't he?" The Colonel's eyes shadowed. "He is almost thirteen, at the age when no one really loves a boy but his mother and she has moments when she wonders if she can keep on. He ought to be away at school, not hanging round the house with a tutor. No discipline. It's always spare-the-rod week with Dorinda. He's a lusty young savage, amidst problem-logged grown-ups who are pressing him into a conventional mold. What chance has he to grow a soul? It is the dream of my life to have my namesake—and incidentally my heir—go to West Point. If he prepared for it, Jock would send him in a minute—but Dorinda hangs on to him. You couldn't talk to her about it, could you?"

"I could, but—I won't, Colonel. Who am I to advise a woman what to do with a child?"

"Who am I, when it comes to that. I have no children, haven't a wife, even." The Colonel bent his white head very near Eve's.

"Anything new about the gold lode?"

"Gold lode? What gold lode?"

He chuckled.

"You couldn't have done it better, my dear. I see that the Senator has begun to train you in the way you should go. He reverses the news picture caption—'Sees All. Hears All.' His secretary is to see nothing; hear nothing and above all, tell nothing. That last is the rock upon which Vera Skinner crashed and went down. She talked too much. Perhaps you don't know whether Señor Alvarez still comes to Jock's office."

"I know that answer. He comes twice a week to take me to lectures on American Literature."

"What does that *caballero* care about American Literature?"

"He says that it helps him so veree much in his Eenglish."

"You ought to go into the *diseuse* business. You are a wonderful mimic. Eenglish! Poppycock! I did a lot of fool things in my youth for the chance of trailing round with a lovely girl, but a lecture course wasn't one of them."

He frowned at Jefferson Kilburn as he approached.

"What do you want, Jeff? Just as Miss Eve and I are settling down to a heart-to-heart, why do you have to come along and make us tune in on another wave-length?"

"Sorry, Colonel. I seem to be casting-director tonight. Mrs. Holden is making up the card-tables. The out-of-town guests must have their little game of contract."

He spoke to the South American who had come up and was bending over Eve in ardent devotion.

"She wants you too, Alvarez."

Alvarez' eyes met Kilburn's before he said to Eve;

"I will come for you at the same hour tomorrow, señorita. I will say more, later, this evening."

Colonel Courtleigh waited until he was out of hearing before he bowed in his best military style.

"There is a saying about Hawaii; 'To have to leave it is to die a little bit.' That is the way I feel about leaving you, Miss Eve."

He crossed the room with the step of a General at the head of an army. Eve smiled at Kilburn.

"Isn't he grand? There's a man! You've played round with me all my life, Jeff, and you never said To have to leave me is to die a little bit. Instead, you used to dodge your sub-deb neighbor when you came home from Tech bringing a bunch of girls and men for a week-end party, perhaps you remember."

She was gay, tormenting. Kilburn caught her wrist;

"What did Alvarez mean when he said he would come for you at the same hour?"

As Eve's startled eyes met his, he laughed, and loosened his fingers.

"I forgot. You are a girl on your own now. I have been seeing too many movies. Aren't you needed at one of the card tables?"

"No. Neither needed nor wanted. I wouldn't attempt to

play with those speed demons. I have concluded that I haven't a card mind."

"Nothing the matter with your mind. You don't like cards, that's the answer."

He parted the hangings at the window and looked out.

"It is a grand night, Eve. The snow has stopped, the moon is cocking one eye at me, and the stars are out. It's too fine to stay in the house. My car is in the garage, top down as you like it. Let's go tourist. Let's see the Nation's Capital by moonlight."

"That's positively inspired, Jeff. I would love it but—suppose Aunt Dorinda should need me?"

"For what? The contract addicts have settled down for the evening. Young Court must be in bed by this time, so you can't coddle him."

"I don't coddle him, Mister Kilburn. I read to him for an hour. You know he has to save his eyes."

"Come on, we won't be gone long."

"It's a date. I'll dash up, get a coat and meet you at the side door. Don't make a sound or we may be stopped."

"Not while I have my two fists," said Jefferson Kilburn and meant it.

xii

A SWIFTLY sailing fleet of clouds broke up the gold patterns the moon was casting and splotched distant white clad hills with purple shadows, as Kilburn turned his roadster into the Avenue which uncoiled ahead like a huge white serpent striped with black. The night wind crooned. Iron riders on iron steeds were capped and caparisoned with snow. Shrubs glittered like tinsel under great arc lights, tree branches linked ghostly arms in a high arch. Occasionally an old-fashioned sleigh filled with laughing, shouting youngsters, jingled past.

He looked at the girl beside him. A silver sequined turban was crushed down on her dark hair, the collar of her ermine coat almost met it. What had Alvarez meant when he had told her that he would come for her at the same hour?

Eve looked up.

"What are you scowling at, Jeff? My coat? Thinking me extravagant for a secretary? You needn't. It's about all that is left of the wardrobe of that one time heiress who was guarded like a truck full of gold being moved from one bank to another. That life seems like a dream now."

"I was wondering if you were warm enough."

Her eyes sparkled like dusky diamonds.

"Warm! I'm roasting. Isn't this a goregous night? You do think of the grandest things to do, Mister Kilburn. There hasn't been so much snow in Washington within the memory of the oldest inhabitant, one of the Senators told me. The Antarctic explorers have discovered that the poles exercise an influence on world weather. The same poles must have mixed signals to have sent such a storm here. Where are we going?"

"The usual sight-seeing round. Lady, we are now passing the Pan American Building, the most beautiful building in the world, each pillar of which stands for a Latin-American Country," he explained in the sing-song of the professional guide.

"You're miscast, Jeff. Instead of being an engineer you should be driving a rubber-neck bus. You'd make a fortune in tips."

"That's an idea. If you forget to tip me when we get back to the house I'll remind you."

He cleared his voice. He must watch his step. Eve's nearness, following his fury as he had watched Alvarez bending over her, was threatening to wreck the apparently friendly campaign he had planned to win her love. It had almost toppled when she had pressed her lips to his cheek. Love. He couldn't doubt after their talk in the boudoir that he had it—of sorts—but it wasn't the kind he wanted or meant to have.

"See the skaters on Mirror Lake, Jeff! The air is so still I can hear the hiss of steel. I'll bring Court here after office hours tomorrow. That boy needs exercise. Something will blow up if he isn't allowed more freedom. I don't know much about children, but I know that. His 'Ho! Ho!'s,' his grip of my wrist, his shout, 'Come with me damsel!' are getting on even my iron nerves. Stop the roadster. I want to look up at the Lincoln Memorial. How the warm, amber light floods the white columns and gilds the shadows!

"That's the way I feel too," she confided softly as Kilburn took off his hat. "There is something about The Great Emancipator enshrined there that makes my heart go down on its knees, even when we are as far away as we are now. I have a theory that every person in the United States should spend at least two weeks of each year in Washington. They would be a lot better citizens if they did. Thirty-six columns for thirty-six states. This country has grown some since President Lincoln's day. I hate to leave, but we'd better go on if we are to get home before we are missed."

They were silent as they drove through the snowy streets

and approached the long hills which were dotted and dashed with toboggans. Shouting, laughing coasters shot down on their sleds and trudged up dragging them.

"It's such a grand night, let's run down to Mount Vernon."

Kilburn's suggestion broke the spell of silence. Eve straightened and pulled the glittering turban low on her hair.

"I was almost asleep. I have been on the jump from one thing to another since seven this morning. It's heavenly to be alone with you in this marvelous air. I hate to be a spoilsport but we must go home before the guests leave. Isn't the flood-lighted, snow-crowned dome of the Capitol magnificent against the dark sky? Not so dark either when it is 'a twinklin' an' a shinin' with stars like it was all buttoned up wid brass buttons.' That's old Reub's flight of fancy, not mine. I wonder if he is keeping Bingo from missing me. I hated to leave that Boston behind but Aunt Dorinda won't have a dog in the house."

"Let's run down to Boxwood in the morning and call on him."

"Just like that. This seems to be 'run-down' evening with you, Jeff. You forget that I'm a working woman. I haven't time to play around with an idle young man."

"Meaning?"

"You. You haven't told me a word about the South American trip. Were you successful with Uncle Jock's business?"

"Yes, that came out all right. About the trip, well, the continent below is booming. It not only has been buying and selling more, it is manufacturing more. Argentina is turning its hides into shoes; Southern Chile is making furniture and paper from its forests; Brazil's cotton is feeding her textile industries and Venezuela's oil wells have been spouting 2,000,000 barrels a month. Asleep?"

"I am not asleep, Jeff. I'm tremendously interested. If Uncle Jock's business is finished, what are you doing in Washington?"

"Did I say it was finished? I may have to go to South America again, and rather soon, too. What am I doing in Washington? Business, Kiddo, business. I have opened an office here. I'm giving expert engineering advice to one of the Commissions, and of course, there's a lady mixed up in the reason for my staying. I'm sold on Washington for the winter. I shall keep my residence at Brick Ends—I wouldn't give up my voting privilege for the most perfect city in the world—but this place is the Nation's brain from which thoughts radiate to every part of the Union. I have no axes to grind and I'll have plenty of work. I have taken an apartment. José arrived yesterday and Snack was sent up from Boxwood."

"Really, Jeff? That's priceless. Now, I'll tell my news. I had intended to let it burst on you like a bomb when you received an invitation to a preview. I have an apartment! It's in a charming old house, with a lift which you run yourself, one of the kind that won't work if the door is left open a crack, sounds prehistoric, doesn't it? I'm moving in tomorrow."

"What! Where?"

"Don't snap my head off. Why shouldn't I be on my own, Mister Kilburn? I have lived in another person's house all my life, except when I was at school, then there was a secret service man parked next door—Uncle Jock's lawyer discovered that my fortune had grown to three millions before it put on its vanishing act—now that I'm no longer in the millionaire class, I'm not worth kidnaping. I can do what I like and believe me, I'll do it. Life, liberty and the pursuit of happiness, will be my battle cry. When I think of my freedom I feel like climbing up to one of those aluminum sea-gulls poised on the top of the Marine Memorial, standing on its back and caroling the Star Spangled Banner."

"Has it been as bad as that?"

"Bad! How would you like to be kept in a strait jacket of restraint? I know how Court feels inside when he lets out one of those ear-splitting yells. If I had had more freedom I wouldn't have made that—that insane proposition to you—and—"

"We've agreed to forget that, haven't we, Eve? You are free, white and twenty-one now. Quite free."

She pressed her head against his sleeve.

"Jeff, you're a dear. I don't know how I lived all these last months without you to talk to. Look out! You almost hit that hydrant."

" 'Smoke in my eyes' probably. I don't like the idea of you living alone."

"But I won't live alone. Remember Annie, the parlor maid with the hatchet chin at Uncle Scrip's? She's coming. She can cook—I can't, never was allowed to try—and I'm to have Bingo, and my Colonial pieces, some of them, which were in the living room at Uncle Scrip's. The apartment is in a building Uncle Jock owns. I suspect that he bought out a tenant that I might have it. I won't have much left for clothes when the rent and my living are paid for, but I'm too happy to mind that. Think of it! A place all my own, and I'm earning it! Can you imagine anything more perfect?"

"I can, but I haven't time to tell you now. Here we are at the house."

"We'll steal in, Jeff, so they won't know we've been away."

In the great hall Kilburn started to lift the ermine coat from her shoulders, brought his hands down on them instead.

"Eve."

She looked up at him.

"Goodness, you're white. Did that hydrant give you the jitters?"

"No. It's about that tip. Think I earned one?"

"Getting mercenary in your old age, aren't you—"

A trumpet call interrupted. A second was followed by the challenge;

"Ho! Ho! Sir Knight. I will cast thee down like thy fellows!"

The shout from the landing was followed by a deafening clatter as a figure in chain armor plunged down the stairs. Clink! Clatter! Creak! Clang! Crash! It hit the suit of plate armor at the foot and flung it down with a rattle and boom that brought the host and guests pell-mell from the card room. A woman screamed. Moya flung herself at Kilburn and hid her face against his breast.

"A bomb! Jeff! Jeff! It sounded like a plane crashing!"

At the foot of the stairs Jock Holden, with Vera Skinner beside him, looked in speechless fury from the mass of iron and steel to the boy on the landing.

Court grinned, waved a tin trumpet. Declaimed;

"Sire, being thy son I am assuredly winning much glory for our house this day. Have I not overthrown and cast down two right valiant Knights?"

He looked at Lady Hyatt, who with her arms about Jefferson Kilburn's neck was sobbing wildly against his shoulder.

"What is this that mine eyes behold? Yon fair dame is swooning with terror."

"Go to your room, Court!" Jock Holden's voice was rough with fury.

"I will do so with all speed, Sire."

Eve ran up the stairs and caught the boy's arm.

"Come along, quick, Court."

He looked back.

"Gee, Eve, I guess my little joke wasn't so funny as I thought. Jeff's girl cracked up and Skinny looks scared stiff. I'm sorry about her but perhaps it will cure her of holding hands with that South American smoothie."

"With Señor Alvarez?"

Eve was hurrying Court along the corridor, always with

her head over her shoulder to see if his father were following.

"Sure. They were in the hall whispering to beat the band just before you and Jeff Kilburn came in. Thought they'd never go and give me a chance to shoot old chain mail down the stairs."

"Did you hear what they said?"

"I heard her say, 'better keep your eye on Kilburn. He has something up—' Then someone came to the door and asked them to sit in on the game and they vamoosed. I don't see why Skinny runs round with that gigolo. She's too good for him."

Eve stopped at the door of the boy's room.

"Hustle to bed, Court. I hope this escapade will be worth all you'll have to take, my valiant Knight."

"I'm going! I'll be seeing you." He stuck his head from the doorway.

"Sst! Eve! Kinder feel as if my little joke didn't make the grade. Do you think Pop's mad?"

"Mad! Your Sire is probably shaking with wild laughter at this minute and thinking what a cunning little boy he has, of the glory he has brought to this house. That's sarcasm, in the manner of King Arthur, in case you care. Go to bed, Court. Quick. I'll do my best to head your father off tonight."

Eve stopped on the landing to look down into the great hall. Women guests in ravishing wraps were saying goodnight to their hostess, who with colorless face and set smile was responding to their assurances that it had been a perfect evening. Jeff and Moya were still standing together.

Eve remembered the jerk of his head, the swift flame of color, his sharp "Don't!" when she had pressed her lips to his cheek in apology. He hadn't jerked it back when Moya had flung her arms about his neck.

He's going without stopping to say good-night to me, she thought bitterly. Moya certainly knows all the tricks.

She reached the foot of the stairs in time to hear Vera Skinner challenge shrilly;

"Now, perhaps you'll dare send that kid away to school, Jock. He's being ruined here."

"So good of you to be interested in our boy, Miss Skinner," conceded Dorinda Holden behind her, "but neither the Senator nor I need your advice. Good-night."

xiii

In her flora printed frock of a soft new orange, Eve snuggled into a deep chair in the spacious living room of her apartment. Squatting on the dark blue rug beside it the Boston regarded her with big round eyes. He sniffed a reminder. She dropped the newspaper with its spine-shivering headlines.

"Hinting for an invitation, Mr. Bingo? Too much of a gentleman, aren't you, to force yourself in. Come!"

The dog jumped into the chair and squeezed down beside her. She stroked his head.

"Let's talk over the house-warming, Bing. Some party, wasn't it? Small but choice with the Senator and Aunt Dorinda and Court and the Colonel and Señor Alvarez and Seth Ramsdell. Ooch, but my slippers are tired!"

She stretched out gold-kid encased feet.

"Not surprising that they are, is it Bingy? I've spent almost every moment during the last two weeks—when I haven't been in the office—getting this apartment settled. I've been up since dawn this morning preparing for the party. I took time out for church, only. I'm going to church Sunday mornings, if I do nothing else during the day, funny-face. The service is like wings under my spirits. It starts the week right. The text this morning was like a crystal clear tide flowing over my mind, clearing it of unrest, 'Be still and know that I am God.' For an instant I had the curious feeling that the world was holding its breath.

"That's like me, isn't it, Bingo? Imagination plus. This room was made for my furniture, it is so old-timey in its size, and the ceilings are so high. Even the baby grand piano Uncle Jock contributed, doesn't crowd it. It belongs to the pre-code age, when residents of Washington had leisure for gracious living. Perhaps the ghost of a lovely lady steals out on the balcony to watch for her lover."

Her hand moved slowly back and forth across the dog's head as she looked around the room. Light from priceless pieces of Ming which had been made into lamps accentuated the satin finish of old-time wood-work, brightened the blue of the damask hangings drawn across the long windows, and deepened the rosy glow of the sunset in the Inness hung in the panel above the fireplace. She had had to borrow vases for the flowers which had been sent by her guests. She would send Annie to the New England storehouse to select more of her belongings. She tweaked the dog's ear.

"Don't go to sleep, Bing, I want to talk. Aren't those yellow roses perfect against the blue hangings? And those long stemmed crimson ones look like Señor Eduardo Enrique Alvarez, don't they? Jeff sent me those gorgeous white lilacs, pink tulips and yellow and violet freesias. Why do you suppose he didn't come? Moya wasn't here either. That's funny. I hadn't missed her before. Hear the guitar! Maybe it is the lover of the ghost-lady serenading her. The music is faint, but it can't be far away. Radio, of course. Makes me feel as if I were back at Uncle Scrip's with José playing in Jeff's garden."

Annie stepped into the room.

"All right if I go out, Miss? There's plenty in the icebox for your supper. The cook at the Senator's asked me to go to church and then have a bite with her and the other servants."

"Of course, Annie. Poke up the fire before you go, will you?"

As the maid knelt on the hearth-rug, Eve asked;

"Does—does church mean a lot to you, Annie?"

The woman sank back on her heels and looked up in surprise.

"Sure it does, Miss. If I've done something I know ain't right and I go to confession, unless it's something too bad to forget, I feel all right and light-hearted when I come away. You seem kind of sober. Got something on your mind troublin' you, Miss?"

"Yes. Have you ever had a splinter so deep in your finger that you couldn't see it, yet felt it every time you moved your hand? I've got something like that stuck in my mind."

"Ain't there nobody—I know you don't belong to my church, so you wouldn't do what I'd do—but ain't there nobody you can talk it out to, Miss?"

"No, Annie. There is no one but myself who can advise me, and I won't listen to my own advice."

Annie rose from her knees and sniffed.

"You ain't the only one as won't listen. It would be a good job if somebody advised Mrs. Holden to take that boy of hers over her knee and spank some sense into him."

"Court? Did he bother you this afternoon? He asked if he might go into the kitchenette. I said yes, because I thought he might help."

"Help, is it?" Annie went completely Irish. "Help, the saints preserve us! He had some kind of a quare key he was trying in the doors. He got two of 'em locked so tight I had to call the janitor up to open 'em."

"I'm sorry, Annie. Court's a dear, he doesn't mean to make trouble, but his curiosity complex works overtime. Go out the front door. That back exit is pokey. Did you pay the woman who came in to help with the dishes?"

"I did, Miss. She was real friendly. She's a sister of the caretaker of this house and what she don't know about the people who live here ain't worth knowing. I guess from what she said the woman on the top floor is a fusser. Nothing ever quite suits her. She says a new young man, handsome as a movie actor, has rented the apartment under this."

"How exciting! Run along and have a good time. You've earned it today. I'm sorry Court bothered you."

"But I liked the party, Miss Eve, and I didn't mind the boy, much. You look tired. You haven't set down today. Shan't I bring you a tray before I go?"

"No, thanks, it will be fun to forage when I'm hungry."

"I'll set the chocolate I made for you on the back of the range. You won't be wanting it right off."

Annie picked up the newspaper and squinted near-sighted eyes at the black headlines which shrieked across the front page.

"Sure, that was a terrible disaster at sea, Miss. Lot of people drowned."

"There were, Annie, but did you read of the boy clinging to the plank who was rescued? Time after time he thought he would have to let go, he was so cold and exhausted, and each time he said to himself, 'Not yet! Not yet!' He belongs to the unstampedables. What is there about some persons that keeps them hanging on, that won't let them give up? They are always rescued."

"Grit, Miss Eve, grit, an' knowin' so long as they hold on, there's always a chance of pullin' through, an' if they give up they're done for anyway."

"Snap out the lamps, please."

The golden gloom shed by two candles on the mantel, the glow from the fire gave a touch of enchantment to the hushed, fragrant room.

Eve nestled deeper into the chair. At last she was on her own. My party! My apartment! My maid! My fire, she exulted. Her mood changed. Why had she asked Annie about church? That question was easily answered. Because all day, beneath her exciting absorption in preparation for her snack party, she had been as aware of Jeff as if he had been present, had been guiltily conscious that she was living a lie. Her marriage was the splinter stuck deep in her mind. She had brought it on herself. Uncle Jock had said: "It's a great world to the valiant." If, instead of making a mad break for freedom that afternoon in Jeff's library, she had, like the boy clinging to the plank, held on for only a few hours more, she would have known that she was free to come and go as she liked, and she wouldn't have messed up Jeff's life. The fact that she had ached to comfort him and help him over his heart-break about Moya didn't excuse her.

Only one thing to do for him now, Reno in June. She loathed the very thought of it, but what else could she do?

He wouldn't ask for his freedom. Freedom! Was there such a thing? She hadn't seen him since the night, two weeks ago, when he had left the Holdens' with Lady Hyatt. Of course he had meant Moya when he had said that there was a lady mixed up in his reason for staying in Washington. His name had been in the newspaper list of guests at many social functions. He must be popular. Why not, he was rich, cultured, entertaining and most important of all, an eligible bachelor—so far as anyone knew.

She watched the burning logs crumble and send scarlet and gold flames up the chimney. The flickering light threw rose and crimson shadows on the white walls, then died and left them a pearly gray.

Hard to keep her drowsy eyes open after that glare of light. To whom was Annie talking? Had the woman who knew everything about everybody come back? After all, what difference did it make if Annie's friends called for her at the front door? She was a jewel, and could she cook? She could.

"Some day when I've forgotten that living picture of Jeff with the fascinating Lady Hyatt hanging round his neck, I'll plan a dinner and invite him and show him what a housekeeper I am, Bingo. I'll-do-it-next—"

Curious. Had she dreamed that she was in Washington? She wasn't. She was in Uncle Scrip's house. She was coming down the broad stairs in her stiff yellow satin frock with her arms full of mimosa, stopping on every other step to keep time to the rhythmic beat of the wedding march.

"Here comes the bride. Here comes the bride."

It was Moya's wedding. She could hear the swish of the bride's white satin gown behind her. The last stair. She looked back. Moya wasn't there. It was her own train she heard. She was the bride. It was her wedding. Whom was she marrying? She could see his back as he stood in the living room waiting for her. He turned. Alvarez! With a red rose as big as a cabbage in his coat lapel. His eyes were great yellow and black glass bulbs. Tiger eyes. How they glared! How they flamed! She dropped her flowers—calla lilies now—as he came toward her.

"No! No! No!" she cried. She tried to run. She couldn't move.

"Eve! Eve! Darling!"

That wasn't Alvarez' voice. She looked up. She sprang to her feet and flung her arms about Jefferson Kilburn's neck.

"Jeff! Jeff! It's you! The relief of it! I thought—I thought I was being married to Alvarez!"

She shivered uncontrollably and drew a sobbing breath.

His arms tightened about her. He laid his cheek against hers. With tender mockery he accused;

"Sleepy-head! You've been dreaming."

She shuddered.

"It was ter—terribly real, Jeff."

He lightly smoothed her hair.

"It's over now, Kiddo. You don't think I'd let you marry Alvarez, do you? Not a chance."

She freed herself from his arms and snapped on the lamps.

"Light will send that dream packing. I've never had quite such a nightmare before. How did you get here in time, Jeff, to play Young Lochinvar and snatch me from the altar, as it were?"

Her eyes were laughing, but her voice was still unsteady.

"Annie was departing in her war-paint just as I reached the door. I came in and found you asleep. Sat down at the piano. The Wedding March hummed through my mind and I played softly so that I wouldn't waken you."

"Then that part of my dream was real. Thank heaven it was the only part."

"What's the idea leaving you alone?"

"Alone! Why shouldn't I be alone? Besides I wasn't. Bingo was here."

"A grand watch-dog, he is. When I came into the room he poked up his head, yawned at me, and snuggled down again."

"Did you expect he would eat you? He doesn't give you credit for having brains, does he, funny-face? He knows that you are one of the family, Jeff. Thanks for those marvelous lilacs and tulips and freesias. Why didn't you come to my party, Mister Kilburn?"

"Couldn't get here. I haven't had a chance before to give you something I brought you from South America. Hold out your left arm."

Eve put her hands behind her.

"You—you mustn't give me presents, Jeff."

"I mustn't give you presents! How long since that rule, or whatever you call it, was put on the books? Have I ever come home from a trip without bringing you a present? Don't be foolish. Hold out your left hand and close your eyes."

His fingers against her wrist sent prickles along her veins.

"All right, look!"

She caught her breath as she saw the bracelet on her arm. Blue moonstones set in silver linked by circlets of diamonds.

"Jeff! How exquisite!"

"Like it?"

"It's perfect. It's like moonlight and stars. But, Jeff—"

He interrupted;

"I like your frock. Going in for yellow in a big way, aren't you? It suits you. I'm no interior decorator but this room is a little bit of all right to me. You haven't crowded it. Not much like that museum in which the Holdens are living. Were they here this afternoon?"

Eve dragged fascinated eyes from the bracelet.

"Everyone was here except you and Moya. But of course I don't have to tell you that."

"Did Court come? Thought perhaps he would be kept locked up on bread and water for a while after pitching that armor down stairs."

"He was here. He has deserted the Age of Chivalry. His sleuth complex is working overtime at present. He came plus the skeleton key, he acquired, I suspect, from one of the stable boys at Boxwood. He made life merry for Annie with it in the kitchenette, where I weakly let him go to get him out of this room. I felt as if he were walking over a slumbering volcano here. There was something in Uncle Jock's eyes when he looked at his son and heir which gave me the shivers."

"The boy will be spoiled if he isn't disciplined. That crashing armor might have frightened someone to death. Did Alvarez and Ramsdell come to your party?"

"Of course. I didn't ask any other young people. This housewarming was for the older ones."

"That the reason I was invited?"

"Don't be foolish. Sometimes you're the very youngest person I know, Jeff. I'm starving."

"Come out with me for supper."

"No, I've been looking forward for years to having a kitchenette where I could get my own. Coming to help me forage?"

"Try and stop me!"

The words were like a charge of electricity through Eve's mind. She had flung them at him that afternoon in her Uncle's library after—after he had kissed her. Did he remember?

She glanced at him from under her lashes. No, he was tapping the ashes from his pipe, he had just happened to say them, that was all. He looked up.

"Why are you staring at me as if you'd never seen me before?"

"I didn't realize that I was. Open that small table and set it in front of the fire, Jeff. We'll bring the chocolate and snacks here. Come, Bingo, and get your supper."

Later as she and Kilburn sat side by side on the couch she set down her cup with a long sigh of satisfaction.

"Heavenly, isn't it, being on my own and having a boy friend here for supper?"

"Nice for the boy friend. Planning to do much of that?"

"Much of what?"

"Supper for two."

"I hope so, but it will have to be Sunday nights. The rest of the week is so full. I don't accept half of the invitations I receive, but I have to go out some. I hear that an exciting young man has rented the apartment under this. 'Handsome as a movie actor' Annie reports. Perhaps I'll meet him then I can ask him to supper. Why don't you smoke, Jeff?"

"Will you?"

She thoughtfully regarded the open cigarette case he offered.

"Would you like me better if I did?"

"No."

"Then I won't, as I don't care for it. Why follow the herd? It isn't that I think smoking wrong—I love to see a man and his wife who look as if they had been comrades for years, smoking together. There's the house phone."

"I'll answer."

Kilburn spoke into the telephone.

"Miss Travis' apartment—Who?—Say that she can't see him. She is dressing to go out to supper."

Eve, with a cup and saucer in each hand demanded:

"Who was calling?"

"Señor Eduardo Enrique Alvarez."

"Why did you tell him I was going out?"

Her indignation was somewhat denatured by the memory of bulging yellow and black glass eyes.

"Because you are, with me. I'm taking you out for a breath of air in the roadster. You've been in this stuffy apartment all day."

"It isn't a stuffy apartment and I haven't been here all day and we'll have it understood right now, that you are not to answer calls to this room and say whom I will see and won't see, Jeff Kilburn. Who is knocking?"

She frowned at the door. Kilburn stepped forward to open it. She reached it first.

"You might say that I was not at home," she flung over her shoulder, and opened the door.

"Why, Moya!"

xiv

MOYA, Lady Hyatt, floated into the room.

"Don't tell me that I'm too late for your party, Eve, precious! Sorry, but people kept dropping in to detain me though I was dying to get here."

She glanced from Kilburn standing motionless, back to the fire, to the partially cleared table, then at Eve. She laughed, her cooing laugh.

"Precious, this room is simply divine. May I have something to eat? I'm starving. You wouldn't turn your cousin—even if she is only a cousin by marriage—out to starve, would you? Jeff, help me with my coat. Hope you're not tired of seeing it, I've worn it every afternoon you and I have been together for the last two weeks."

Kilburn did not move. His eyes were on Eve. She said crisply;

"Take the lady's coat, Mister Kilburn. New, isn't it, Moya? I adore black caracul, it's perfect for widow's mourning. Jeff must have been thrilled to beau you around in anything so swank. Of course you may have something to eat. There's lots of cold party left, in spite of the fact that Court Holden was one of the guests. Sometimes I suspect that boy is hollow from his toes up. I'll take out these cups and bring hot chocolate for you."

"Why did she have to come?" Eve fumed under her breath, as in the kitchenette she arranged tomato and anchovy-canapes, mushroom sandwiches and bits of smoked salmon on wafers of toast, with Bingo watching her in absorbed attention. Had Jeff been waiting for Moya? If he had, he hadn't moved like a ball of fire when she had ordered him to take her coat. Imagine dictating to Jeff. One might as well try to push over the Washington Monument.

She filled a slender silver pot with hot chocolate and added it, with a cup and saucer of eggshell delicacy, to the tray. She looked at the bracelet on her arm, unclasped it and laid it carefully in the drawer of the table. "That will save answering a lot of questions," she said aloud. "Moya has the eyes of a ferret."

Kilburn banged open the swing door.

"Give me that." He took the laden tray from her hands. "Why did you ask her to stay?" he demanded furiously.

"I ask her! That's the joke of the week. I couldn't very well turn her out when you had been waiting here hours and hours for her, could I?"

"No, I suppose you couldn't when I had been waiting 'hours and hours.' Sorry the time seemed so long to you. Hold that confounded door open, will you? It's likely to swing back and hit this tray."

Eve laughed. The memory of his furious "Why did you ask her to stay?" was like wings under her spirit. If he were terribly in love with Moya he wouldn't have said that.

"Funny that a man never can do anything alone," she flouted. "Ask him to help and he has to have someone hold the tacks, or tell him if the picture is straight, or put a finger on the cord if he is tying a package. Annie carries that tray through by herself every day."

Kilburn grinned engagingly. "But I'm not Annie. I'm high-priced help, you won't know how high-priced until you come to pay me for my services. Perhaps I'd better collect a payment on account now, prec—"

"Jeff Kilburn, don't you dare call me that. If Moya does again, I'll throw something at her, preferably something that smashes. Do you realize that we are keeping a starving female waiting?"

"Let's go. Be a good sport and hold that door open will you, Kiddo?"

"With pleasure, Mister. You can't come, Bingo."

Moya looked more doll than woman as she sat in the deep chair in which Eve had dozed a short time before. The firelight cast rosy shadows on her face, tinted the pearls about her white throat, deepened the violet of her eyes to pansy purple. She pouted carmined lips.

"Doesn't Eve keep a maid that you had to help, Jeff? You've been gone ages."

"It's evident that you are not a housekeeper, Moya. If you were, you would know that Sunday is the maid's evening out," Eve explained, as she placed a Chinese teapoise beside the deep chair. "Set the tray on this. Doesn't Jeff buttle superbly? Quite as if he had done nothing else all his life."

"Perhaps you'd like to engage me permanently Mrs.—Miss Travis?" Kilburn suggested smoothly.

"That chocolate smells delicious. Do set the tray down, Jeff. You and Eve are always having your little jokes, aren't you? As if you were sharing a secret." Lady Hyatt's voice confirmed its prophecy of peevishness.

"Our secrets are not always a joke, are they, Eve?"

The gravity of his question sent Eve's heart to her throat, her eyes to his. Her cheeks grew warm. He wouldn't tell—

"I won't," he said aloud as if by some curious telepathic transmission he knew what she was thinking.

"What are you two talking about?" Lady Hyatt demanded. "This chocolate is divine, but it isn't quite sweet enough. Will you bring me some sugar, Eve, precious?"

"I'll get it."

"You don't know where it is, Jeff. I'll go."

In the kitchenette Eve took her time finding the sugar. Of course Moya didn't want it, she was too afraid of losing her size-sixteen figure to touch sweets. If she put on flesh she would look like a ball which would roll either way. What she wanted was to have Jeff to herself. She could have him. Couldn't he see what a lightweight she was? Why were men so dumb when it came to a blonde? Apparently he had helped with that black caracul coat for the last two weeks. Well, as had been said before, Moya could have him.

This was a grand chance to wash great-grandmother's egg-shell cups and saucers she and Jeff had used. Lovely things. They must have been tenderly handled to have come down through the years unchipped and unbroken. She placed them in the cabinet. That was that. What next? Back to her guests? She couldn't dawdle round the kitchenette forever. After all, it was her living room. If Jeff and Moya wanted to be alone together they could go somewhere else.

She shook her head at the Boston who, with ears pricked, was regarding her with big round eyes.

"Don't look so grieved, Bingo. Moya doesn't like dogs—you'd know to look at her she wouldn't—the moment she goes, I'll come and get you, funny-face. Bye-bye!"

On the threshold of the living room she stopped abruptly. Moya, Lady Hyatt, was kneeling and holding out rosy tipped hands to the fire. She was gazing up at Kilburn who, with arm on the mantel, was looking down at her. She complained;

"Jeff, their conversation was so highbrow—all about policies and politics—that I just managed to tread water that was all. Mrs. Holden is always in the Senate gallery when a debate is on. Of course, she is beautiful—if one cares for her type—but men don't like her. She's too intellectual. Men don't really like women—Eve, precious, how you startled me, stealing across the room like that. Jeff and I had forgotten you were in the world."

"I never forget that Eve is in the world, Moya," Kilburn contradicted. "Don't touch that tray, Kiddo. I'll take it out for you later. Moya drank her chocolate without more sugar as you can see."

Lady Hyatt held out a hand.

"Help me up, Jeff. I must go. I'm due for supper at one of the Legations. I was asked to bring you, and I promised I would, though I told the hostess that you were literally snowed-under with invitations. That's what you get for being a rich, fascinating bachelor in the Nation's Capital."

She looked up and leaned against him as he held her coat. He had been quick to pick it up. Was he anxious to get away with her, Eve wondered. She reminded dryly;

"I'm still here, Moya."

Lady Hyatt laughed and blushed in pretty confusion.

"Of course you are, precious. Jeff and I—"

"Is your car waiting, Moya?"

"It is, Jeff. My chauffeur is a treasure, but you wouldn't have hired him for me if he hadn't been, would you? I don't know what I would do without Jeff to advise me, Eve. I consult him about everything. He's like a great big brother. You should have seen him block Señor Alvarez when he tried to be devoted on the ship coming from South America. Poor man, he has such romantic eyes. I was inclined to be nice to him. I've loved your little party, precious, it's been divine. Sorry to take Jeff away, but he's my No. 1 man for festivities, such quiet little festivities as a widow in deep mourning may attend. Good-bye!"

Kilburn held the door open suggestively. As she stepped into the hall he spoke to Eve.

"I'm coming back."

"Don't trouble. You're not my No. 1 man, you know, I don't consult you about everything," she reminded.

He needn't come back, she told herself as she carried the silver tray to the kitchenette. She took the bracelet from the table drawer, regarded it thoughtfully, and clasped it about her wrist.

"Come on, funny-face." She knelt and put her arm around the dog. "You love me, don't you Bingo?"

She paused in surprise as she entered the living room.

"I thought you'd gone!"

"You heard me say I was coming back." Kilburn flung a log on the fire.

"You didn't come to help me, I hope. I don't need you."

"You don't have to tell me that, Eve, but you can help me."

"Help you, Jeff? What's the matter?"

"Nothing to make you as frightened as you look. I mean you can help me resist temptation until—"

He poked the fire till the wood blazed.

Eve's eyes traveled from the Ming lamps to the damask hangings shrouding the long windows, to the glowing sunset above the mantel, to Bingo in his basket, on to the man standing back to the fire. Was he trying to tell her that Moya was a temptation, that it was better for him not to be with her much until after his marriage had been annulled? The thought hurt intolerably. Moya was such a, such a moron!

"I understand, Jeff. Cheerio. Love conquers all," she encouraged and hated herself for her flippancy.

"Do you understand? I wonder. Someone is rapping."

"How do people get in downstairs without ringing my bell first?" Eve protested indignantly. The indignation was a vent for her emotions. She opened the door. Vera Skinner faced her, her eyes big with incredulity.

"Why, Miss Travis! Think of finding you here! Are you calling on Lila?"

She glanced at Kilburn standing back to the fire and brought her thin hands together in a gesture of surprise.

"Isn't this Lila Glenn's apartment or am I dreaming?"

"This is my apartment," Eve corrected with the dignity becoming a young woman for the first time in her life on her own. "Be quiet, Bingo."

Miss Skinner retreated a step before the furiously barking dog. She achieved the not easy feat of keeping one eye on him and one on Eve as she conceded;

"Stupid of me, wasn't it? Lila's apartment is the one under this, of course."

"Wrong again," Kilburn corrected. "I have rented that."

Eve regarded Miss Skinner with the expression a woman's face takes on when she is politely waiting for a caller to depart. She even tried to hurry the departure by suggesting:

"Doubtless you will find your friend in another part of the building."

Vera Skinner's laugh was as sharp as her thin features.

"Another part of the building! My dear child, I occupy the suite above this and a superannuated invalid is the tenant on the ground floor. I didn't know that Lila had moved. If I haven't found her, I have found something else. You seem to have changed your mind about going out, Miss Travis. I'll tell Señor Alvarez, who is in my living room, that you are at home. Good-night."

Bang went the door. Eve looked at it before she returned to the small table.

"This seems to be just one of those days, doesn't it? If Miss Skinner didn't know that I was living here how did she know that Alvarez had been told that I was going out? I wonder what Uncle Jock had up his sleeve when he put me in the house with her. He told me once that Aunt Dorinda accused him of everlastingly trying to manage other people's lives. Is he trying to manage mine? Don't stand there staring into space, Jeff, as if a Gorgon-eyed female had turned you to stone. I'll take out these dishes. Please put away the table."

She returned to the room with the dog trotting at her heels. At the window she parted one of the long hangings.

"Perfect night. Isn't the Dipper clear? Scientists say that it is breaking up, that the middle five of its seven stars are moving out of it at the rate of ten miles a second, but that it will be 50,000 years before we'll miss them. This long, tree-fringed avenue has developed just as L'Enfant planned, hasn't it? There's magic in the moonlight on the city. Hear the church bells calling the faithful. The dome of the Capitol looks as if it had been carved from a mammoth pearl. Are you really living in this house, Jeff?"

"I am. I'm the exciting young man who has rented the apartment below this. You would have known it if you hadn't been absorbed in getting settled. You may find me useful—in case of nightmares. Come away from that window, I want to talk to you."

Eve faced him and clenched her hands behind her.

"I've something to say to you first. Is your living in this house a keep-an-eye-on-Eve movement? If it is, just understand that I will not be watched. You have dictated to me all my life. I'm on my own now. If you have taken that apartment to—"

"Wait a minute! You're confusing the issue, as they say in Court. You know that from a slow moving village Washington has swelled to a crowded teeming city, fairly bulging with people who have jobs or who have come here to stay until they put across a program, scheme or have succeeded in getting a code modified. It is almost an impossibility to find a place to live. When Senator Holden told me that one of his tenants was planning a round-the-world tour if he could sublet, I snapped up the apartment."

"Didn't you know I was coming here?"

"I did not when I hired it. When you told me the other night that you had rented a suite in a house owned by the Senator, I suspected it. When I received that swanky card from you inviting me to a snack party, of course I knew."

"Why haven't you told me before?"

"We all put off an unpleasant task. I knew you wouldn't like the arrangement. Get this, if I had the choice I would prefer not to live in the same building with you, but—" the doorbell rang.

"Shall I answer it?"

Eve whispered;

"It must be Alvarez." She shivered. "That dream still haunts me. Let's not move and he'll go away."

Kilburn laid his arm across her shoulders and held her beside him. He reminded in a low voice;

"I told you that you might find the exciting young man in the apartment below useful. Let's gumshoe down the service stairs and go for a walk. It's a grand night."

XV

MONDAY morning! Spring in the air. A hurdy-gurdy in the street. It was that kind of a day.

Eve looked back at the house she had left, an old, brownstone house, fallen from its once aristocratic estate into apartments. It was a pity that the decorative balconies and wrought iron trellises on the back weren't visible from the street.

She curbed a ridiculous impulse to throw a kiss to it. At last she was a girl on her own. She was happy this morning. Jeff had been his old friendly self last evening. They had stolen down the back stairs, out the service door. The soft winter night had dropped around them like curtains of purple velvet mellowed with a golden glow where street lights penetrated. They had walked and walked, not talking much. They had passed the White House. The light from its many windows warmed even the shadows under the trees. They had watched the play of light and shade on Washington Monument, had seen the aluminum cap gleam like silver as the moon dodged from behind clouds. The questioning and unrest of which she was so deadly tired had been swept from her mind. She had been utterly content. When Jeff had left her at the door he said;

"You know where to find me when you want me, Eve. Burdened as he is with national affairs our Senator still has time to play casting-director. I'll say he has put on a pretty good show. The possibilities of drama in this house are something our old friend Shakespeare might have thought of to say nothing of the moderns. There's excitement in the air. Good-night."

Heavenly morning. Had the Senator planned to get Jeff and his former secretary and herself under one roof? If he had, why? Did he think that she might find out what Vera Skinner and Alvarez were planning? Could she? Her uncle knew that she would be eager to help if she could.

Gorgeous air! Scented with spring fragrance. She drew a deep breath of it. What a day for a canter through Rock Creek Park with its miles of bridle paths! The blue of the sky was almost sapphire, its depth illimitable; against it the government buildings shone like mother-of-pearl. It was a day when anything might happen, something adventurous if she were given a choice. Hadn't Jeff said that excitement was in the air?

"God's in His heaven and Eve Travis is on her own," she

paraphrased gleefully as she swung into the broad avenue which teemed with busses and street cars. It was crowded with Government employees on their way to work, queues of private cars en route to the Captiol and administration buildings, and hundreds of sightseers faring forth on pilgrimages. A boy passed whistling the latest song-hit. A plane thrummed overhead with silver wings rocking. So early were portions of the tourist bloc seeing Washington from the air. And behind all this stir and bustle lived the permanent residents in their sumptuous or modest homes who watched these birds of passage—if they saw them at all—with a mild, somewhat amused, aloofness.

With a little croon of pleasure Eve stopped before a flower shop. The sidewalk beneath the windows was banked with potted-plants. Ageratum by the lavender score; clumps of forget-me-nots; jonquils in glory; tulips, rose purple, white; hyacinths as blue as the sky above. Inside were templar roses, vases of crimson perfection; carnations, dozens of them; masses of sweetheart roses; iridescent glass bowls of purple violets; more bowls of orchid and salmon and scarlet sweet peas; freesias, yellow, white, pale amethyst; and afloat in a low black dish waxy pink japonicas. The door was flanked by mammoth orange pottery jars full of sprays of white lilac, blue iris and tall spikes of pink snapdragon. By the curb a [illegible]y painted cart was piled high with blossoms which a [illegible]y in Sicilian costume was selling.

Eve bought a single flower which matched to a tint her geranium color hat and bag.

"Perhaps it doesn't look businesslike," she thought as she pinned it to the jacket of her tailored navy blue wool suit, "but it goes with the day."

From a passing bus droned the voice of a guide;

"Straight ahead you see the Capitol Building. George Washington laid the corner stone with a silver trowel. It is one of the architectural triumphs of the world. Notice the massive dome with the bronze statue of Freedom on the top, the stately columns, its noble dignity."

Quite a burst of oratory for a guide, but even that didn't adequately express the beauty of the building looming against the cloudless sky, Eve thought, as she looked ahead to where Freedom split the heavens.

She stopped on the upper terrace of the Senate Office Building, from which she could look down upon the city. She could see the portico of Arlington House on the brow of a hill, a hill whose slope stretched half a mile to the placid Potomac. The blur of color was the Stars and Stripes floating from a staff before the house. Far away loomed the white tower of the Soldier's Home; toward the south the spires of Alexandria pricked the luminous sky.

Seth Ramsdell stopped her as she was passing through the outer room of Senator Holden's suite of offices. His brow was furrowed, his eyes were anxious.

"Any idea where we can get in touch with the Senator?" he asked. "He hasn't appeared nor sent a message. He's always at his desk by eight-thirty. Likes to get his correspondence out of the way before the job-hunters descend on him. There'll be the dickens to pay if he doesn't come today. His committee will break loose. The trouble-shooters are set to kill that bill of his."

"I don't know where he is. He didn't say yesterday afternoon that he wouldn't be here. Have you 'phoned Mrs. Holden?"

"'Phoned! She's incommunicado. I've done everything but break into her room. The only satisfaction I got from my calls was to be told that she cannot be disturbed. Is she sick?"

"I didn't know it. I'll go to the house during lunch hour—"

"Call for you, Miss Travis," the overblown blonde at the switch-board interrupted.

"I'll take it in my office," Eve answered.

It was only one more call for the Senator. She cradled the telephone. Where was he and why was his wife incommunicado? Had what had seemed a rift between them split into a ragged chasm of hatred? Was marriage bound to end in that? She wouldn't believe it. Marriages of that sort made the front pages, one heard nothing of the millions who carried on in dignity and beauty. Suppose she and Jeff Kilburn really were married, what would they have made of it?

She pushed her chair back impatiently. They weren't. Why should she spend a moment considering what might happen if they were? They were friends. Friendship was better than marriage. When Jeff's arms had closed about her after that hideous dream yesterday, she had felt that nothing could hurt her while he was near. She'd better get to work. There was one advantage in having the Senator away, she had more uninterrupted time. The switch-board girls turned calls over to Seth. She ought to file the reports on the gold mine. She knew now why José had been brought to Washington. The Senator had given her Jeff's note-book to file with the rest of the data. Did Alvarez really believe that the son of his father's one-time partner was dead or did he suspect that he was in hiding?

" 'Better keep your eyes on Kilburn's apartment.' "

Why should Vera Skinner's suggestion which Court had

overheard flash through her mind at this minute? Why hadn't she remembered to tell Jeff last night? It was a wonder that she had remembered anything after the surprise of hearing that he and the Skinner menace lived below and above her. Was her subconscious prodding her to warn him to keep José out of sight? He was right. The situation was drenched in drama. What a plot for a motion picture. That wasn't news. The air of Washington fairly buzzed and flared with motion picture plots.

"More work and less imagining, Miss Secretary." Eve reminded herself crisply.

As she laid a folder of papers on her desk, the door from the outer office was flung open. She sprang to her feet.

"Aunt Dorinda! Why are you here?"

Dorinda Holden closed the door and leaned against it as if she needed its support.

Her eyes look as if they'd been rubbed into her head with a dirty finger, Eve thought as she noted the heavy shadows. Aloud she urged;

"Do sit down. Do you want Uncle Jock? He hasn't come in yet."

Seated on the edge of a chair, Dorinda Holden clenched her hands in her lap. She made a desperate effort to steady her quivering lips.

"I know that, Eve. He's gone. He went after we left your party. He has taken Court away. They went in Jock's plane."

"Away! Where?"

"I don't know. You were at breakfast the morning after Court pushed the armor downstairs. You remember how angry his father was?"

Eve remembered. If she lived to be an hundred, she would never forget the expression of her uncle's face. She nodded.

"After you left the room, Jock told me that I had had my chance at bringing up our boy, that it was his turn now, that I was making a sissy of Court by coddling him."

Eve thought of the plunging, clanking, crashing suits of armor.

"No sissy could push over our chain-mail friend of the vintage of 1195 and live. Court, a sissy! That's the funniest thing I ever heard."

Color tinted Dorinda Holden's white face.

"Your gay little laugh helps me, Eve. I was sure you would feel that way about him. You know that Court can do anything other boys do, except football and baseball, and rough games like those. I think Jock has taken him to a school. It is more than two weeks since he threatened to and I thought he had forgotten. I should have known better. He never forgets. You don't think Court will be better off at school, do you?"

"Sorry not to agree with you, Aunt Dorinda, but, I do. He needs other boys with whom to compete and fight, if necessary. I was raised in a hot-house. I know what desperate lengths a person will go to smash a way out. Uncle Jock is doing it for Court's good. Can't you see that?"

"I wonder. Is he doing it for the boy or because Vera Skinner taunted him, 'Now perhaps you'll dare send the kid away to school, Jock!' "

She crossed to the window, came back and demanded passionately:

" 'Jock!' How dare she be so familiar before those Committee men and their wives? Jock was furious when he found that I had invited her to that dinner. I did it to show her that my clothes are not out of date, that I am not too highbrow to carry on socially for our Senator, and more important than my two silly personal reasons, to stop the whispers going the rounds that she and Jock were—were—"

"Perhaps she never had called him that before, Aunt Dorinda. Perhaps his name was jolted from her tongue by that fiendish crash. At least she didn't hang around his neck." Eve forcibly crushed down the memory of Jeff Kilburn with Moya clinging to him. "The clang and clatter gave me the jitters and you'll have to admit that I am not a jittery person. You just naturally dislike Vera Skinner, don't you? But you believe what Uncle Jock told you about the pearls?"

Mrs. Holden drew a silver fox cape closer about her shoulders.

"I believe him—because I want to. I love him. Some day you will find out, Eve, that the greatest proof of the reality of love is its invincibility against the battering of reason."

"In this case reason had better stop battering. If Uncle Jock were—were even foolish about Vera Skinner he wouldn't have me live in the same apartment house with her, would he? You know he wouldn't."

"You may be right, Eve. Perhaps, because of my miserable inferiority complex, I have made a nightmare out of a troubled dream. I don't know why I came to you with my anxiety, dear. I had to do something. I couldn't stay at home and wait and wait not knowing what had happened to my boy. If only I had answered Jock, when he accused me of spoiling Court. I couldn't. When I am deeply moved I freeze inside. I can't show what I feel. I set up a barrier and walk alone on one side of it and Jock walks on the other. Perhaps he doesn't walk alone. That's the tragedy of it. If it isn't Miss Skinner it may be—

"Jock! Where is he?"

She caught the arm of her husband as he entered the room. He pulled off his broad-brimmed black Stetson, and closed the door behind him.

"I handed you a rotten deal when I hustled Court away, 'Rinda," he admitted gravely, "but I knew that if I told you I was taking him to school, you would fight against it and I would give in as I have given in a dozen times before and let him stay at home to be coddled. I'm going home with you now. On the way I will tell you where the boy is."

He opened the door to the outer office, waited until his wife had left the room before he said to Eve;

"I'll be back in an hour. Round up the members of the appropriation committee. Tell them to be here at one sharp. That will give them an hour after Congress goes into session. After they assemble we are not to be disturbed by anything short of a call from the White House. Get that?"

The door banged. Eve felt as if an able-bodied cyclone had dumped her in the desk chair after having swept her along in its centre. Court in school! "Jock" had dared send "the kid" away! Aunt Dorinda had wrenched off her mask that Eve might know her as she was! It was incredible.

She shook herself mentally. Cyclone or no cyclone she must collect that committee.

She was telephoning when Seth Ramsdell entered with a bunch of papers in his hand. She smiled and nodded to him, then insisted crisply to the person at the other end of the line;

"You must get him, Miss Grant. In the Senate Chamber? You can't interrupt him!—You won't—all right, I will."

She snapped the instrument on its stand.

"That was Senator Cantor's snooty secretary, Seth. I've corralled all the others. She won't give him my message. I'll see that he gets it. Did you see our Senator?"

"Yes. Don't go with that message, Eve. I'll send a boy."

"Nothing doing. I may not have learned much but I have learned that when you want a thing done your way, do it yourself. I want Senator Cantor and I'm out to get him."

She knew that he followed her to the door of the outer office, but she wouldn't look back. Thoughts of him accompanied her as she hurried along the corridor to the elevator which led down to the underground railway which connected the Senate Office Building with the Capitol. Seth was becoming uncomfortably intense when they were together. She hated to hurt him, she liked him immensely but she didn't love him. Should she have stopped his pursuit of her long ago by telling him that she was married? The word still stuck in her throat. But she was so little married, and the slight bond between her and Jeff Kilburn would be broken so soon. Hadn't Jeff intimated last evening that waiting was becoming unendurable? No, she wouldn't tell him. She preferred to wear a hair-shirt over her conscience when she was with him.

At one of the doors of the Senate Chamber she beckoned to a page.

"Take this note to Senator Cantor and don't come back without an answer," she directed.

The snub-nosed youth with puckish eyes, grinned;

"You couldn't have picked a tougher nut to crack," he protested before he pushed open a door letting out the easy drawl of a man's voice and letting himself in.

As Eve waited, two of the members of Jock Holden's committee strolled by arm in arm. They were shaking with laughter as they looked at a scrap of paper one of them held. A group of women with determination surrounding them like an aura hurried by. There was a man-hunt glint in their eyes, and acrimony in the set of their tight-lipped mouths. Were they stalking their Senator? Messenger boys, some in blue, some in gray, darted past. A court stenographer came out sorting his notes. A group of tourists stopped and were directed to the gallery by a door-keeper. Elevator doors clanged. Lights above them flashed floor numbers or letters. A Senator emerged with his forehead glistening with perspiration. Had he been addressing the Senate? A woman joined him, a smartly dressed woman. Instantly he was all smiles and urbanity. He put both his hands over hers before he caught her arm and guided her toward the stairs up which panted and swarmed sight-seers.

The page appeared.

"Senator Cantor says he'll come, Miss."

"Thanks lots."

As Eve entered the office the overblown blonde at the switch-board, who was outlining her mouth heavily with red, suspended operations long enough to inform;

"Skinny's just left, Miss Travis. And was she mad? Gosh, how I hate that dame!" The words vibrated with venom.

"What did she want?"

"Search me. She asked if the Senator was in. I told her he'd just gone out with his wife. Girlie, her eyes burned like green traffic lights. Then she went into your room, which used to be hers, said she left something there. She didn't stay long. Came out looking's if she'd swallowed the canary."

Eve flung open the door of her office. She shut it behind her and crossed to the desk.

She drew a little breath of relief. The bulging folder marked Gold Mine, Alvarez, was on her desk as she had left it. There had been a horrible second when she had suspected that Vera Skinner might have taken it. That had been a silly idea. Why should she take it? Hadn't she handled all the correspondence? Didn't she know the reports from A. to Z.?

She did, all but the note-book which contained memoranda in regard to José's claim, which the Senator had turned over for filing yesterday! Had she been after that?

Hurriedly Eve riffed the papers. No note-book! It must be here! It wasn't. Perhaps the Senator had taken it? No. It has been in this folder before he came in. Now it was gone and Vera Skinner had it.

"I heard her say, 'Better keep your eye on Kilburn. He has something up'—"

Court's words fitted into place like the missing piece of a picture puzzle. Vera Skinner in some way had heard of José's claim. Now she had stolen Jeff's notes about it. He must be warned.

She glanced at the clock. He might possibly go on to his apartment for lunch. She would phone. It was only a chance but she would try it, at least she could speak to José and tell him to have Jeff call her as soon as he came in.

Phone him! His number wouldn't be in the book, he had so recently moved into the apartment. That needn't stop her in this city. She dialed Information.

"Operator? Senator Holden's secretary speaking. I must talk with Mr. Jefferson Kilburn—he has recently taken an apartment—he must have a phone—I'll hold the line—"

Eve's eyes were on the clock as she waited with the receiver at her ear. Every moment counted. Suppose he were not there? What would she do next? She couldn't leave the office—she—

"Jeff! Jeff, is it really you? This is Eve. Anyone in the room? Then listen."

XVI

JEFFERSON Kilburn laid down the telephone. Lucky he had returned to the apartment for papers, otherwise he would have missed Eve's call. Vera Skinner had warned Alvarez to keep an eye on him, had she? Apparently she had stolen his note-book containing the facts in regard to José's claim to ownership of the gold mine, and what a mine it had turned out to be! Claim! It was more than a claim now. José Manuel Mendoza was the rightful heir.

He threw open the French window and stepped to the balcony. Snack, the shepherd, followed, crouched on his haunches and pricked his ears, as if listening to a sound in the street below. Kilburn puffed at his pipe as he looked at the panorama spread beneath him. Tree buds were swelling. Was it the hint of spring in the air which gave him this on-the-crest-of-the-wave feeling? Mirror Lake in the shallow valley reflected both the rugged strength of the Monument and the Grecian perfection of the Memorial. In the west clouds were piling up till they looked like crenelated castles, gold-plated by the sun.

He glanced at the ornate iron trellis which connected his balcony with the one above which was Eve's. He thought of her panic when she had awakened from her dream. The memory of her clinging arms, the fragrance and feel of her soft hair against his cheek set his pulses racing. Would she have clung to him like that if she didn't love him? Later when they had walked and talked she had seemed utterly content.

Suppose some night when the stars were twinkling and the moon was shining, she were to lean over and call him? Could he climb that upright to her balcony? Could he? He had certainly gone Romeo-minded. Weren't there stairs in the house? Thoughts like that wouldn't help him carry through the best-friend program he had laid out for himself.

Had she been annoyed at his proximity? Would she suspect, as he did that his being in the same building with her, was a carefully worked out plan of Jock Holden's? In spite of having been warned to keep hands off, the Senator was trying to stage-manage Eve's life and his.

He'd better stop thinking of Eve and decide on his next move. He must put José on his guard. Even with his claim filed, if Alvarez found out from the stolen memoranda that the rightful heir was alive, that same rightful heir's life wasn't worth a nickel. It would be so easy to accuse José of being mixed up in the late revolution, and so difficult for José to make anyone believe that he had disappeared from his own country because of a woman.

"Which conclusion shows what I think of Señor Eduardo Enrique Alvarez," Kilburn confessed to the distant hills. "I'll bet that the Senator and I have only touched the edges of that situation. Let's get busy, Snack."

He left the balcony and closed the French window behind him. He crossed to the fireplace with the dog at his heels.

Nice room, he approved, as he refilled his pipe. The soft pine walls and heavy green hangings were restful, the chairs were deep and inviting. Not much around. A few choice things from the Orient. The swords in exquisitely wrought scabbards on the stand on the teakwood table set one to wondering. How many heads had fallen before the headman's sabre? What tragic self-accusations had the keen *harakiri* blade silenced? What tales could the dagger in its lacquer fan-sheath tell? If this were his apartment, he wouldn't have such things around even if they were priceless examples of workmanship. Much as he liked to have Court drop in with his tutor he had been uneasy each time the boy had been in the room. The swords had a sinister fascination for him.

He touched a bell.

As quickly as if he had been waiting outside José appeared on the threshold.

"You ring, *señor?*"

Kilburn thoughtfully regarded his fine face and the dark eyes which suggested banked fires. He was slim and straight with a patrician lift to his head. Pure Spanish, he had all a Spaniard's fire and gayety. No Indian blood in him. Anyone with half an eye for human values would know the José Manuel Mendoza had not been a servant always.

"Anyone been here today, José?"

The man approached with the gliding tread of a panther.

"Sí, señor. I glad you come back. It was for you to hear, something told me."

"All right, shoot."

"Shoot him! You say that, *señor?*"

"No! No! No! José. Don't look so infernally pleased. I didn't mean shoot with a gun. I meant go ahead, tell me who came."

"Pardon, *señor*. I think I know English very well when I come to this country but sometimes I do not understand American, I try most hard to learn it. It say so very much in so very few words. A *señora* rang the bell just before you came in."

"A lady?"

Even as Kilburn asked the question his mind ran the gamut of his female acquaintances. Who could it have been? No one whom he knew socially of course. A friend of the previous tenant, perhaps, possibly a saleswoman who had sneaked into the building.

"Was she trying to sell something, José?"

"No, *señor*. She looked at me straight, then she laugh and say;

" 'Is this Mr. Kilburn's apartment?' "

"Then what?"

"She asked were you at home. When I say, 'No, *señora*' she say she come again."

"Coming again! Remember what the woman looked like, José?"

"*Sí, señor*. Hair like a Titian *señorita* and—"

"Red hair! Was her face thin, white?"

"*Sí, señor*. Very thin. Very white."

Kilburn frowned. Vera Skinner was losing no time. But why come to him?

"I know who she is, José. That woman is hand in glove with Alvarez. I mean she is helping him."

"Is she then too trying to steal the mine which my father left to me?" José's upper lip curled back like that of a snarling dog.

"Take it easy. Alvarez has doubtless told her, as he told Senator Holden, that you are dead—recently he has been at your old home trying to prove it—and that upon your death, your father's mine passed to him, the son of his one-time partner."

"But, *señor*, I am not dead. I am here! Here!" José struck his breast with grand opera abandon.

Kilburn suppressed a chuckle.

"Sure, you're here, but from your own confession you encouraged the belief among your townspeople that you had been swept away in your boat, didn't you? If you wanted your mine, why let them think you drowned?"

José lifted imploring hands to heaven and dropped them to signify despair.

"As I told you, *señor*, it was because of a girl. You know how it is. A girl thinks you are, what you are—what shall I say?"

"You mean she thought you intended to marry her?"

"*Sí, señor*. That is it. I jus' mak luf—you call it, she pretty, she dance, but give her *el nombre de mi padre?* No, *señor*. She say she keel me, so I go on the river—turn over boat an' swim ashore. Someone told me the gold mine was a —a—what you say dud, that it was worth nothing. I leave it behind. I come to this beeg country where *señoritas* are gay, an' laugh and do not keel when I walk away. Then one day I hear that Alvarez sell my mine. I do not hear for how much. I take job with you."

"And now you want to come back to life and claim your mine. It will take some doing, José. The Titian haired woman tipped off Alvarez to keep an eye on me. He may come to this apartment."

"If he come—" José's hands clenched.

"Now get this. If he comes, you won't know him—"

"I not know that robber, that—"

"Do you want to enjoy the money from your gold mine?"

"Sí, señor. Sí! Sí!"

"Well, don't cry about it. You sold it to Senator Holden. He has had an offer for it and will treat you on the level if the deal goes through. But, you've got to do exactly as we tell you, understand?"

"Sí, señor. Está bien."

"If the bell rings, don't open the door until you know who it is. If Alvarez should come, stare him straight in the eyes and pretend you never saw him before. You are dead. Understand?"

"Sí, señor. I understand. But that 'you are dead' make me all ice in the blood."

"And you'll do as I tell you?"

Sí, señor.

"All right. That's all."

After the man left, Kilburn stood before the fire smoking. Snack on the rug at his feet blinked heavy lids. Except for the muffled hum of the traffic from the highway below the room was quiet. In the fireplace red embers shimmered, and little flames from the burning logs licked at the chimney. The tall clock was a ticking shadow in the corner. There was a warm scent of tobacco and wood smoke in the room.

Why the dickens had he mixed into the row between Alvarez and José, he asked himself. He answered his own question. Because he was always interested in the underdog, even when he knew that nine times out of ten, the under-dog was under because he hadn't drive enough to fight himself to the top. In this case, it was because he had run away from a woman.

He packed fresh tobacco into his pipe and frowned unseeingly at the old clock. He thought of the dancer with her beauty and her jewels, of the toy revolution which started in Alvarez' country so soon after his arrival and he thought of the five thousand dollars which Jock Holden had paid the South American for an option on the mine. In that country an able-bodied revolt could be financed with that amount.

He had been tremendously interested when the Senator had engaged him to check up on the value of the mine. And he had gone, but first—he paced the floor—but first he had gone through that empty ceremony with Eve. He should have known better. Instead of taking her seriously he should have laughed her out of her foolish idea of marrying to obtain control of her fortune. It would have been better had he told her that she had no fortune. He was wholly to blame. If only he could go back to that afternoon in the library at Brick Ends. Well, he couldn't. Life was a one-way road. No turning back. He must go on. He and Eve were friends again. Friends! That word was a joke when applied to himself. He loved her. Love was a weak word for what he felt for her. He was lucky that he hadn't lost her friendship. She "adored him in evening clothes," he thought of "the grandest things to do." She had flung herself into his arms when frightened. Not too broad a foundation upon which to build love, but it would have to serve for the present.

José spoke.

"A *señora* to see you *señor,*" his voice said, but his eyes flashed. "The same one," before he stepped aside with a low bow. Snack sprang to his four feet, wide awake now.

Vera Skinner brushed past José. In contrast to the unrelieved black of her tailored suit her face was chalky. Her flaming hair, about a close caracul turban, and her green eyes provided striking color accents. She looked around the room.

"You do yourself rather well here, don't you, Mr. Kilburn?" She frowned at José lingering in the doorway. "Why is he waiting?"

"For orders. What will you have?"

"I want nothing except to talk with you."

"You needn't wait, José. Call Snack."

The dog followed the man reluctantly, stopped on the threshold to look back and made a low sound in his throat.

"Go on, Snack!" As the dog obeyed, Kilburn invited; "Won't you come nearer the fire, Miss Skinner?"

"No. I shan't be here but a moment, I hope. I've come to trade."

"Trade?"

"A note-book, just note-book. Re: Alverez gold mine. No use adjusting your poker-face. You know and I know that Senator Holden has an option on a mine Alvarez inherited, that this José Mendoza of yours claims it. I have the data you gave the Senator right here. Will you trade?"

"I don't trade in stolen property."

"What do you mean, stolen?"

"Less than two hours ago you took that note-book—just note-book—from a folder on the desk in the office of Senator Holden's secretary, didn't you?"

"How do you know that?"

"You have spent your life in Washington and you are registering surprise. I'm amazed at your ingenuousness, Miss Skinner. Don't you know that for every resident in this city there are two little birds who carry news?"

"Cut the sarcasm. I'm in a hurry. Will you trade?"

"For what?"

"I'll turn over to you these notes about your man José's claim to the gold mine—as yet Alvarez knows nothing of them—if you will get back for me my job with Senator Holden."

"Even if I would trade, which I won't, you exaggerate my pull with the Senator. Besides, those notes are now of no value to our case."

"What do you mean? They will prove José Mendoza's claim, won't they?"

"Sorry to disappoint you but your trade isn't worth the breath you are spending on it, Miss Skinner. You should have thought the matter through before, in the hall at the Senator's the other evening, you advised Alvarez to keep an eye on me."

"In the hall! There wasn't a person within—" She bit off the damaging admission.

"Within hearing, you were about to say? Dear Miss Skinner, you have forgotten the little news-birds which crowd the air of the Nation's Capital."

"Does that mean that you won't say a good word for me with the Senator? That you are willing I should—break him by other methods?"

"It does."

"Then it's war between you and me. Good morning." She turned at the threshold.

"Alvarez swears that he will have the girl you are in love with—your eyes tell tales when you look at her—I know something else, too. I'll help him get her. Think that over, Mr. Diplomat!"

The entrance door to the apartment closed. Kilburn drew a bunch of papers from his pocket. He glanced through them and nodded satisfaction.

All there. After he had called Vera Skinner's bluff there had been a horrible instant when he had wondered if one of these pages had been left in the note-book she stole. Lucky he had followed his hunch to hold on to them. Even one in her possession might throw a monkey-wrench into the Senator's plans.

"So, she'll help Alvarez get the girl I'm in love with, will she?" his thoughts ran on. Had Vera Skinner seen Eve's terror when she woke from her dream that she was about to be married to the oily South American, she could tune in on another wave-length. Alvarez was out of the running. If only he were as sure that Seth Ramsdell would be turned down. He and Eve were together in the Senator's office every day. Proximity was responsible for a lot of marriages.

He said aloud;
"That boy has me worried."

xvii

"COURT is my child and I want him at home," flamed Dorinda Holden.

"He's my child and I won't have him spoiled," countered her husband. "I've shirked my job, 'Rinda, but I'm through shirking. I want our son to have a sense of duty and integrity. He'll never acquire it coddled at home with tutors. He needs the contact and competition of boys of all ages. He must be trained to be captain of his soul and body. If, when he grows up, he elects self-indulgence as his master it won't be because his father was too soft to insist that he have his chance. He will remain at the school where I have placed him."

Jock Holden delivered the ultimatum as he faced his wife in her boudoir. Her silver fox cape flung on a chair was an ultra modern touch in the room keyed to the late Victorian era. They had not spoken from the time they left his office until now. He hated to hurt her, he thought, as he noted her pallor and the little lines etched at the corners of her blue eyes, but better now than to have her hurt by Court later, and a spoiled, thwarted boy was bound to break loose and twist the heart of the person who loved him most.

"Where is the school?"

"I shan't tell you. It is not so far that you couldn't get there within a few hours if Court needed you. The Headmaster prefers to have parents keep away for a couple of months at least; he thinks it is unsettling for a boy to have visitors until he is well fitted into the routine."

"Two months! How will you know if Court is happy? How do you know he won't be abused."

"Abused! Don't be absurd, 'Rinda. He is at one of the finest prep schools in the country, not a reformatory. The boy is bright enough to play the rules."

"Was he—he terribly unhappy when you left him?"

"Unhappy! You know his grin. I thought it would split his face in two parts when the Headmaster called in a stocky lad and told him to show 'Holden' around. Court went over well with the boy. He will be a good mixer."

He approached her as she stood straight and rigid against the mantel.

"Let's be friends. I'm sorry it had to be done this way,

but I was determined that Court should have his chance at a normal well-rounded boyhood."

She looked at his outstretched hand and clenched hers behind her.

"I suppose Vera Skinner knows where Court is. Perhaps she helped you select the school."

Jock Holden put his hands into his coat pockets.

"Perhaps she did, but it's possible that I am capable of selecting it myself. What's been done with that lot of junk that was left after Court's juggling act? I've been so rushed with work I had forgotten about it."

"You mean the armor? I told Cato to pile it in a closet. I didn't know what to do with it."

"I'll send an expert for it. Unlike Humpty Dumpty, it has got to be put together again, it doesn't belong to us. Something tells me that when our son 'for the glory of our house, cast down two right valiant Knights,' he put a more expensive punch into our party than the party itself."

He picked up the telephone in answer to a ring.

"Yes. Speaking—What's that, Eve?—Go slow. I can't understand when you're so excited. Yes—Yes—How did she get them?—You did. What did he say?—Hm, he'd better get in touch with me at once, I'll be at the office within half an hour. Wait! Wait! Did you round up my committee? All of them?—Okay."

"What has happened, Jock?"

"Nothing, nothing to the boy, 'Rinda. Don't look so white. Some papers missing in the office, that's all."

"Important papers?"

"Important enough to mess things up if they get into the wrong hands. When I say that, I say plenty. I must get back to the office. Don't stay in and brood over Court, 'Rinda. Go out and play cards."

"I don't brood, Jock, and I don't play cards." Before the mirror Dorinda Holden drew her smart turban lower. "Now that you have relieved me of all responsibility of our son, I will go out. I'll telephone the Colonel and ask him to take me to lunch. He is so distinguished and such a shrewd political prophet that I feel mentally stimulated when I am with him." Her defiant eyes met her husband's reflected in the mirror.

" 'Rinda!" Holden turned as a voice outside the door said impatiently;

"If he's here, I'll find him, Cato."

Holden opened the door. Kilburn stood outside with Snack beside him.

"It's a break, Senator, that I've caught you before you left. Vera Skinner has stampeded with—"

"Come outside, Jeff."

Dorinda Holden caught the door before he could close it. "Come inside, Jeff and tell me what has happened." Her voice was gracious, sweet.

Kilburn looked from wife to husband.

"Come in, Jeff. What Dorinda doesn't know will worry her more than what she knows. Women are like that. Spill it and spill it quick."

"Sorry to chisel a dog in, I know you don't like them, Mrs. Holden," Kilburn apologized as Snack followed him into the room, "but I have to exercise this fella. Things have been happening fast, Senator."

He told of Eve's telephone message, of Vera Skinner's visit to his apartment. He said gravely;

"I couldn't promise to ask you to take her back, Senator, that would be butting in on your business. Of course that's all rot about 'breaking you.' "

"It may be rot and it may be the truth. She—"

"Jock! You don't mean that that vicious Vera Skinner can affect your career? She can't! You've never done a crooked thing in your life. It's absurd," Dorinda Holden protested.

There was a curious light in Holden's eyes as he looked at his wife.

"Thanks for the vote of confidence, 'Rinda. After that, she can't. You can help me block her. You've sidestepped social obligations. Don't do it any more. You know the rules here, make the calls you should make, have a fixed reception day. Unbend. Folks have the idea that you're a highbrow. You may be, but it is fatal to have them think it if you're out to be a social success. Get the women and men to talking and tell me what you hear. Will you?"

"I will, Jock."

"Shake." He held her hand tight in his. "We'll have a new campaign slogan. Instead of 'Miss Skinner or your wife?' we'll make it 'Holden and his wife!' Bring Eve to dinner tonight, Jeff. I want to talk with her."

"I will—if she's free."

"She's got to be free. We haven't a dinner date have we, 'Rinda?"

"No. If she hesitates, Jeff, tell her that we are to have mushrooms, marrons, and meringues with ice-cream. She has the appetite of a school-girl for the things she likes."

"I'll do my best to sell her your menu, Mrs. Holden. Ready, Senator?"

In the car on their way to the Senate Office Building, with Snack in impregnable dignity beside the chauffeur, Holden said;

"I'm glad you came, Jeff. I wouldn't have told 'Rinda about this gold mine mess—I haven't told her my problems for months. Somewhere she and I took a wrong turn, she doubted me unjustly—I may have acted like a darnfool but there never has been any woman in my life but her—and I bitterly resented it. But, if I know her, and I am sure I do, she'll go side by side with me through deep water."

"Deep water! You don't believe that Vera Skinner and Alvarez can make trouble for you, do you, Senator?"

"You never can tell. Alvarez' Embassy has been nosing round about that revolution which started in its country while you were there."

"While I was there! They don't suspect me of financing it, do they?"

"Better not laugh—yet. Heaven only knows what they suspect, but I suspect that Alvarez will draw you into it if he can. When it comes to vindictiveness he's in a class by himself. He could get away with murder almost, he's so smooth and sleek. He'll drag me along with you. All your data about the revolution was in that note-book, wasn't it?"

"As it happens it wasn't. I had a hunch that it would be safer in my pocket than in your office."

"That's a break. Some of the boys on Capitol Hill would give their shirts to see me discredited. Vera Skinner's blow-up in your apartment will serve one purpose at least. I'll bet that at this moment, instead of brooding over the deep-lying tragedy which is involved in sending a boy to prep school, 'Rinda is donning paint and feathers in preparation for the social war path. Here we are. I'll be swallowed in committee the moment I enter the office. See Eve. Find out if Skinner took other data besides the note-book. And Jeff, while we're on the subject of Eve, how long are you going to let her keep this farce of being a spinster on her own?"

"As I told you once before, Senator, just so long as she gets a kick out of this freedom stuff—that is, within reason."

"You're wrong. She's yours. Make her admit it. You are thinking that you neither need nor want advice about managing your matrimonial affairs from a man who has messed up his own, aren't you? But Jeff—this isn't advice, it's a suggestion—watch out for wrong turns, they're so infernally easy to take, and if you miss the deliriously happy stretches, and tender intimacies, matrimony is a long laborious road. That's all about that. Tell Eve to chuck everything else overboard and come to dinner tonight—and let me know what you find out. I won't have a minute until then."

Eve was speaking into the phone when Kilburn entered her office and closed the door behind him. She looked up, then said hurriedly to the person on the other end of the wire;

"Yes.—Yes—Yes. That's all, now. Good-bye."

"What's happened, Jeff? Snack, you darling!" With the dog's forepaws in her lap and his head snuggled against hers she asked eagerly;

"Did you find Uncle Jock?"

"Yes. I like that crisp white school-girl collar you're wearing, Eve."

He sat on the corner of her desk. How lovely she was. How vivid. Radiant health was the answer to that. What talking eyes. They flamed, warmed, deepened, sparkled with laughter. Marriage with her wouldn't be a long, laborious road, there would be tempestuous interludes, perhaps,—not all of them April showers, either—and sobering responsibilities, life was like that, but there would be devotion, the deliriously happy stretches, the tender intimacies of which Jock Holden had spoken.

Even as he thought of these things he told her of Vera Skinner's call at his apartment; asked her if she were sure that the note-book was missing; questioned her as to the length of time she had been away from her office. He sounded like a cross-examining district attorney, he felt like a man staring at a "KEEP OUT" sign on the gate of Paradise.

"What do we do next?" Eve asked when he stopped talking.

"Next, so far as you and I are concerned, is dinner with the Holdens tonight."

"Can't."

"In the lexicon of youth which fate reserves for a bright womanhood, there's no such word as 'can't,'" Kilburn paraphrased lightly. "See Bulwer Lytton's Richelieu, Act II, Scene 2, if you don't believe me."

"You've gone more Dictator-minded than ever, Jeff."

"To use any capacity is to develop it."

She sprang to her feet as he came behind her chair. Snack regarded them with inscrutable eyes. She put her hand to her throat.

"What's the matter Kiddo?"

"N—Nothing. Don't look at me as if I had bumped my head and you thought I was going to cry. I wish you would stop calling me Kiddo. I'm not a child. I am grown up."

"Think I don't realize that? What time will you be ready to go to the Holdens'?"

"Am I going to the Holdens'—with you?"

"You are," he announced pleasantly but uncompromisingly. "The Senator commanded me to bring you, and Mrs. Holden seconded him by asking me to tell you that there would be mushrooms for dinner—"

"Mushrooms!" A small reluctant smile tugged at her lips. "I feel myself going."

"And marrons—"

"Going—"

"Meringues with ice-cream."

"Gone! My sales resistance is lowered to the point of juvenility when it comes to those heavenly triplets, mushrooms, marrons and meringues. Why does Uncle Jock want me to dine with him?"

"To learn all you know about the missing memoranda. Said he wouldn't have a minute till then."

"That's different. Business before pleasure. The mail must go through! That goes for you too, doesn't it? Doubtless you had another engagement."

"Meaning?"

"Now don't put on your dumb expression, Jeff Kilburn. With Moya, the lovely Lady Hyatt, of course. Didn't you tell me last evening that she was a temptation and didn't you put your arms tight about her the night Court threw the armor downstairs?"

"What would you have a man do with his arms when a lovely woman throws hers about his neck? Let them hang limp as a scarecrow's?" Kilburn's eyes shone with laughter as he took a step toward her. "Try it and demonstrate what I should do."

She backed away from him. The color mounted to her hair. "I gave a demonstration last evening, didn't I? You seem to be the answer to a frightened maiden's prayer. First Moya and then I." She glanced at the papers on her desk. "Now that you have delivered the Senator's message—"

"You needn't say any more, I'm going. I'm shipping Snack back to Brick Ends, the gardener there will take care of him. His barking annoys the invalid in the apartment below mine. Next, there will be an objection to José's guitar, I presume. I'll call for you at seven-thirty."

"Evidently I am to go to the Holdens' with you whether I want to or not?"

"You've got the idea."

"I'll be ready at seven-thirty. Good-bye, darling!"

Kilburn wheeled;

"Speaking to—"

"Snack, of course, foolish. What's happened to you, Jeff? You seem all bubbly inside as if you had heard wonderful news."

"Can't say that I've heard good news. It's spring in the air. It's that kind of a day."

He pushed Snack ahead of him and closed the door.

xviii

DARK palms, in tropic splendor, reached to the glass roof of the cool white stone patio of the Pan American Union; a lighted fountain twinkled in the centre; at one side of it a red, green and blue parrot made guttural sounds and blinked lidless yellow eyes. It was very colorful and as murmurous with voices as a forest shaken by the wind.

Up and down the great stairways beautiful women and some not so beautiful, trailed frocks of gold or silver, frocks of all tints and shades of the rainbow; sparkled with jewels, tapped dazzling sandals to the seductive rhythm of strings. Beside them men in sombre black and white, men with jeweled orders on their coats and brilliant ribbons across their breasts, men in glittering uniforms, bent their heads in devoted attention. Around them the hum of many accents, Spanish, German, French, Italian; the sibilant English of the Japanese, ebbed and flowed like a tide. Representatives from Peru, Chile, the Argentine, Venezuela, Lima, brushed elbows with Senators and Congressmen from within the area bounded by the Pacific, the Gulf of Mexico, the Atlantic Ocean and the Canadian line.

A gallery was splashed with the scarlet and orange costumes of musicians. The melody from their guitars conjured memories of turquoise skies, frothing emerald seas, hot golden suns and silver moons, woke a desire for love in body and soul.

Alvarez, in the last word in evening clothes, a red ribbon across his shirt-front, was waiting at the foot of the stairs, as Eve came down with Dorinda Holden, regal in amethyst velvet and pearls. He offered his arm.

"Que diclia! What luck! You will dance, señorita?"

Eve shrank back for an instant as the yellow and black glass eyes of her dream glittered in her memory. She rallied a smile.

"How can I help it? The music has made me go completely Spanish."

As they reached the softly lighted ball room, Alvarez declared ardently;

"Never have I seen you so ravishing and you are to me always beautiful. The shimmering fabric of your gown, not quite red, not quite rose, must have been woven for you by a magician. Shall we dance?"

Violins, poignant, ecstatic, horns gleeful and windy and insolent, trumpets high and silvery, were played with a swing and dash which swept every nerve and muscle of Eve's body into their rhythm.

Alvarez expertly guided her into a dimly lighted alcove where the orange satin of cushions on a marble seat made a brilliant spot of color against the glossy green of palms.

Eve conquered a panicky impulse to run. She had determined to find out what Vera Skinner and Alvarez were planning. Perhaps they were not planning. A week had passed since the note-book had been stolen. Nothing had happened to Senator Holden yet. This might be her opportunity to find out what was in their minds if she could stave off Alvarez' torrid love-making. She nodded toward the musicians she could see above the heads of the dancers and said lightly;

"Two orchestras. I like the red capes the leader and ensemble are wearing who are playing the guitars. The bullfighter motif. So appropriate for this ball."

Alvarez leaned toward her. She controlled a shiver and drew away as his sleeve touched her bare arm.

"I brought you here to tell you I adore you, to ask you to marry me, señorita, and you talk about the capes of the musicians."

Fiery sentiment crisped his voice. Eve regarded him with cool, laughing dark eyes.

"You should make allowances for the lady from New England who never before has attended such an exotic affair. For me this will hold the all-time record for balls. Is your friend—Miss Skinner here?"

Her quick change of subject disconcerted him.

"Why do you question me in regard to her? Why not ask Senator Holden? He is the señorita's best—friend is he not? Those pearls she wore—do office secretaries as a rule wear real pearls? It is not in a spirit of criticism I am asking, it is for information."

Eve opened her lips to answer hotly. A seventh sense nudged her. She swallowed the words. Something furtive in his eyes, a suppressed eagerness in his bland voice, set the grade-crossing bell to jangling in her mind. "Watch your step!" it warned. "Watch your step!" She said reproachfully;

"Are you suggesting that it is poor taste for me, being one of those aforementioned office secretaries, to wear real pearls?" She touched the strands of her softly gleaming necklace. "Just to set your mind at rest I'll tell you that I didn't earn these, they were—"

"A gift from Señor Kilburn," Alvarez finished smoothly.

His statement sent the color in a rosy wave to the widow's peak of dark hair on Eve's forehead and her eyes to the moonstone and diamond bracelet on her arm.

"Jeff? Of course not, I inherited them."

Would that give him the idea that she was still an heiress? She would destroy that illusion. She said regretfully;

"My pearls, with a few other jewels are all that is left of my once able-bodied fortune."

"You are jesting, señorita. Your office work it is for fun, is it not? American women work, it is a fad. All Washington knows that you are a very great heiress."

"Does it really? All Washington should catch up with its newspaper reading. You might tell the interested parties that my fortune was snatched up in the tail of the late economic typhoon and that even scraps of it can't be found. To return to Miss Skinner, is she your secretary now?"

"Señorita Skinner has been engaged by the Embassy. She is most valuable to us—after having been trained by Senator Holden."

What did he mean by that sleek cat-and-canary smile? Eve asked herself. Aloud she said;

"The Embassy is lucky to get her, I have heard of her efficiency till I'm ready to tear my hair in despair of ever being so good, and what's more, your Embassy must need her now. I read in the paper tonight that the recurrence of a well-organized revolutionary movement which broke out last winter, had been thwarted by the arrest of thirteen persons suspected of participating in the conspiracy, two already have been executed, that seized documents revealed that the revolt had been organized in the United States, that the leaders were in this country and would be arrested soon—"

"So-o, that is out? It is what you Americans call a news leak, is it not? Why did you read it, señorita?"

The yellow in his eyes predominated as he asked the question. Eve controlled a shiver.

"I'm an omnivorous newspaper reader. I read everything from ads to long reports on conferences. To be sure, much of what I devour is contradicted the next day, but I keep on reading."

"May I suggest that you read no more reports about my country? You might see something that would trouble you."

"Something about your country that would trouble me! You're joking, aren't you? Do you know what I call you to myself? The Mystery Man of South America. Perhaps you are one of the leaders of the revolution."

"Señorita!"

Eve had read of eyes that flashed fire. The phrase had seemed the amusing exaggeration of a thrill-minded writer. Now she knew it to be true. She said quickly;

"I'm sorry. You shouldn't take me so seriously. Remember, I'm new to the world of diplomacy, I'm a fairly good secretary only. However, I'll learn. I am young and honest and working for Senator Holden is an education in itself. He's a tonic person. When I'm with him I can't believe that people can be mean and timid and discouraged. Have you noticed what an extraordinary talent he has for talking about things that matter—to the person to whom he is talking?"

Alvarez repointed his waxed mustache.

"I have, señorita. Also have I noticed that he has what you call an extraordinary talent for buying cheap."

"Has he? I wouldn't know about that."

"Has he?" Alvarez mimicked her voice to perfection. "Of course you know about that. You know that he took an option on my gold mine for fifty thousand dollars. Now I want to buy it back and he is asking one million."

"Only a million! Does anyone deal in an amount as small as a million in this billion decade?"

The eyes watching her glowed as if fires had been lighted behind them.

"It is not a joking matter. If the mine is worth so much money, I should have it."

"Did you buy it originally?"

"I inherited it, from the last owner, my father's partner."

"Had he no children?"

"One son and he is dead."

"Are you sure?"

"Very sure. I shall be able to present the proof to Senator Holden tomorrow."

Eve's pulses broke into double-quick. Tomorrow! Had he known that Vera Skinner had the memoranda in regard to José's claim, he wouldn't have said that. He might suspect, but he didn't know, that the heir was still alive. Perhaps he did. There had been something sinister in his voice when he had said he would present the proof of the heir's death to Senator Holden. Did he mean to put José out of the way? Perhaps he intended to prove that José had been one of the revolutionary leaders who had been executed. Where was Jeff? He had said that he would be at the ball. She must tell him. Alvarez mustn't know what she suspected. She said gaily;

"Why are we spending a moment talking about a stuffy gold mine? Listen to that enchanting music. The rhythm gets into my sandals. I can't keep them still. Of course if you don't care for my dancing, señor—"

In answer he put his arm about her.

"Your dancing is like yourself, señorita, perfection."

"Then you'd better begin at once. I'm sure he is one of the guitar ensemble playing for dancing."

"José! You're dreaming, Eve."

An olive-skinned page in the scarlet of a Legation uniform touched his arm.

"Señor Kilburn?"

"Yes."

"A call on the telephone for you, señor, of great importance, the señora said."

"Of great importance! Who is it? Did you get the name?"

Vera Skinner is after Jeff to make terms! Eve thought exultantly as she listened eagerly for the page's answer.

"*Sí, señor*. She very careful that I do. She said Lady-H for Henry—Hyatt."

The name loosed something in Eve's soul, an emotion terrible, devastating. She said under her breath. "Moya! Darn her! Darn her! Darn her!" She could feel her heart beating against her side, its loud thumping filled her ears.

"Señora say she hold the line until you come, señor," the page reminded.

"All right." Kilburn took the plate from Eve's hand. "Take this. Show me where the phone is. Wait here until I come back, Eve. After I answer the call I'll give those musicians a look over. I can't believe that José would do such a fool thing as to come here where he might run into Alvarez, but there's no accounting for the Castilian temperament, and he's pure Castilian. I'm uneasy about him. I am responsible for his being in Washington. I'll take you home—"

Eve said above the sound of her pounding heart;

"Here comes Seth. I promised I would go home with him, didn't I Seth?"

She slipped her hand within that of the slightly dazed Ramsdell and said sweetly to Kilburn;

"Better not keep your ball and chain waiting, Jeff. You may lose her. Legation phones are the world's busiest. Come, Seth."

She heard Kilburn say something but she didn't care what. The thought that she had turned him down was fiercely satisfying. She caught Ramsdell's sleeve.

"Here comes Alvarez, Seth. One might think he knew Jeff was going. I don't want to see him. Someone has stopped him. A lovely lady. See him preen. Now is our chance to dodge him."

Later as they entered the patio with its cool walls and palms, the set of Ramsdell's mouth, the gloom in his eyes tugged at her conscience. She asked;

"You don't mind taking me home, do you, Seth?"

"You know I want to take you home. You know I love you. What you don't know is that from now on I refuse to pinch-hit for Kilburn. This is the last time you will have a chance to work off your anger at him on me."

This was her chance to show Jeff that there could be another man in her life besides him, that she was absolutely independent of him. She said softly;

"But, suppose, suppose I love you, Seth. Suppose next fall—"

He stopped and looked at her with kindling eyes.

"Are you intimating that you will marry me next fall?"

Eyes on her hands she said;

"Perhaps."

"Eve! Beautiful!"

She held him off as he drew her toward him.

"Not here, Seth, please. Get the car and I'll be waiting outside the exit door."

"I'll get it and then—"

He pressed his lips to her hand before he hurried away.

Must be getting to be a habit with her, this telling men she wanted to marry them, Eve mocked herself, as she waited by the marble balustrade for Seth's lemon yellow speedster to glow in the seemingly endless line of shining cars which rolled up the curved drive, collected their owners, and rolled on.

Why had she been so furious with Jeff? Once she had seen a dam burst and release a roaring cataract which swept everything before it. It had been that way inside her when the page had delivered Moya's message. Even the memory of it turnd her hands to ice.

She shrank into the shadow of a pillar as a group came from the doorway. She couldn't be seen but she could hear a man's voice;

"Have you heard what they're saying about the fair-haired boy, Holden? That he's owned lock, stock and barrel by one of the South American republics, that he financed its last toy revolution; they say they can prove that his engineer Kilburn touched the match to it. He has traded his reputation for a gold mine or two. Can you beat that? Esau and his mess of pottage."

Eve drew a long incredulous breath. The Senator and Jeff involved in that revolution! Whoever had broadcast that rumor had gone completely mad or vicious. Were Vera Skinner and Alvarez responsible?

She ran to the speedster when Ramsdell drove up. She said breathlessly;

"Seth! Seth! Someone has started a story about Uncle Jock and Jeff. Go back to the ball and find them."

"What sort of story?"

She told him. A horn behind sounded a reminder.

"We're blocking traffic. Jump out, Seth. I'll drive myself home, lock the car and leave it at my apartment house door. Give me the key. Hurry! Hurry! The Senator and Jeff ought to know at once."

You're not a ball of fire when it comes to quick thinking, Eve told herself as fifteen minutes later in her softly lighted living room she looked down at the key in her hand. How would Seth get it? She glanced at the clock. Two. She would sit up and wait for him.

She patted Bingo when he lazily descended from his basket to greet her. She changed from her evening frock to a rose velvet house gown. She returned to the living room and poked the embers into a blaze. If she were to sit up until Seth came she wanted the fire for company.

To her impatient fancy the minutes dragged on as slowly as cars in a traffic jam. Why didn't Seth come? It ought not to take all this time to find Jeff and the Senator. Suppose they should prove that Jeff did touch a match to that revolution—of course he didn't—but they might make a Court think so. What would happen to him? Nothing should happen to him. It didn't bear thinking of. Life wouldn't be worth living without Jeff. She stood rigid, frightened, said under her breath over and over.

"It couldn't happen! It couldn't!"

If she had gone to South America with him she could have proved that he had had no hand in the revolution. Another time when had she held on, she might have saved the situation. Unstampedable. It was a great quality.

She dropped to her knees in front of the fire and held out icy hands to the warmth.

What was that queer sound outside? Someone tapping on the glass? Of course not. Must be a vine. She sank back on her heels. Rather pokey here alone. She had sent Annie to the New England store-house for china she wanted, curious how empty the apartment seemed without her. Bingo was pricking his ears. He heard something! She listened. Held her breath. There it was again. Was someone on the balcony or was she just hearing things?

She stood with her hand pressed hard against her clamoring, hammering heart. Had she imagined the sound? No. She was awake. She wasn't dreaming. Someone was tapping cautiously at the long window.

xix

LADY HYATT had not been on the line. The operator knew of no call for him, Kilburn had discovered when he reached the telephone. He'd bet that Alvarez had sent the page with the message. Why? That question was easily answered, to make Eve think that he, Kilburn, was so devoted to Moya, Lady Hyatt, that she had him paged at a ball. The trick had worked. Never had he seen her so angry. Did it mean that she cared? Had the Senator been right when he had said, "She's yours. Make her admit it?" She had greeted Seth Ramsdell radiantly. Just as well that he had taken her home, she was in no mood to listen to anything he, himself, had to say. Meanwhile he would take a look-see at the musicians.

From the shadow of an alcove he scrutinized the faces of the leader and ensemble who occupied one of the galleries at the end of the ball room. All had glossy black hair, all were dressed in scarlet and orange, each one wore the flowing cape of a matador. Not surprising that Eve had thought she recognized José, the men were his type and looked alike. He was not one of them. That was a relief. He hadn't realized before how much he had José's safety on his mind. It was a mean break that he had had to send Snack away. He had felt that the man was safe as long as the dog was in the apartment.

Safe! Of course José was safe, he jeered at himself. Alvarez wouldn't dare touch him, wouldn't dare have him put out of the way. As for that idea of Eve's that he was preparing to accuse José of being a ringleader of the revolution, it was bunk. When her imagination got started it was apt to snatch the bit in its teeth and take her common-sense for a ride. Just the same, he would be easier in his mind if he went home and made sure.

In the checking room he ran into Seth Ramsdell leaving his coat.

"Where's Eve? Thought you took her home. What are you doing here?" he demanded.

"Thank goodness you haven't gone, Kilburn. I've been wondering how I would get hold of you. Got something phoney to tell you. What is there about that to turn you white? Eve's all right. She is at home by this time. She sent me back to find you and the Senator. Better park your coat."

In the corridor Ramsdell repeated what Eve had overheard.

"I'd like to get my hands on the man who started that about the Senator," he concluded with a break in his voice.

"You don't need anyone to take care of your part in the yarn, I'll bet."

"Ten to one it wasn't a man who started it. It was a woman. Vera Skinner threatened to 'break' the Senator if she didn't get her job back, for some reason she's dragging me in. We're wasting time, Seth. We must find Holden. If he isn't here, go to his house. If he isn't there, come to my apartment. I'm beginning to suspect that this story about him and me is part of a plot which leads eventually into a gold mine."

"All right. Let's go."

Kilburn made the rounds of the rooms. Many guests had left. Ramsdell hurried up.

"I asked the door man if he had seen the Senator. He said that he and Mrs. Holden left ten minutes ago. Alvarez is with the Embassy staff smiling his oily smile at departing guests. Gosh, how I hate that guy."

"That makes it one hundred percent. Get after the Senator, quick. Rout him out of bed if necessary. Meanwhile, I'll try his club. It isn't far from here. We can't phone. Phones have ears. We've got to tell him. Somehow he must stop that rumor."

"I'll hop a taxi. Eve has my car."

Kilburn walked to the club of which both he and Holden were members. The Senator had not been there during the evening, the doorman informed him. He walked on to his apartment. The distance was not great and the taxis that passed had fares. The fresh air cleared his mind. Would Vera Skinner dare start a rumor which would hurt the Senator?—his own part in it didn't count, it was too absurd—the answer to that was easy. A jealous woman of her type would stop at nothing to get what she wanted and she wanted her job back. She wouldn't reason that if Senator Holden were discredited he would not need a secretary in Washington. He wouldn't need Eve either. She had been beautiful tonight. Once when she had looked up at him he had jerked his head back just in time to keep his lips from hers. Suppose he had kissed her? Suppose while she was in his arms he had told her that he was to sail for South America in eight days, that whether she wanted to go with him or not, she was going. That was a thought!

A sleek yellow speedster shot away from the curb in front of the apartment house a moment before he reached it. Ramsdell's car. Why hadn't he waited for him? He must have found the Senator. Perhaps he had left a note.

He pressed the button for the lift. Nothing doing. Someone had left the door open. He walked up the stairs. In his living room he snapped on the light. No sign of a note. Evidently Ramsdell had been unable to rouse José who was a sound sleeper. Probably he would telephone. No use going to bed until he heard from him. Must be near daybreak.

He started toward the window. He stared incredulously. One end of the pole above the balcony doors had been pulled from its socket, one green hanging was missing. A chair near it had been overturned. A fight? Was Eve right? Had Alvarez sent a man after José? Something drew his eyes to the sword stand. The fan dagger was gone!

He dashed to José's room and pounded on the door. He flung it open. The room was lighted. The gay spread on the army cot bed was unwrinkled, but a guitar lay there as if dropped in haste. José might be in the kichenette. He called. No answer. The man was gone. He sprinted to the living room.

Where was the key to the balcony door? He looked down at the floor. It couldn't be lost. José might have put it in his pocket when he locked up, before he had been surprised, but it wasn't probable. Perhaps it wasn't locked. He rattled the knob. Something clinked to the balcony. The key! The door had been locked from the outside! Why? It was like a nightmare. Why waste a second wondering?

The key couldn't have poked itself through the hole and locked the door, could it? Someone had left this room with that hanging, evidently. There was no one on the balcony. Had José gone that way? Had he been pushed out, over the rail? What a thought! What a gosh-awful thought!

He seized a chair and swung it against the door. Glass cracked. Splintered. Shivered into bright fragments. He put out his hand. Groped for the key. He had it. He thrust it into the lock and flung open the shattered door.

For an instant he looked at the hills, monuments, buildings, looming like shadowy shapes in the foggy dawn, then clenched his teeth and looked over the railing. No dark shape below that he could see. He extracted a sliver of glass from his thumb as he looked up. His heart stopped. Swinging from the balcony rail above was the red cape of a matador.

Fury blinded him. Had José dared to go to Eve's apartment? "Steady," he warned himself. "Steady!" José had no red cape, unless, unless, Eve had been right, and he had been among the musicians at the ball. Had Alvarez sent a man to get the rightful heir to the gold mine? Had they fought? Had the victor climbed to the balcony above? The Skinner woman had threatened to help Alvarez get Eve! Had she been kidnaped? He was mad to let such a thought into his mind, he must keep it cool and clear.

Why was he mumbling to himself while Eve might be in danger?

He dashed into the living room. His thumb was bleeding like a stuck pig. He wound his handkerchief about it. The phone! It would ring furiously just now. Perhaps it was Eve. He didn't dare ignore it.

He answered breathlessly;

"Kilburn speaking—What's that Seth—Stop and get your breath—The Senator took Mrs. Holden home? Cato gave him a message and he left the house pronto. Right?—Why is Mrs. Holden frightened?—Kidnaped! Who would kidnap the Senator?—Of course it would be the first thing she thought of—Of course you shouldn't leave her. Bring her to my apartment. I—I can't leave here. Get hold of the Colonel and bring him—O.K."

He dropped the phone into its cradle. Now what? He wasn't so sure that the Senator hadn't been kidnaped; he was one of the richest men in the country. If he had been it would be a smashing climax to this nightmare scenario. People went haywire when a man was missing. The word was a dagger thrust into imaginations scraped raw by horror. It was a crazy thought. The Senator might have stepped out to keep a rendezvous with a woman, though in all the years that he had been in public office, there had not been the slightest whisper that he had the rendezvous habit. Why was he spending a moment's thought on a man who was able to take care of himself when Eve might be in danger?

The door bell buzzed like a thousand and one bees advancing in close formation. A million icy feelers crept along Kilburn's nerves, as he flung open the entrance door.

A police officer faced him. His jowl and waistline were above par, his chin jutted as if eager to outrun the gimlet eyes above it, the fingers he removed from the bell were cushion-tipped. His voice rasped;

"Say, what's going on here?"

"What do you mean?"

"I mean this. I was standin' across the street ringin' in to headquarters, when somethin' made me look up. I'll be gosh-darned if a man didn't come out of a balcony door in this apartment, climb up the iron work like 'twas a fire escape, an' he a monkey, to the one above."

"Did he go in?"

"Cripes, I don' know."

"What have you been doing all the time since that you didn't find out who it was, and if he got in?"

"Wait a minute! Take it easy. He was swingin' a cape an' I figgered it was some dumb rich boy puttin' on the Romeo act an' that 'twasn't none of my business, but the further I got away from the buildin' the more I wondered. I got home and told the wife and she sent me back, an' here I am. My name's Kelly."

While the officer talked, Kilburn formed and rejected plans with lightning rapidity. Eve's name must be kept out of this. If José had climbed to her balcony, he had been driven to it. She was safe with him, he would stake his soul on it. Many a time the Spaniard had played his guitar in her garden. Would he, himself, have allowed José to go there had he not been sure that the man could be trusted? If it were someone else—

"Come in, officer. I've got a hunch that I know who Romeo is. Watch this room that he doesn't come back and I'll go to the apartment above."

"Okay with me. I'm off duty an' I ain't got no right to be buttin' in on this. Say! What's happened to the door?"

"Found it locked when I came home. Hanging pulled out by the roots. Key on the outside. I smashed the glass with a chair."

"I'll say you swing a nasty chair, boy. Glass took a crack at you, didn't it. Your hand's bloody."

"That's nothing. Sliver of it in my finger. Wait here will you, Kelly, till I come back? No, you'd better come with me, but understand, whatever we find is off the record. You're not on duty. You're in my pay from this minute. Get me?"

"Sure. I get you. Scram!"

Kilburn scrammed. He ran up the stairs. Behind him, like a tugboat under steam, puffed the police officer. Before he could touch the entrance door of Eve's apartment, it swung inward slowly as if luring into the dark hall. Uncanny! Infernally uncanny! Kelly was popeyed.

"Something's wrong," he whispered. "Turn on the juice."

Kilburn closed the door behind them, groped for a button and flooded the hall with soft light.

"Anyone at home?" he called.

No answer. The two men stood tense, listening. From somewhere came a weird sound. A rustle. A crackly rustle, as if a garment were being dragged and stopped, dragged and stopped across the floor.

"What d'you make of that?" Kelly rasped close to Kilburn's ear.

"Great Scott, don't whisper! Talk," he commanded in a voice which clattered through the still place.

With Kelly close at his heels he stopped in a doorway and flashed on light at dressing table, bed and desk. Eve's room. The glistening frock she had worn at the ball hung on a clothes pole. Had she changed to go out? What was moving under the puff flung over the bed?

He jerked it off. Bingo looked up at him, yawned, stretched, tucked his nose between his paws and blinked red-rimmed eyes.

"Where's Eve?" Kilburn demanded. "You're a grand watch dog, Bingo. Did you see her go? Where is she? Where is she?"

Kelly touched his arm.

"Don't stand there talkin' to the pup. There's somethin' phoney goin' on here. Try the next room."

He lighted the adjoining room. He knew by the crucifix on the wall that it was Annie's. Where was she?

Cr-ee-eep! Cr-ee-eep! Cr-ee-eep!

The weird sound was nearer. He could feel the heat of Kelly's hot, pudgy hand through his sleeve. The officer pointed;

"It's there!"

Together they tiptoed to the threshold of the large living room. Light from Ming lamps shed a soft glow on the satin finish of old mahogany, brightened the blue of the damask hangings, deepened the rosy glow of the sunset in the Inness above the fireplace, which was flanked by Renaissance candlesticks by the fragile pair. A couch was near the fire. A typewriter on a small table was as out of character as a bi-plane in a Roman forum. The balcony door swung open. Air riffled the corners of a pile of papers beside the machine. Kelly drew a long breath!

"Cripes! That's the queer sound we heard. The Saints preserve us! Look at that!"

Kilburn's eyes followed his pointing finger. Set in the dog-basket was a bowl of reddish water, beside it a first-aid kit.

"Say, did the dame live alone?" Kelly demanded in a hoarse whisper.

"Yes, except for a maid and a dog."

"Then I'll bet it was a gangster who'd been plugged I saw shinning up to this balcony. He broke in here and made the girl bandage his wounds."

What color there was in Kilburn's face left it.

"You don't belong on the force, Kelly. You ought to be writing for the movies. A speedster shot away from the door downstairs just before I came in. Your gangster made his getaway in that. Suppose Miss Travis did dress his wound, she would be here now, wouldn't she?"

Kelly swelled visibly with importance.

"I guess you don't read the papers, boy. He wouldn't leave her behind to tell tales, would he? If he was a bright guy—and those fellers are mostly bright guys—he'd take her with him, wouldn't he?"

XX

IT seemed to Eve that she stood for hours, listening to the tap-tap on the window while she stared at the blue damask hangings which shrouded it. How could a person get to that balcony unless he were a Human Fly? Perhaps he had been prowling in the apartment and had sneaked out when she came in. If that were the case, why didn't he walk in now without tapping? She forced her fascinated eyes to the clock. The long hand had checked on one minute, that was all. Perhaps she had been asleep. Perhaps this was a nightmare like that horror when she had dreamed that she was about to marry Alvarez. Perhaps she was getting the nightmare habit.

The sound again! She started for the door. She would run down to Jeff. She stopped. No! She had boasted that she was a girl on her own. She would see this thing through without calling for help from the exciting young man in the apartment below. Unstampedable. Curious how that word kept recurring to her.

"Why don't you bark, funny-face, and show them that there's a man in the house?" she whispered to Bingo who was sniffing at the damask curtain.

Hand over her heart to still its pounding, she crossed the room. Face close against the damask she asked in a loud voice;

"Who's there?" then with with a flash of inspiration, "I'm sure I heard someone, Jeff."

"Señorita! Señorita!" a low voice outside implored.

Only one person called her that. Had her heart parked in her throat for keeps? How could Alvarez get to her balcony? She—

"Señorita! Señorita! It's José. Let me in, I beg you, señorita!"

"José!"

The name was wrenched from taut nerves. She conquered an urge to laugh till she cried. She was no more afraid of José than she would be of Court. She pushed back the hangings and unlocked the window. The Spaniard tumbled into the room. He was dressed in scarlet and orange. A lock of black hair fell over one eye, the knuckles of one hand were blood-stained. He leaned against the mantel as if spent, his breath came in gasps. Bingo sniffed at his leg, wagged his short tail and padded to his basket where he rolled up in a ball and disclosed the lipstick-red lining of his mouth in a prodigious yawn.

José smiled engagingly, if palely.

"He know me, señorita. *Està bien.* He know that I am here not to hurt you."

"Sit down, José. You look all in."

With the air of a Spanish grandee, José waved a hand.

"If you will be seated first, señorita."

Eve didn't need the suggestion, she was glad to lean back in a corner of the couch. The stiffening had suddenly and unaccountably left her knees. José perched on the edge of a chair facing her. His breath came more evenly, his white teeth glimmered in a smile. He said ingratiatingly;

"You wish to know why I am here, señorita?"

She remembered the acrobatic feats her heart had staged when she heard the tap at the window. His matter-of-factness was maddening.

"Surprising as it may seem, I do. Hurry up and tell me, José, for you can't stay here, you know."

"But where shall I go to be safe, señorita?"

"Safe! What do you mean? Who will harm you?"

Even as she asked the question she knew. The son of his father's one time partner, of course, Eduardo Enrique Alvarez. Perhaps this was her chance to block Alvarez and Vera Skinner. Perhaps José had been divinely inspired to come to her. She clasped her hands tightly on her knees and leaned forward.

"Begin at the beginning and tell me why you came here, José."

"Now your voice is kind again, señorita. It was *la guitarra* which brought trouble to me last night. In a paper I read, 'Wanted; guitar player for evenings, queek.' I am much alone evenings. I think I meet people to dance and sing. I answer, by phone, what you call the ad."

"Hurry, José. You can't stay here. Perhaps I can help you to go somewhere else."

"Si, señorita. I make haste. I get the job. I play at beeg party at Pan American Building."

"Then I did see you when I was dancing with Señor Alvarez?"

"Sí, señorita. I put my head down queek. Then when I saw you with that grandson of a *peòn* who's trying to steal my mine, I stood up and muttered curses. It was not good for the music. The leader whispered, 'Throw him out!' I did not wait. I went. I had what you call, given myself away. I had what you call also, a hunch, that if I had, that

thief, Alvarez, would get the gold mine which *mi padre* had left by his will to me. I speak fast. Do you get my Eenglish, señorita?"

"I get it. You're not speaking fast enough, José. Go on."

"I reech the apartment of Señor Kilburn. The service door was just not closed. 'Aha,' I say, 'why is thees? Alvarez, maybe?' I go on toes down back stairs, I go softly up front stairs, a key was in the lock. That queer, I think. *El señor* never come home what you say—tipsy-tight. Something tell me to tak' care. I unlock door gently, put key in pocket, steal in. I feel someone there. Someone hidden. I think queek. He is there to get me. Will I fly? No. No. He might stay and harm Señor Kilburn who has been so kind to me. I wait. I put heem out. Where is he? I heard a sound! Hst!"

The sibilant "Hst!" sent chills coasting down Eve's spine. She sprang to her feet.

"Don't stop to act it out, José. What next?"

José swept back a lock of hair with grand-opera technique.

"Next, señorita, I look in mirror in living room. It reflect a bit of cloth like man's sleeve at edge of hanging at *el balcon* window. Again I think queek, very queek. I who have keeled my bull, I know what to do." He strutted across the hearth rug.

"I make mad rush. I put my arms round hanging—I feel man in them! Aha, I think, you not beeger than me. I get you. I pull like a devil. Hanging comes down. I wind it round the man I hold, like the cape of a matador. He struggles. Kicks! I feel preeck in arm. I push and drag him to service door. I send him wound in hanging rolling downstairs, I bang door. I lean to get my breath. I think. Alvarez sent him! He will come back! I must go. Where? If I leave building he may be in wait outside. Like movie, flashes picture of vine lattice on balcony. I remember that you live above. I will hide on señorita's balcony. I lock door behind me. I climb! Once I look down!"

He swayed. His eyes half closed. He gripped the mantel.

"It makes me deezy when I remember. I cannot go high places. I thought I fall. I prayed to all the saints to help me. *Está bien!* I am here. I burn candles to them to—"

He pitched forward. Eve caught him.

"Sit down. Pull yourself together, José. You must get away! You're not safe in this house!"

She ran to the kitchenette, with Bingo at her heels, and came back with water. She raised José's drooping head and held the glass to his lips. He drank eagerly.

"Gracias, señorita. Está bien. My brain it no longer—" he rotated his fingers.

"Stop, José, or you'll have me deezy, too. There's blood trickling down your hand!"

"I told you, señorita, I feel preeck. The man behind the hanging had a knife, something tell me."

"A knife! Keep still, José. Don't move! That bleeding must be stopped before you leave here."

She dashed from the room and returned with a bowl of water which she set in the dog-basket. She opened a first-aid kit and expertly slit José's sleeve. At the sight of the wound above his elbow, his eyes closed, his head rolled back.

Eve scoffed;

"You, who have keeled your bull! Can't you see that it's not much more than a prick, José?"

While she expertly bathed and bandaged his arm, she made and rejected plans for his safety. Should she try to get hold of Jeff? No, Jeff was with Moya, hadn't she sent for him? Much as she hated the thought, it relieved her of anxiety about him, he was safe from the man who had attacked José. The Senator? No. That would mean dragging him into the mess and he had enough to combat in the whisper going the rounds that he was mixed up in a South American revolution. He might be accused also of trying to get rid of José to secure his mine. There was Seth—no, she would depend only on herself. This situation might have been staged by Vera Skinner, the Vera Skinner who had said of her;

"Pretty, but dumb!"

In spite of her anxiety, Eve chuckled;

"I'll prove that I'm a better gal than you are, Gunga Din."

To boast was easy, to make good was another thing again! What would a person in danger in a strange country do first? Appeal to his Embassy of course. His Embassy! But suppose José were one of the ringleaders of the revolution who was being trailed? He wasn't, of course he wasn't. Hadn't Jeff brought him to Washington to prove his claim to a gold mine? She would suggest the Embassy. If he were guilty he would protest, if he were not that was the place for him. Neither Alvarez nor his hired thug would dare touch him. Suppose he met Alvarez there? No danger of that at this time of night. Alvarez lived at a Club outside the city, and tomorrow Jeff would look after José. Seth's car was at the door! He could go in that!

Tingling with excitement Eve fastened the slit sleeve above the bandage. She mixed a dose of aromatic spirits of ammonia and forced some of it between José's lips. The first trickle down his throat brought his head up with a jerk.

"Sapristi! Quin es? Señorita! You give me fire! I—" he choked as she forced him to take another swallow.

"Sorry! Perhaps I made it too strong, José, but you must get away to your Embassy. You'll be safe there. Quick! See if you can stand."

He pulled himself to his feet and clutched the arm of the chair.

"I stand fine. The Embassy. It is the place!"

Not guilty, Eve exulted. That settled that.

"But how I get there? My head it go round and round."

"Stop waving your hand, José, or mine will whirl too. Mr. Ramsdell's car is outside. You drive it to—"

"Alas, señorita, it is what you call a swell plan, but I cannot drive with one hand—"

"I suppose you couldn't, even to save your life," Eve flamed. "I suppose I've got to get you there, my brave *caballero*. Wait until I put on my coat."

"You can't come, Bingo. Bad enough to have one of us mixed up in this," she told the Boston who had followed her to her room. "Where can I put you that the big, bad, bandit who knifed José won't find you, if he should suspect that José came up here? Hop on the bed, funny-face, it's against the rules, but no one will look for you here."

She threw a puff over the dog. Slipped into her ermine coat. She steadied José to the lift, decided that it was risky to take him that way and left the two doors open so that it could not be used. She helped him down the stairs. Her breath caught at every sound, her heart stopped at every shadow. She half led half pulled him across the sidewalk to Seth Ramsdell's speedster. She pushed him in, jumped in beside him and started the engine. It promptly back-fired.

"That sound contributes to the gayety of nations," she said aloud as the car shot forward.

Almost morning. The haze was lifting. Stars were fading. Behind the hills a faint pink fused into the indigo above making a luminous streak of amethyst. Houses were taking on shape and color. From somewhere near came the "clap-clap" of a horse's hoofs on macadam as a lonely milk-man made his rounds. Just where the white marble obelisk touched the sky, pale unearthly lights flashed to warn flyers of the Monument's location. There was the warm scent of freshly stirred fires. The world shimmered with opal tints. Dawn was stealing across fields and river.

Lucky she knew where the Embassy was, Eve thought as she stopped in front of the imposing building on the broad avenue, arched with interlocking branches of giant elms. She looked at José slumped in the corner. It was one thing to get him here. Another to get him out of the car. He appeared to be in a daze. Perhaps a servant would help her.

She ran up the steps. Pressed the bell. Behind her the motor purred softly. Someone would come to help her. Someone must! The door opened. A servant in livery stared at her. She whispered;

"Quick! Help me! One of your countrymen—" her voice caught in her throat and gurgled into silence. A man had stepped into the hall. A man who looked back at her with amazed kindling eyes, Señor Eduardo Enrique Alvarez.

xxi

FOR a breathless instant Eve stood as if bogged down by the blaze in Alvarez' eyes. But only for an instant. Before he could speak, she turned. She dashed to the speedster. As she jumped into it, he called from the threshold. He was on the steps! In her excitement she shot the lemon yellow car forward with a suddenness that jolted a groan from José.

Just in time she saw Alvarez in the middle of the road holding up his hand. She jammed over the steering wheel, but the running board was so close to him that her blood turned to ice. All that was needed to complete the nightmare of the last few hours was for her to run down somebody.

"No hitch-hikers!" she called over her shoulder and laughed.

"Lucky you are queek on the wheel or we run down that man begging for a ride, señorita. Why did you not leave me at the Embassy?" José asked faintly. "My arm, it shoots full of fire."

"Leave you? Don't you know who came to the door? Don't you know whom we almost ran down? It was Alvarez."

He said something in Spanish, something so fluent, so vindictive, so sibilant that Eve suspected it of being not one curse, but a string of them. Must be wonderful to relieve one's fury like that. In comparison, English seemed childishly inadequate.

"Where you take me now, señorita? It soon will be day."

"You are right and we can't drive on like this forever, José. I've been trying to figure out what is our best move. If we return to Mr. Kilburn's apartment someone may be lying in wait to grab you. I'll take you to Senator Holden's.

He will keep you safe, at least until you and he get that gold mine business settled."

"But, already it is settled for me, señorita. *El* Senator ask me to say nothing yet until the papers pass. It might make the trouble because my country wish to control all mines within its borders."

Through Eve's mind echoed the words;

"Heard what they're saying about the fair-haired boy, Holden? That he's owned lock, stock and barrel by one of the South American Republics."

"It isn't true! Of course it isn't true," she assured herself passionately. It was just a hateful rumor started by Vera Skinner to make trouble for the Senator. Why had the woman dragged Jeff into the mess? Why worry about Jeff? Was any man in the world better able to take care of himself? She remembered her anguish of mind when she had seen him in his library at Brick Ends with the automatic in his hand and she remembered to what a mad proposition her terror had led. If she had had more faith in him then her face wouldn't burn like fire now.

A sound snapped her attention to her surroundings. A car behind. Coming fast. Alvarez? She must land José somewhere before he overtook them. If she could dispose of the dark-haired *caballero* beside her without Alvarez knowing it, she would have the time of her life leading that tiger-eyed diplomat on a wild-goose chase. The mere idea of it set off little ripples of laughter.

"Look back, José. See a car?"

"Sí, señorita! It has stopped for the traffic light."

"Grand! Listen, José. I'll cut through the side street to the next Circle, detour and come out on the Avenue near Senator Holden's house. I'll shoot into the drive and stop a second at the service door. The minute the car stops, jump out."

"But, my wounded arm, señorita. It will hurt much."

"Be your age, José, don't baby that little scratch. It will hurt more, a whole lot more, if Alvarez gets you, to say nothing of your mine. Keep your eyes on that car behind us. If it gains on us tell me quick. Understand?"

"Sí, señorita, but I do not like the way you speak to me."

"Stop sulking, José, or I'll put you out now. Darn that traffic light! Car coming?"

"Two, señorita. *Está bien!* They stop for signal, also."

"Thank heaven. We're off!"

She cut the corner with a speed that drew a groan from José.

"For a big, he-man fighter you're a tender flower," Eve scoffed. "Car in sight?"

"Not yet."

"Good! We've made the Avenue without being seen. A girl's best friend is the traffic light. Now for the Senator's. Tumble out the moment I stop. Hide in the shrubs near the service door. If I can make the Avenue again without being seen coming out of the drive it will be safe for you to ring the bell. Tell whoever comes to the door that I brought you. Understand?"

"*Sí, señorita.* I will be safe, but you? Have you not fear? You are gay. You laugh.

"When in doubt, laugh! That is Colonel Courtleigh's prescription, not mine, but it's a good one. What have I to fear? I have done nothing but break the speed law, besides, I have been safe for so many years, José, that I'm having the thrill of my life. I feel as if my hands were on the throttle of the engine of a streamline train beating the rush of a thousand wild horses across a prairie."

"You are very beautiful when you talk so queek, señorita, it makes me luf you more and more."

Eve's mind skidded. She stared at the man beside her, at his dark, limpid eyes, at his lips parted in a fatuous smile above his gleaming teeth. Had the night's excitement made him quite mad?

"One more word of that, José, and you'll be dumped right here for Alvarez to pick up. Keep your eyes on that back window."

"I keep them on it, señorita, no car coming. Why are you angry that I luf you? *Soy un español de familia noble.* I forget you do not understand my language. It mean I am a Spaniard of noble family. My grandfather was *un gran general,* a noble. The grandfather of Alvarez, with whom you dance, was *peón.* I luf you when I play *la guitarra* in your garden, then I am servant. I tell you nothing. Now I am Don José Manuel Mendoza. I will have money, much money—"

Eve shot the roadster into the drive of the Holdens' house and stopped it with a jerk.

"Out! Out! Quick, José. If you don't mind landing in court for cutting by traffic lights, I do."

As he hesitated on the step of the car she gave him a little push.

"Hide! Hide!" she whispered.

At the exit of the service drive she looked cautiously up and down the street. Nothing in sight. The yellow speedster shot on to the broad Avenue.

Better take it easy now, she thought. If I hurry, I may arouse suspicion. Evidently I've thrown Alvarez off the track. Did he send a man to Jeff's apartment to get rid of José? I thought my heart had stopped forever when he stepped into the hall at the Embassy. Lucky it is strong or it wouldn't have kept on beating after the shock of José's love-making. Lucky that Jeff hasn't suspected the state of his butler's affections.

She tramped on the brake just in time to avoid collision with a black sedan. She saw the word POLICE in the lighted panel at the top, and shut off her engine.

"Here is where I pay the piper for trying to rescue a foreigner in distress," she told herself. Three men jumped from the car. What would she say to them? Tell them where José was of course and why she had helped him. She would have that first-aid kit open in her living room for evidence. Would a police officer wear evening clothes with a soft hat pulled down over his eyes and a tweed top-coat?

"Jeff!"

Kilburn put his hand on the door of the speedster. Two men in uniform closed in behind him.

"Alone, Eve?" he demanded.

"Of course, I'm alone."

"Where's the gangster?"

"The w-what?"

"The gangster whose wound you dressed?"

"Gang—gang—" For the first time in her life Eve was threatened by hysterics.

Kilburn caught her shoulder.

"Stop laughing, Kiddo, or I'll shake you. Tell these men quick what has become of the man whose wound you dressed."

Eve swallowed a little gust of nervous laughter. She looked from Kilburn's stern face to the uniformed men behind him. One of them had blue, Irish eyes set in sun-bursts of fine lines. She addressed her explanation to those eyes.

"It wasn't a gangster, Sergeant, it was Mr. Kilburn's man José—if you believe him, he's a Spaniard of noble family. Someone attacked him when he entered Mr. Kilburn's apartment. He climbed to mine. I tried to take him to his Embassy, then—then changed my mind. Don't glare at me like that, Jeff. If you don't mind, I'd like to go home."

"That's where you're going. First tell these men where you left José."

Eve told them.

"Why didn't you stop at the Embassy, Miss?" the Sergeant inquired suspiciously.

"I did. But when the door opened I saw a—a—man, well, a man I don't like standing in the hall and I ran." Eve's shiver of revulsion was real. Kilburn turned to the police;

"Pick up José at Senator Holden's, will you? Put him where he'll be safe until morning. Then I'll come and get him and tell you the whole story. Move over, Eve. I'll drive."

He answered a question of one of the officers before he started the car. As it shot forward, Eve snuggled into the corner of the seat with a long sigh.

"Never in my life was I more glad to see anybody than I am to see you, Jeff. When that black sedan suddenly appeared in front of me, I didn't know what was coming. Who would believe that a night which started with that gorgeous party at the Pan American Building would end in melodrama. I suppose that attack on José in your apartment would come under the head of melodrama, wouldn't it?"

"What attack? Remember I don't know. I know only what you told the police, that he climbed to your apartment, that you dressed his arm. I've suffered the tortures of the damned since I entered your living room and saw that—" he cleared his voice. "Tell me what happened."

The early morning air blowing in through the open window of the speedster was fragrant with the scent of swelling buds. Eve drew it deep into her lungs. Ahead stretched the Avenue. Empty. Mysterious. Silent. Haunted by the spirits of great men who had passed that way on the road to fame or oblivion; by phantom parades and pageantry. It was so quiet now that she could hear the swish of naked branches of trees, the beat of her heart. A few pale stars stood at their post as if on guard until the city waked and the great river of workers surged toward the white buildings now tinted with the faint rose of dawn. Kilburn's profile was grim and clear-cut. Nothing Latin about him, thank heaven. In a little rush of emotion she pressed her head against the rough sleeve of his top-coat. She spoke in a hushed voice as if she feared to disturb the ghosts;

"You're so nice and tweedy, Jeff, American style. I'm fed up with these exotic *caballeros.*"

"*Caballeros!* Did José annoy you, too?"

"Don't shout! Depends upon what you mean by annoy. If tapping on my balcony window at two A.M. comes under the head, he did. He would have to make his entrance that way, he wouldn't have thought of coming up the stairs. He reacts instinctively to the dramatic. Promise not to blow up until I've finished and I'll tell you about it."

"I promise. Go on."

Eve began at the moment she had heard the reference to Jock Holden and himself as she waited for Seth, dramatically described her reaction to the sinister sound at her window;

"I'll never again doubt that a person's blood may freeze in the veins, Jeff. Mine was full of ice. My mind kept on working, though. I thought 'I'll run down to Jeff!' 'You won't,' I snapped at myself, 'you're a girl on your own, remember.' "

Kilburn made no comment. Eve's voice was hurried, uneven, as she told of opening the window, of her amazement when José tumbled into the room. Not until she described her glimpse of Alavarez in the hall of the Embassy did he interrupt. His voice sent a shiver of nerves through her body.

"Having proved that a girl on her own had the courage to open that window why didn't you 'phone down to me that José was in your apartment?"

"I thought of it and then I thought you were probably with Moya—"

For the first time since he had taken the wheel he looked at her.

"With Moya! At two o'clock in the morning! What do you mean?"

"She sent for you, didn't she?"

"As it happened she didn't. Now I'll tell my side of the story."

He began with his discovery that there had been no telephone call for him; he ended with his call to Headquarters to have every cruising police car put on the trail of a lemon yellow speedster.

"And we found you," he concluded huskily as he stopped the car at the apartment house curb.

"Thank heaven!" Eve responded fervently.

"That goes double with me. Come."

"Where do we go from here?" The question instead of being as gay as she intended was shaky.

"To my apartment. Ramsdell was to bring Mrs. Holden there."

"Aunt Dorinda! At this time in the morning! What's happened, Jeff? What are you keeping back?"

Kilburn put his hand over the hand clutching his arm as they entered the lower hall.

"Nothing that need frighten you, Kiddo. Who the dickens is using the elevator at this hour? We'll walk up. I'll bet this old house is popeyed over the events of the last twenty-four hours. Take the stairs slowly—you can't help your aunt by running up—while I tell you what happened when the Senator reached home after leaving the ball at the Pan American. Old Cato, his butler, his face a dirty gray instead of a shining black, called him aside and gave him a message. Without a word to his wife, Holden dashed out of the house. Stop on this landing and get your breath, darling. I won't say a word more until you do."

"I've stopped. I'm out of breath only because I'm terrified, Jeff. Go on! Please go on. Where did he go?"

"We don't know. Ramsdell arrived a short time after he left. Mrs. Holden was walking the floor. 'Jock's been kidnaped!' she kept saying. 'It's because of the gold mine! I've always felt that Alvarez was a snake in the grass. There was something strange about that message. Cato's face was gray.' Ramsdell cornered Cato in the pantry and tried to get the truth out of him, but all he could learn was that someone, someone sobbing so they could hardly speak, wanted Massa Senator to come at once. I suspect that Cato recognized the voice, but Seth couldn't third-degree the truth out of him. He knew of course, but he was protecting someone."

"Hurry! Hurry! Jeff. Aunt Dorinda must be wild with anxiety."

The door of Kilburn's apartment was flung open as they reached it. Dorinda Holden still in violet velvet and pearls stood on the threshold, but she was not looking at them, her eyes big and purple and incredulous stared beyond them. The door of the elevator was open. Jock Holden pushed a woman ahead of him as he stepped out, a woman with a white face and flaming red hair. His face was livid, his voice hoarse, as he said:

"Our boy is lost, 'Rinda."

XXII

JEFFERSON KILBURN looked about his living room and touched the mantel behind him. It wasn't dream-stuff, it was wood. The window was still minus a green hanging, the sword stand minus the fan sheathed dagger. He was awake, wide awake and the people about him, motionless, as if held under an hypnotic spell, were real. Eve, in a corner of the divan, Dorinda Holden clutching the arms of a deep chair, Colonel Courtleigh leaning on the back of it, Ramsdell behind Eve and in the centre of the room, white-faced Jock Holden clutching the shoulder of Vera Skinner, were real. The woman's slender body was shaking.

"Sit down, Miss Skinner."

Kilburn pushed a chair toward her. Jock Holden kicked it away.

"She's able to stand until she tells her story. I'll tell my part first. When I reached home after the ball, Cato told me that the Headmaster of Court's school had been on the line, that the boy hadn't come in after practice. I got him from my office. Didn't want Dorinda to be frightened. He said that a boy had seen Court run up to a car driven by a woman, get into it and drive away. That at midnight a woman had 'phoned that I had sent for Court. He couldn't believe that I would take him away from school that way and had been trying to reach me ever since.

"At first I thought you were the woman in the car, 'Rinda, then I knew you wouldn't do it. Eve wouldn't do such a fool thing. Next I remembered that Cato had told me when I came in that Miss Skinner had been trying to get me on the phone. I suspected then who had taken Court. My hunch was right. Tell them what you did, Skinner."

The woman's face was livid. Her black gown was wrinkled and dusty, her toque had slipped back on her red hair. Her lower jaw trembled. Holden's grip tightened cruelly.

"Go on," he ordered through stiff lips.

"I didn't mean to lose him, really I didn't, Senator," Vera Skinner pleaded.

With a low cry Dorinda Holden sprang to her feet.

"What difference will it make what that woman says? Why isn't someone hunting for the boy?"

Colonel Courtleigh pressed her gently back into the chair.

"Remember, Dorinda, that Court is thirteen years old and smart as a steel trap. He'll find his way around."

Dorinda Holden shuddered.

"Will he when I've never given him a chance to find his way around? His father is a rich man. Our boy may be held for a reward. Why are we sitting here waiting? Waiting! Waiting for what? Is anything being done to find him, Jock?"

"Every police station in the District of Columbia and within a hundred miles has been notified, 'Rinda, a net-work of cruising cars has been thrown out. They'll have him safe at home before breakfast, see if they don't, honey."

Holden gave Vera Skinner's shoulder a reminding shake.

"Talk!" he commanded. "Tell the truth. It may help you later. You know the penalty for kidnaping."

"But I didn't kidnap him, I didn't Senator. I told you that my plan was to take him away from school for the evening only, just to give you a little scare. You've been so lucky. I thought if your heart could be twisted for even a few minutes—"

"Leave my heart out of this. You drove to the athletic field, beckoned to Court—then what?"

"I told him I had a message from his father, that if he'd jump into the car I would drive him as far as the school bounds while I told him about it.

"He said, 'Okay, Skinny. No rule against going that far. I won't be missed in that bunch of athletes. I'm no good in sports but you bet your life I'm going to be.' "

Her voice thinned to a whisper. She put her hand to her throat.

"Go on," Holden prodded stonily.

"That's just what we did, we went on. I kept Court so interested that he didn't notice when we passed the school bounds. When he realized that we were beyond them, he said;

" 'Hold on, Skinny! Slow down. We've passed the school line! What's the big idea stepping on the gas like this?"

"I said, 'I thought you might be homesick, Court. I'm taking you to your mother.'

"He said, 'You are? Suppose I don't want to go. I'm crazy about school. You turn around now like a good fella.'

"I said, 'No, Court, you're going with me. It's a party. You've always liked my parties, haven't you?' " The telephone rang. "Perhaps they've found him! Perhaps they've found him!"

Holden seized the phone. He still gripped Vera Skinner's shoulder. The room was so quiet that the crumble of a burnt-out log had the nerve-racking effect of an explosion.

"Holden speaking. No news from anywhere? He hasn't come back? All right. Yes, I'll stay here."

He looked at his wife sitting forward in her seat, white knuckled hands clutching the violet velvet of her frock.

"They'll find him, 'Rinda, they'll find him, dear. As for you—" he clenched his teeth as he looked at the white face of the woman beside him—"Do you know what I'd like to do to you—"

"Jock!" Dorinda Holden's voice was sharp with fear. "Let her go on."

"There isn't much more to tell," Vera Skinner said wearily. "Court didn't say much, but I talked and talked. When we were about five miles out of the city, he said;

" 'You're a humdinger of a driver, Skinny. I wonder we haven't been pinched we've gone so fast. I'd like your party better if the Headmaster knew where I was. He may think I'm dumb enough to beat it because I'm homesick. Call him from the next telephone station we come to, will you?'

"I said I would. By that time my anger at you had cooled, Senator, and I realized what I had done. I did 'phone the school, told them that you had sent for the boy in a hurry. I gave them no time to answer as I realized that I had made matters worse, that they would know that a man like you wouldn't take a boy away from school in that way. When I went back to the car, Court wasn't there."

"Where was he?" Dorinda Holden demanded icily.

Vera Skinner lifted her thin hands and dropped them in a gesture of futility.

"I don't know. It was a filling station. Some car may have picked him up."

"He went back to school. Of course he went back to school. Say you think he did, Jock."

"If he did, he hasn't arrived, 'Rinda. Sit down, dear. That was the Headmaster calling. Go back to your apartment, Skinner. Stay there until the boy is found."

"But, but I want to stay here. You don't understand, Jock. I love Court. He and I have been pals. I wouldn't hurt him—"

"Well, you have, haven't you? Get out!"

Vera Skinner looked at Kilburn. He ignored the anguish in her eyes.

"You'd better go, Miss Skinner," he advised.

He went with her to the lift. She was so dazed that he didn't dare leave her. He unlocked her apartment door, led her into her living room.

"Better rest," he suggested.

"How can I rest? I'm wild with anxiety. Promise you will telephone if they hear of Court, promise, Kilburn. The Senator won't. He never will forgive me."

Memory flashed like a zig-zag of lightning through Kilburn's troubled mind. Court wasn't the only person she had hurt.

"Why should I believe that you're really sorry for what has happened to the boy? You've done your best to hurt his father, haven't you?"

"Hurt his father! Hurt the Senator? What do you mean?"

Whatever compassion Kilburn had felt for her turned to anger.

"Didn't you threaten to 'break' him?"

"I threatened, yes, but I didn't do it. I—I couldn't hurt Jock. I took Court to give his cold-blooded mother a jolt. I—"

"Do you mean that you don't know that the ball tonight was buzzing with the report that Senator Holden is in the pay of one of the South American Republics, that I, as his agent, started that toy revolution the papers are playing up?"

She sank into a chair as if her legs refused longer to hold up her slender body. She dropped her head into her thin hands.

"I didn't know it! I didn't."

"Did you give Alvarez the note-book with the memoranda about José?"

She looked up. Her eyes were emerald green.

"Do you think I am utterly a fool? Would I have any hold over him if I gave it up? It is in that desk.

"Then give it to me."

"And why to you, Jefferson Kilburn?"

"Because it is my property you stole. I furnished that information."

"Try and get it."

She was insolent, assured. Kilburn turned toward the door.

"Believe it or not, I shan't put up a fight for it. Good-evening."

She caught his sleeve. Her chin trembled.

"You will 'phone me if Court is heard from?"

"Certainly not. And what's more, I don't believe in this act you've put on. You know where Court is. You're having him held for ransom. I'd be willing to testify to that in court!"

There was an instant when he thought her fingers were tensed to strangle him, then they dropped.

"You don't believe that. You know you don't, Kilburn."

"Why shouldn't I? You steal papers. You start rumors—"

"That's a lie! I have not started a rumor. To prove it I'll give you that note-book."

She crossed the room to a secretary desk of red chinese lacquer, unlocked a drawer, and came back with the small loose-leaf note-book in her hand.

Killburn took it.

"Sure the pages are all there?"

"Quite sure."

Something in her voice, a touch of vindictiveness in her eyes roused his suspicion. He picked up the telephone on the stand near the door and dialed his own number. A voice answered. He said;

"Ask Miss Travis to come to Miss Skinner's apartment at once. No. No! It is not about Court."

He snapped the instrument into its stand. His voice was rough with fury;

"When I think of the anguish you've caused, I think that boiling oil would be too easy a punishment for you, Vera Skinner."

"I suppose you've never done anything you're sorry for, Kilburn? I suppose every page of your life is snowy white. Why did you send for Eve Travis? Why should she butt in? Isn't it enough that she has my job? I won't let her in."

"I will."

"You'll be sorry, Kilburn, if you open that door."

He opened it in response to a sharp knock. Eve stepped into the room. The reflection of light from her rose velvet frock touched her pale skin with pink. Her eyes were dark with anxiety. She asked breathlessly;

"Have you news of Court, Jeff? Something terrible that you didn't want them to hear?"

Kilburn was aware of Vera Skinner leaning against the red lacquer secretary, aware of the contemptuous twist of her lips as he answered Eve.

"No. No. I want you to look over the note-book that was taken from the gold mine files. Anything missing?"

Eve turned the pages, looked at the numbers in the corners.

"All here, Jeff. Are you sure that she hasn't cheated you and had copies of these pages made?"

Vera Skinner laughed, a brittle laugh. She riffed the edge of a paper she held.

"Not of those, Miss Travis. Perhaps now you'll be kind enough to okay this. Know what it is? It's copy from a marriage register. You may be interested in the names. Eve Travis and Jefferson Kilburn. Did I hear you mention the word 'cheat,' Miss Travis?"

xxiii

"CHEAT!"

The word clanged through Eve's tired mind. It started a queer inconsequential train of thought; Vera Skinner's apartment would be like this. Good housekeepers had a word for it, slack. Tilted pictures, soiled silk pillows on the sagging divan, trays full of cigarette stubs, wilted carnations in a waterless vase, newspapers on the floor beside a chair, ashes, trails of them, as if the smoker had paced back and forth, back and forth between telephone and fireplace.

Her eyes rested on the woman regarding her with triumphant mockery. She wanted to appear sophisticated, gayly indifferent, amazingly witty; instead she felt like a robot with an echo complex as she repeated;

"Cheat!"

"Right the first time. C-h-e-a-t. Ever heard the word before?"

If Vera Skinner but knew it, she had, Eve thought, Jeff had called her that. Why didn't he say something now? How could he? Hadn't she refused to acknowledge their marriage? If only he would give her a hint as to what he wanted her to do, instead of standing with an arm on the mantel staring down at the hearth littered with torn papers and burnt-out logs. Evidently he didn't intend to help, it was up to her. "When in doubt, laugh," the Colonel had said. She laughed.

"*Awe!*—that's Hawaiian for 'ah well' in case you care—the course of deception is full of uncharted rocks. Hope you don't mind being indexed as an uncharted rock, Miss Skinner."

Eve's gay bravado threw Vera Skinner off her course. Her green eyes flashed to the man by the fireplace.

"Don't look at Jeff for confirmation. Miss Skinner. From first to last the responsibility for concealing the mar—marriage is mine."

"Then you acknowledge it?"

"Why not? What's more I feel immensely flattered that you should have stored the fact in your mind along with the really important business of our Senator's;

" ' And still the wonder grew
That one small head could carry all she knew.'

"Those lines were written for you, Miss Skinner. Don't look at me as if I'd gone out of my mind, Jeff. I haven't. It's just my exuberant self rising from the bog of deceit. Phoenix from the ashes motif. I'm sorry only that Uncle Jock should be annoyed by publicity about my affairs just now."

"And why should there be publicity about your affairs?" Vera Skinner cut in sharply. "You flatter yourself. Do you think I will add to the Senator's trouble by starting it? When he dictated letters to Kilburn in South America he always devoted a paragraph to you. It roused my curiosity. I did a little sleuthing and unearthed the record of your marriage. That's all there is to it. So far as I am concerned, you may be known as Miss Travis for the rest of your life."

She tore the paper she held to bits and flung another untidy contribution toward the fireplace.

Kilburn opened the door.

"That being the case we'll go. We don't know what has happened since you left my apartment, Eve."

"You'll phone me if you hear any—any news, won't you?" Vera Skinner pleaded unsteadily.

"I will. Good-night, good-morning, rather."

On the stairs he said to Eve;

"First and last that woman has stirred up a heap of trouble, but she rates some consideration for keeping silent about our marriage."

"Are you so afraid to have the truth known?"

"Not afraid, but I don't care to have it broadcast by Vera Skinner. There is one person only who should make that public." He went on as if the subject of the marriage had ceased to interest him. "She's a queer combination. She's not really malevolent, she's just selfish and wrong-headed and twisted in her point of view because she cares for a man who adores another woman. Love's too big for her, that's all."

"Do you mean that she loves Uncle Jock? Whom does he 'adore'?"

"His wife, of course. Can't you see?"

"I can't. If you are right, I'm afraid I don't appreciate his subtle method of showing it. When I'm adored, I'll expect it to be with the soul of a poet and the passion of a Romeo," Eve said flippantly.

Kilburn caught her in his arms and silenced her startled protest against his shoulder.

"This is rather a public place to begin to fill that order, but—"

It was a lingering kiss, it woke something in her body and soul.

"Eve," he whispered, "Eve."

The door to the apartment was flung open. Jock Holden stared at them.

"Only you! I thought I heard something. I thought it might be—" his voice broke.

They followed him into the living room. Had no one moved since she had left to go to Vera Skinner's apartment, Eve wondered. Dorinda Holden still sat on the edge of the big chair, her nervous fingers crinkling the violet velvet of her gown. The Colonel still stood behind her. He looked tired and for the first time he looked old. Jock Holden paced the floor. Seth Ramsdell, watch in hand, sat at the telephone table.

"They told us to call again in five minutes. Almost time, Mr. Senator."

No one spoke after that. Seated on the divan, Eve looked at Jeff Kilburn. She bit her lips to steady them. She thought of the hours and days they had spent together in happy comradeship, and she thought of the instant it had taken in the hall to tear a veil from her heart, to show her that she cared more for him than for anyone else in the world. She loved him as a girl loves the man she marries. Her heart stopped. But he loved Moya. Hadn't he said that after June—

Dorinda Holden sprang to her feet. Her voice was shaken as she demanded;

"Are we wood and stone that we sit here waiting, waiting, waiting while Court may be—" She shivered. "I'm going out on the street to look for him. I won't—"

Her voice broke on a high note.

"What was that sound?" she demanded hoarsely.

Eve whispered;

"Did you hear that thump on the service door, Jeff? Did you hear it? José threw the man who stabbed him down the back stairs! Be careful! He may be after you!"

Kilburn dashed out of the room. His sharp exclamation was followed by the appearance of a figure in the doorway, a figure trailing a green hanging, with a dagger in one hand.

"Good-evening, boys and girls of the radio—"

"Court! Court!"

With a broken cry Dorinda Holden dropped to her knees beside the boy. She caught him close, pressed her face against his breast. Her husband made queer noises in his throat. The Colonel rested his head on his arm on the mantel. Eve sat down suddenly on the divan. Jeff Kilburn snapped at Ramsdell whose eyes were popping.

"Call off the police, Seth! Quick!"

Ramsdell dialed noisily. Court smoothed his mother's hair.

"Mom! Mom! What's the matter? Did you think I'd croaked?"

"Court! Court!" Dorinda Holden shuddered.

Her husband laid his hand tenderly on her shoulder and drew her to her feet. He kept one arm about her as he said, with an attempt at jocularity more moving than tears;

"Well, son, with that black eye and your shirt torn open you look as if you'd been through the war. Tell us what happened."

"Gee, Pop, I don't know what happened after—"

"After Miss Skinner left you to phone the school."

"How did you know that?"

"She told me."

"That's a break. Do you mind if I sit down? I'm sunk."

He dropped to a chair Kilburn pushed behind him. He flung off the green damask hanging which had clung to his shoulders and dropped the dagger to the floor.

"I guess if it hadn't been for that curtain your angel child would have had his neck broken, Mom. I wish you'd all sit down, it gives me the hebe jeebes when you stand there staring at me." There was a hint of tears in his boyish voice.

Dorinda Holden returned to the chair. Her husband leaned on the back of it. Ramsdell still occupied the stool by the telephone, the Colonel dropped to the divan beside Eve and nervously polished his monocle with a sheer handkerchief. Kilburn left the room. Court grinned. The fast darkening skin about one of his blue eyes gave its twinkle a demoniac touch.

"All set to hear the story of my young life? Gee, Jeff, that looks good," he approved as Kilburn entered with a tray. "I'm ready to eat raw dog. Haven't seen any food except the snack I snitched from your icebox, since lunch at school."

Eve hurriedly placed a small table beside the boy's chair for the tray containing a glass of milk and a wedge of chocolate layer cake.

"That's all I could find to fill a rush order, Court," Kilburn explained. "If José were here—"

"Say listen, Jeff. Where is José? I thought when I came here I'd find him, instead of that I ran into a wild man—rather he ran into me."

"Court!"

Jock Holden touched his wife's shoulder.

"Let the boy eat first, 'Rinda. Then we'll hear all about it." His shaky hand as he opened his cigarette case belied the lightness of his voice. "While we watch the animal feed, Seth, get the school."

Morning light stole in through the uncurtained window. The clock rhythmically ticked away the seconds. The fire crumbled. Ramsdell phoned in a low voice. He said finally;

"We don't know the whole story yet. I'll tell him, sir. Good-bye."

With a sigh of repletion, Court set down the empty glass.

"I guess that little snack will keep me going for a time."

"Now son," his father prompted. "Tell us what happened after you and Miss Skinner parted. We know what came before."

"Do you, Pop? I'm glad of that. After I left Skinny I tried to think how I could explain without getting her in wrong. She's been grand to me, you know."

"We know. Go on, Court. Your mother has been terribly anxious."

"You say you know how I came to leave school? Well, after we'd passed the bounds and Skinny said she was taking me on a party, I looked at her sharp. It was dark by that time but I thought she looked sort of funny, her eyes glittered like green glass, her hair was stringy, and she—she seemed kind of wild."

"Were you frightened, dear?"

"Frightened of Skinny, Mom? No, I wasn't frightened, but as the car picked up speed—she drove awful fast—I kept thinking and the more I thought the more cockeyed the thing seemed. I knew she'd lost her job with Pop and I thought perhaps it had gone to her head. Every day in the papers you read of someone doing something queer."

"Why didn't you make her stop and let you phone, Court?"

"I thought of that, Pop, and then she seemed so kind of wild that I didn't know what she might do if I left her. You know, Skinny's been great to me, I couldn't leave her alone so far away from anyone who knew her, could I?"

Jock Holden cleared his throat.

"I suppose you couldn't, son. Go on."

"That's just what we did. Went on and on. I didn't realize the school was so far from Washington when we flew there. When I began to recognize places and knew she would be safe, I planned. I hadn't the slightest intention of being taken wherever she intended to take me. I decided to hitch-hike to Jeff's."

"Why not home?"

Court looked straight at his father.

"Well, you see, Pop, it was a pretty stiff yarn I had to tell and I thought you might not believe me. Jeff's kind of young, he makes a fella feel that he understands. Get me?"

Dorinda Holden laid her fingers tenderly on the hand on her shoulder. Her husband's face crimsoned. He said gruffly;

"I get you. Go on!"

"Finally I persuaded Skinny to phone the school. The minute the door closed behind her, I jumped from the car. Not until I had sprinted down the road toward the city—I knew by the pink haze in the sky where that was—did I remember that I hadn't a nickel in my pocket. I fished through them to make sure. Nothing but my locker key, a knife and that skeleton key I had such a whale of a lot of fun with before I went away. Couldn't trade that stuff for a ride. Oh boy, oh boy, now I'll hitch-hike, I thought, I've always been crazy to try it. The first car that came along stopped. A tough looking guy was at the wheel. Now don't be frightened Mom, I didn't get in."

"I'm sorry I made a sound, Court, but, for a second I saw you—"

"I'll bet you did, a whole movie of me laid out flat. I just slid into the bushes and the man went on. Next a honey of a limousine came along, with a big black chauffeur. This is where I get in, I said, and held up my hand just the way it's done on the screen. The darky pulled up and I asked for a ride. It might have been old Reub talking, when he said sort of roughlike and yet respectful;

" 'What's a young gentlemans like you doing out this time of night?'

"I didn't answer, I just climbed in. I told him a yarn about being kidnaped that made his teeth click like telegraph keys. He left me in front of this house after I'd told him that if he let on he'd seen me the big bad kidnapers might get me. Gee, you should have seen his eyes roll."

"And then—" Kilburn prompted.

"Then, Jeff, I got as far as the door of this apartment, the entrance door downstairs had been left on the latch. I rang the bell and rang and rang. No answer. I began to get a little edgy. Suppose you and José were away? I felt in my pockets. The skeleton key! Was I pleased when I saw that? I'm telling you."

"The same key with which you almost drove Annie out of her mind?" Eve asked to give the excited boy a chance to get his breath.

"The same. It worked. The apartment seemed spooky when the door closed behind me. I called 'Hey there! It's me! Court!' No answer. I snapped on the light in the hall. Tiptoed to the living room. Lighted that. And then I heard someone move in the kitchenette. You won't believe it, but I felt my hair rise the way Snack's does when he hears something he doesn't understand, the sound was so—so sort of underground. I didn't move. A door closed softly.

"I listened. Then I began to think what a chump I was to go haywire over a sound. Of course, José had closed that door. He'd probably slipped out the back way and would come bouncing in the front to give me a scare. He's a sort of kid sometimes, isn't he Jeff?"

"I'll say he is. What happened? Did he come back?"

"Not then. I looked in your room to make sure you hadn't gone to bed, then I beat it for the icebox. I was darn near starved. I polished off a cold chicken and had a hunk of cake. Then I prowled back to the living room. I'd just taken down the fan dagger and was running my finger along the blade, when I heard the apartment front door open. Thinks I to myself,

" 'I was right. José beat it down the back stairs and up the front. He thinks he'll take a rise out of me. Nothing doing! Here's where I give that snooty bull-fighter the scare of his life.' He's opened up high and wide and handsome to me, with yarns of the number of bulls he's thrown, sometimes when I've been waiting for you, Jeff. I'll bet he never stepped into an arena."

"I've had doubts myself, Court. Go on, what next?"

"I slipped behind the long curtain at the window. I was gurgling so over my little joke that I thought that *hombre* sure would hear me. I heard him sort of grunt, then came the storm, as they say in the movies. And was it a storm! Somebody grabbed me! Twisted the hanging round me! I heard it rip from the pole. I started to yell. Couldn't make a sound. I kicked. I tried to put over that clinch you taught me, Jeff. Couldn't get a grip. Then I knew that it wasn't José who had me, that it was a big, bad, bandit. I managed to free one hand and jabbed with the dagger. The man grunted in Spanish. I was picked up. Carried. Pitched down some stairs."

"Court! Court!"

"Sit down, 'Rinda. You can see the boy wasn't hurt. Go on, son."

"I don't know how long I huddled where I fell. I moved my legs and arms and neck. Nothing was busted. That was all right. I decided to stay where I was. I wasn't afraid to go back, but, well, I was comfortable and warm and darn sleepy." He yawned prodigiously.

"What next?" Dorinda Holden asked anxiously.

"That's all. There isn't any more. When I woke up, I decided to try the back door—and here I am. Gee, but I'm tired."

"Come on, son. We'll take a taxi and go home."

Dorinda Holden rose.

"No, Jock. I'll take Court back to school. He can sleep on the way. You'd rather go, wouldn't you, dear?"

The boy caught her in a mighty hug.

"Would I? I'm telling you I would. You do understand a fella, Mom."

Eve never had seen such beauty of expression on a human face as that on Dorinda Holden's as she said;

"Thank you, Court. Will you phone our garage, Seth, and while we are waiting for the car, if you don't mind Jeff, I'll see if I can find something more for Court to eat."

"Swell, Mom! I'd like one more shot at that cake."

The boy and his mother left the room together. Jock Holden brushed a hand across his eyes.

"So, 'Rinda will take the boy back. She's a grand sport."

"Who was the person whom Court heard in the kitchen?" Eve demanded. "It wasn't José. He found the back door on the latch and stole round to the front. It was after that that he mixed up with Court. Alvarez must have sent a man here to get—"

She shivered.

Jock Holden put his arm about her shoulders.

"Whatever he came for, honey, he gumshoed off the premises before he did any harm. We'll do a little sleuthing tomorrow and find out the truth. Meanwhile, I'll go with 'Rinda and the boy—"

"But you can't go! You can't, Uncle Jock. Seth has been trying to find you all night to tell you what I overheard. Tell him, Seth."

Ramsdell told him. Holden looked at Kilburn.

"What do you make of this, Jeff? Has Skinner—?"

"She swore that no one saw the book she stole. I have it in my pocket. The notes about the revolution were not in it. I have carried those with me."

"Then Eve misunderstood what was said, Seth. You and she have been dreaming."

"She heard them all right, Mr. Senator. As to dreaming—I'm the one who should be pinched to make sure I'm awake. Eve's promised to marry me."

"What?" roared Jock Holden.

"Is that true?" demanded Kilburn. The cold scorn of his voice, the blaze in his eyes terrified Eve. Her voice stuck in her throat. She nodded, whispered through stiff lips;

"Yes."

xxiv

FROM the window of her office Eve looked across the river. She could see the Stars and Stripes floating above the portico of the House of Arlington. The sunset gun from Fort Myers echoed from shore to shore and the blur of color slid slowly earthward.

The Senator had sent word for her to wait until he could talk with her. What had he to say? Perhaps he didn't want her any longer. Perhaps he didn't trust a girl who told a man she would marry him, when already she was married. Had only a week passed since that early morning when Jeff had demanded if Seth's exultant announcement were true?

She hadn't seen him since, for that matter she hadn't seen Seth either. He had been sent to the Senator's home city to confer with some of his constituents. When she saw him, she would tell him the truth. The door opened.

"Seth! When did you get back?"

"About an hour ago. Sorry to see me, aren't you? Telling

me at the Pan American ball that you would marry me was just stringing me along, wasn't it? Coquetry. What every woman knows."

Eve looked away from his hungry, baffled eyes.

"It wasn't coquetry, Seth. At that moment I—"

"You're telling me! I know. At that moment you were furious with Jeff Kilburn. I knew it, but when you said you would marry me, like a poor chump I forgot it. Then when I bubbled over in his living room and proclaimed the glad tidings, I saw your eyes and knew that you'd just taken me for a ride."

"I hadn't, Seth! Really, I hadn't. I like you enormously and I thought for a minute that that might be love."

"Sure that it wasn't?"

"Sorry, but I'm sure, Seth. I—I wish I could care."

"Thank you, but you may consume your own sympathy. I don't want it. I'll ask the Senator to give me a job in his home town. I have a brother who would give his ears for a chance in this office. He can take my place, then I'll be out of your way."

"No Seth, no. You were made for Washington. I'm the one to go."

"You'll stay right where you are."

"Not unless you keep on here."

"All right. I'll stay. I can take it. I—"

Eve answered the buzz on her desk.

"Yes, Mr. Senator."

She picked up her note-book.

"Uncle Jock wants me. He wants you too. We're friends, aren't we, Seth?"

Ramsdell's grip crushed her fingers.

"Sure, we're friends. If ever you need me—" his laugh was bitter— "The old formula."

"But it still clicks. It's a grand thing to remember, Seth."

Why hadn't she told him that she was married? Eve asked herself. How could she until she was sure that Jeff would not object?

As she and Ramsdell entered Senator Holden's private office, he shot a keen glance at them before he looked up at suave, silky Alvarez who stood near his desk. He had a red carnation in the lapel of his blue serge coat. He had murder in his black and yellow eyes. He protested;

"Why do you call señorita Travis into this conference, Senator Holden? You don't need her when Ramsdell is here, do you? Charming as she is, it is no place for her. I have much to say that will be unpleasant for her to hear."

"Hear! She isn't supposed to hear. She's my secretary.

Good secretaries don't hear their employers' business. They just take it down. I judge you've been unfortunate in some you've known. Seth, have you the papers I want? Okay! Ready Eve. Now, Alvarez, go on with your complaint. If I get the gist of your monologue, you are accusing me of having cheated you."

"I know you cheated me, Senator. You offered fifty thousand for my gold mine. You paid five thousand dollars for the option. I hear that already you have sold it for millions."

"Keep your shirt on, Alvarez. Only two millions. You seem to have forgotten that you sat on my doorstep, figuratively speaking, until I took the option on that mine. I wanted you to wait until I had sent my expert to examine it, but you couldn't wait. And now you want to take the profit out of gold. There are others. You had nothing but a few samples of ore and a trumped-up deed to show that you owned the stuff. I took a chance."

"You call taking a chance offering fifty thousand dollars for what you can sell for two millions?"

"Quite a chance when one considers that you had no right to sell it." Holden touched a button on his desk.

"No right! What do you mean! I inherit the mine—if the son of my father's partner is not alive. He is dead. I—"

His eyes flamed, went cold, as he looked at the two men who entered the room. Eve's heart stood still. Jeff and José—José in the last word in afternoon clothes. They glittered with newness. Would Jeff look at her? Evidently not. She bent her head above her note-book. Holden prodded;

"Sure you inherited the mine, Alvarez?"

Alvarez swallowed. Wet his lips. Glared at José.

"He is a dead man come to life. I was sure José Mendoza was dead."

"Your mistake. The man you sent to Kilburn's apartment the night of the Pan American ball didn't kidnap him—as you had ordered—but, we got the man and he's come clean. He has told why he was sent there, what he was to do and how, hidden in the kitchenette, he heard someone come into the next room, lost his nerve and beat it down the service stairs."

The face of Alvarez turned the color of old wax. José took a menacing step toward him and muttered something in Spanish.

"Keep your hands off him and talk English, José," Holden commanded. "Jeff, as Alvarez seems to have forgotten the terms of the will of José's father, you might refresh his memory."

"I have the terms here, Senator." Kilburn drew a note-book from his pocket. "Alvarez knows that his father sold out his entire interest to José's father, that in his will, Don Mendoza left the mine to Alvarez should his own son die without heirs. José did not die as you've known for months, Alvarez. There is a certain dancer in your home town who has kept you informed of his whereabouts. José was fool enough to write to her." There was a hint of amusement underlying the clipped assurance of Kilburn's speech.

The eyes of Alvarez narrowed.

"I could kill you for that, señor Kilburn. I can endure losing the mine—but you, you have blocked me at every turn. You, it is who go to South America—you stay there till you find the will of Don José Manuel Mendoza. You dig up a dead man. On the ship home you make passionate love to Lady—"

"Keep her name out of this, you—"

"Stop, Jeff! I'll take care of this. How about that five thousand you obtained from me under false pretenses, Alvarez?" Holden demanded.

Eve didn't hear the South American's reply. Her eyes were on Jeff's white face. He must love Moya if the mention of her name made him look like that. He had made passionate love to her on the voyage home, had he? After that, why should he treat her like a pariah because she had told Seth Ramsdell she would marry him—sometime? What had he meant when in the hall outside his apartment he had kissed her? The memory sent her blood racing through her veins, set every nerve alive. She felt again his lips warm and tender on hers. She loved him, she knew that now. It made no difference if he did love another woman. Aunt Dorinda had warned,

"Some day, Eve, you'll find that the greatest proof of the reality of love is its invincibility against the battering of reason."

She had found it out. She—

"Getting this, Eve?" Jock Holden snapped.

She nodded and bent her head over her note-book. Of course he had seen her looking at Jeff with her heart in her eyes. Equally of course, he knew why. He knew everything. She must have lost Alvarez' answer to the last question, for he sneered;

"Doubtless you paid this present Don José Manuel Mendoza the magnificent sum of five thousand dollars for his mine, Senator Holden? Perhaps he knows what you sold it for?"

Not the words, but his sombre insolence stopped Eve's breath. The letter opener which Holden was bending back and forth between his strong fingers snapped. He dropped the pieces to the desk.

"Yes. He knows. You'd say that I had paid you five thousand dollars wouldn't you, José?"

"Sí, sí, señor. You have been magnificent. I am reech. Reech." José's manner was gay, typically Latin.

Holden waved a deprecatory hand;

"You must make allowance for José's enthusiasm, Alvarez. After he's lived a while in a country which thinks and talks in billions, a mere million won't seem much to him."

"A million dollars for him? He—" Fury cut off Alvarez' voice.

"Sure, José accepted my offer to go fifty fifty with him before Kilburn went to investigate the mine. I told you when I bought what you so picturesquely called 'Your mine' that I was buying a pig in a poke, didn't I? Well, it proved to be a right fat pig. I turned over the property yesterday at your Embassy. Your country wishes to conserve its natural resources and bought the mine as an object lesson, as a stimulus to native-worked companies. The national army will occupy the gold zone."

Holden rose.

"There's one thing more, Señor Eduardo Enrique Alverez. I understand that a whisper is going through the cloakrooms that I'm in the pay of one of the South American Republics, that Jefferson Kilburn at my instigation and expense set the financial match to that toy revolution down in your country. Now, I may buy a pig in a poke, but I find out all about the poke. You'd better spike that rumor and spike it quick."

"And if I don't, Senator?" Alvarez defied insolently.

Holden brought his big fist down on the desk.

"If you don't—well, first, there's a bunch of press boys waiting in the outer office for an interview. This stuff will be meat to them. Next, the pages Miss Skinner didn't get of that little note-book of Kilburn's will be turned over to your Embassy. They are chock full of dynamite, loaded with proof that you backed that little scrimmage at home. In case that isn't enough of an incentive for you to stop the rumor you've started, I'll go to your boss with a bill of sale of a mine you didn't own—that you knew you didn't own—signed by you."

Alvarez' eyes burned like coals in his waxy face. He bowed from his waist.

"The rumor will be spiked. *Servidor de v. cabellero,*" he acknowledged suavely and backed out of the room.

Jock Holden glared at the closed door.

"What in thunder did he mean by that?"

"That he was your servant, señor Holden," José explained.

"Huh! Here's your cheque, José. I suppose you'll go home, buy back the ancestral acres, marry a dark-eyed señorita and raise a big family."

José looked from the slip of pink paper in his hand to Eve, and then at Jock Holden.

"No, señor. You have, as they say in this country, got me wrong. I stay here and spend my money. I marry here. Señor Holden, I ask your consent to pay my addresses to your niece, señorita Travis."

"José!" Eve whispered.

"José!" Kilburn thundered.

Jock Holden shrugged.

"In this country we let the girl answer for herself. How about it, Eve?"

"No! No! I told you José the night I tried to help you escape from Alvarez' assassin—who wasn't an assassin at all —that—"

"Did José annoy you that night?" Kilburn's face frightened Eve.

"He did not, Jeff. The excitement had gone to his head, that's all. I don't intend to marry anyone. I don't like men. I don't trust them. One moment they pretend to love you and the next they're rushing someone else. I wouldn't marry an angel from heaven if he were to lay his halo at my feet."

Red stained her cheeks as her eyes met Kilburn's dangerously cool. She said unsteadily;

"I'm sorry, Mr. Senator, to have inflicted you with an emotional jamboree. It won't happen again, I promise."

"Hold on, Eve, don't go. I want you to take a letter. Seth, see that Señor José Manuel Mendoza gets through the outer office without being mobbed." Holden held out his hand to José. "Good-bye and good luck. Watch your step, spending that money. Even a million has its limit."

"*Sí, señor.*" José's eyes registered despair as he turned to Eve. "Señorita, I go with a broken heart." He bowed in the general direction of the two men," Señores, I'll be seeing you."

Ramsdell opened the door. Beside him José left the room with shoulders back and jaunty step. Holden laughed.

"Those press boys outside are waiting for him. Promised 'em a break if they'd let up on me for twenty-four hours. Can't you see the headlines, SPANISH BUTLER COMES INTO A FORTUNE? Sit down, Eve. Stop staring out of that window, Jeff and listen. I've made reservations for you on a ship sailing day after tomorrow—"

"Sailing! Where?"

Eve could cheerfully have bitten out her tongue for assisting at the shocked exclamation. Kilburn went back to the window. Holden selected a cigar from the lacquered box on the desk. He regarded her above the flame of the lighter.

"He's sailing for South America. When I sold the gold mine I agreed to have my consulting expert go back and give the new owners all the dope he had dug up about it—first asking the aforementioned expert if he were willing. He is and he's going at once. Got to move fast when dealing with one of those countries, where the government is here today and gone tomorrow, if you get what I mean. Now take this letter."

Eve grasped her pencil. She must keep her mind on her work, she must. How could she when Jeff was going? Was he so disgusted with her for encouraging Seth Ramsdell that he wanted to get as far away as possible? Let him go. While he was gone she would get that silly marriage annulled. How could she without money? Money! Money! Everlastingly the question of money. The whole country was mad about it. She had spent part of her shrunken principal moving her furniture. Her balance at the bank—Bank! That was a thought! Why not use the money Barrett had deposited to her account, the cheque book he had sent her? She would use it for the annulment. It would be like giving it back to Jeff, wouldn't it, if she gave him his freedom?

"That's about all."

Jock Holden's voice snapped her out of her reflection. Horrified at her inattention, she looked at her note-book. The page was covered with short-hand hieroglyphics. Had she written her thoughts or what the Senator had dictated?

"When do you plan to leave Washington, Jeff?"

"At midnight, Senator. I can make a quick get away. I've been paying farewell calls and arranging to close the apartment during this last week."

"Say listen, Jeff. You and Eve ought—"

Kilburn's eyes flagged him.

"Hands off my life, Senator."

Jeff had known for a week that he was going and had not come near her in all that time. Eve bit her lips to steady them. How could he do that to her when they had been such friends? Was Moya back of his indifference? Was she influencing him?

"Send final instructions to the ship, Senator. I've planned to stop at Brick Ends before I sail. Good luck to you, Kiddo. I shan't be away long and when I return we'll straighten out things for you—and Seth. He's a great boy. In the words of the Colonel, 'There is a saying about Hawaii; "To have to leave it is to die a little bit."' That's the way I feel about leaving you, Eve."

Eve's eyes lingered on the door he closed behind him. She asked unsteadily;

"Did Jeff mean that, Uncle Jock?"

"You're asking me. You know him better than I do."

"But he hasn't been near me for a week. Not since—"

"Not since you admitted that you had told Seth Ramsdell that you would marry him. You didn't expect him to come after that, did you?"

"But, I'm not going to marry Seth, Uncle Jock."

"Have you told Jeff?"

"No. I haven't had a chance, besides, how could I? It would be almost like asking him again to marry me, wouldn't it?"

Holden swung round in his chair and scowled at Eve.

"Well, suppose you did. You owe it to him, don't you? Don't be afraid to tell him. Don't be afraid of anything. You'll find it's a great world to the valiant. Look here, honey, you've known Jeff Kilburn all your life, haven't you? He's as square and honorable as they make 'em, isn't he? Do you honestly believe that any argument would have induced him to marry you, if you hadn't been the dearest thing in the world to him?"

"He's never told me that he loves me."

Eve watched lights blossom on the bridge across the Potomac, followed the red glow of a plane shooting across a sky fusing from blue to purple, before she confided;

"I thought Jeff loved Moya, I really did, Uncle Jock. That is why I wouldn't go with him to South America last September."

"And you have been playing round ever since as if you were free. That isn't honest."

"Do you think I don't know that? That it hasn't been in my mind almost every minute? You can't blame me any more than I blame myself, Uncle Jock. I have hurt myself more than I have hurt anyone else. Selfishness, thinking only of oneself, does that, doesn't it? It eats and eats till a person's character is full of holes. Mine must look like a sieve."

Holden laughed.

"I guess there are still parts of yours which are whole, honey. You say you haven't told Jeff that you don't love Seth? He believes that you do. Men in love aren't mind-readers. They don't think much, they just feel. Sorry I can't help. You heard Jeff order me to keep my hands off his life. I'm a brave man but I'm a little afraid of him—although

I did make the ship reservation—it's one of those de luxe cruise ships—for Mr. and Mrs. Jefferson Kilburn."

"Uncle Jock! Did you really? About Mr. and—Mrs. Kilburn, I mean?"

"I did. I see you've got the idea. Your eyes are shining like stars. Come home with me now and talk with your Aunt Dorinda. Day after tomorrow isn't far off."

"You dear! Can you spare this not too efficient secretary?"

"I might, on a pinch. Get your hat and come along."

Eve held him by the lapel of one coat pocket as she asked anxiously;

"But, you are so busy. You need someone in my place. Why will you do, Uncle Jock?"

"Do?"

Senator Holden rammed the broad-brimmed black Stetson down on his head and glared at her:

"What will I do? Shoot the first person who dares recommend a woman secretary."

XXV

AT the ship's rail Jefferson Kilburn watched the crowd on the pier shouting, crying, waving handkerchiefs. Flowerhawkers, messenger boys, friends of passengers thronged the gangplanks. Lights were blossoming in distant buildings, red and green and blue neon signs were flaring and fading against the jagged skyline. A red sun rested for an instant on the tip of a spire like a mammoth golf ball on a gigantic tee, then sank out of sight. Distant taxis honked. A plane thrummed overhead with lights winking.

Why was he standing here as if he were expecting someone? he demanded of himself. He pulled the brim of his soft cap lower over one eye, thrust his hands deep in the pockets of his topcoat and crossed the deck to the harbor side of the ship.

Arms on the rail he thought of Eve. Why had he been so stunned when she admitted that she had told Seth Ramsdell she would marry him? Hadn't he always suspected that she cared more than she realized for the boy? Probably at this minute she was having tea with him somewhere. Well, if she loved him she would be safe with him. He could leave her more easily knowing that Alvarez had been sent back to his own country. He might have annoyed her. Vera Skinner was out of the picture too. She had left the city. Her apartment in the converted brown stone house was for rent.

She was out of Jock Holden's life. The estrangement between him and his wife ended the night their son was missing. A great boy, Court. He was making good at school with his heart still set on West Point. He would get there. The army needed the sort of man he would be. Colonel Carter Courtleigh was in danger of bursting with pride over his namesake.

"Visitors ashore!" a voice shouted.

The ship's whistle blew a warning. The deafening sound brought Kilburn's numb heart tinglingly, achingly alive. Why was he leaving Eve? What if he had been intolerably hurt because she had told Seth Ramsdell she would marry him? She was his, wasn't she? Arrogantly he had waited for her to come to him, now he wanted only to get to her, to hold her close, to tell her he loved her, always had loved her, always would, that never while life lasted would there be for them another parting. His pride had trapped him.

Anger at himself made his brain light, his face burn. He wouldn't stay trapped. He would return to Washington and camp on her trail until he had made her love him, made her want to be his wife. The gold mine could go to thunder. He was the world's Number 1 quitter to have left her. It wasn't too late. It didn't matter if his luggage was aboard. He would go back to Eve.

He dashed across the deck. The ship bellowed a final warning. Chains clanked. A hand grabbed him. A sailor with eyes as a-slant as his cap shouted;

"Can't make it, Mister! If you've forgotten something radio for it."

Furious with himself because of the attention he had attracted, Kilburn returned to the harbor side of the deck. He lighted his pipe with fingers that shook and folded his arms on the rail. He felt the faint vibration of the ship as the turbines swung into action. Ahead where sea and sky met lay a silver mist faintly tinged with pink. Vessels swung with the tide, their top-masts burning like flames in the afterglow which set afire the brass rail of a gig bouncing beside an airplane carrier swaying in the dark current of mid-channel. White capped sailors were piling into it for shore leave. In the west, crimson rays shot suddenly to the zenith as if the sun had burst to pieces when it dropped. Sea-gulls soared and dove with ceaseless cries. Wind clouds with ruffled rose and violet edges piled up in the east. A broken moon like the half of a newly minted silver dollar, hung above them. A single brilliant star pricked through the sky. From somewhere came the music of an orchestra and a man's voice singing. A foolish little song full of lilt and laughter, it carried enchantment in its train as if drifted out to sea.

The broad deck was deserted. Passengers were settling their belongings in their cabins for the long voyage. A long voyage. Why hadn't he gone by plane? Why had he allowed Jock Holden to make arrangements for him? That answer was easy. He had been too sick at heart about Eve to care how he went. It would be a perfect night. If only Eve were with him. He'd better sign off on that line of thought.

A uniformed boy touched his shoulder.

"Mr. Kilburn? Radio for you, sir."

His throat tightened. Was it a message from Eve? He waited until the boy had vanished into a companionway before he opened it. He frowned down upon the words:

"Ever see a movie The Man Who Played God?

"J. H."

Kilburn reread the message and thrust it into his pocket. Jock Holden had a queer sense of humor if he thought that was funny.

"This is station X X Y Z." The resonant voice came from the Lounge. "Our Washington correspondent says, 'Senator Jock Holden, the fair-haired boy of Congress, today announced—' "

The salute of a near-by vessel drowned the voice. By the time the ship's answer had thinned into an echo, an advertisement was being broadcast.

What was Jock Holden announcing? Kilburn wondered. Not Eve's engagement to Ramsdell? Of course he wouldn't until she was—

"I couldn't let you go alone, Jeff. I—I was afraid that a man-eating widow—"

He stared unbelievingly at the girl beside him. Was she a vision conjured by his longing? No, a vision wouldn't speak in a voice half laughter, half tears, wouldn't materialize in a green wool suit. He whispered incredulously;

"Eve! Eve!"

"Are you sorry I'm here, Jeff? You're white as a sheet. Have I crashed in on your life a second time and spoiled it?"

The hurt-little-girl look in her eyes brought a blinding mist to his. His pounding heart quieted. Eve had come to him. He'd better watch his step. He laughed.

"You couldn't spoil my life, Kiddo, by coming to me. Don't back away as if you were afraid of me. Come here."

He caught her hand and drew her toward him. "I like that green beret, you're wearing." He tucked a dark curl behind her ear. "How did you get here?"

She disengaged her hand and rested her arms on the rail. "Uncle Jock's plane to Curtiss field yesterday morning; shopping madly for cruise clothes—I have some of the most adorable evening frocks, simple, yet swank, if you get what I mean—and—and here I am."

"I meant how did you get on the ship?"

"Walked. You didn't expect me to come in a wheel chair, did you?"

"I didn't expect you at all."

"Didn't Uncle Jock radio that—that he was announcing our—our mar—marriage? He promised—"

"He radioed. I'll take that message up with him later. Did you consent to the announcement?"

She nodded with her eyes on a bobbing gig full of white capped sailors.

"Look at me. Why?"

"Dictator! Going to make me tell all, aren't you? If you must know it was because I was fed up with deceit. I wanted to be free. Free! That's a joke. I haven't felt free for an instant since I left you in Uncle Scrip's living room. I tried to ease my smarting conscience by thinking you loved Moya."

"You knew I didn't. Alvarez accused me of making passionate—that was the word he used, wasn't it—love to her. I didn't. Believe me, darling?"

"You admitted that she was a temptation."

"That was some of my cockeyed diplomacy. Tried to make you jealous. We'll take that up later, too. Did the Senator know you were coming—to me?"

"Know it? Haven't you sensed the size and luxury of the royal suite he engaged for—for you? He has phoned me every few hours since I left Washington to tell me what to do."

"Did you do it?"

"I did not. I just said, 'Uhuh,' and did what I liked. I have been absolutely on my own. When you see the boxes in your cabin and the dent I've made in my bank balance, you'll think so, Jeff. I've scattered Eve—Eve Kilburn cheques all over New York."

"Eve Kilburn." He cleared his voice. "Nice name. Don't be so breathless, darling."

"I can't help it, Jeff. My heart is pounding so it tightens my throat. All the way to the ship I kept thinking suppose, suppose he really doesn't want me? Your face was so strange when you saw me that I thought, I thought—"

He caught her close. Bent her head back.

"Can't have you thinking that," he said huskily and kissed her lips, her throat, her eyes.

"Here comes the bride! Here comes the bride!" chorused men's voices to the accompaniment of the put-put of a motor.

Eve twisted free. Her cheeks were scarlet as she looked

over the rail. The gig from the airplane carrier was passing in a shower of spray. Blue coated sailors were standing, laughing, and swinging white caps as they repeated lustily;

"Here comes the bride! Here comes the bride!"

"They saw us, Jeff! They sang that to us," she whispered. "Even the sky is blushing furiously, it's crimson with embarrassment. I don't wonder."

Kilburn laughed and waved his soft cap.

"Happy landings!" he shouted to the men who already were fading into the dusk which was dropping like a violet-grey curtain between them and the glittering back-drop with its jagged skyline.

"Good luck!"

The words drifted back across the water.

Eve's eyes shone like stars.

"That was a beautiful wedding send-off, Jeff. Better than rice and confetti, wasn't it?"

"It was. And speaking of weddings, let's go to the royal suite and unpack that trousseau of yours. Hope you brought a white evening gown. I adore you in white. But first, hold out your left hand."

He drew a diamond circlet from his waistcoat pocket and slipped it on her finger. He pressed his lips to it.

"Always carried it with me in case I had a chance to use it. Belongs there, doesn't it?"

She nodded with her eyes on the ring.

"Like it?"

"Love it."

"Know what it means? That for better for worse, for richer for poorer, in sickness and in health, you go wherever I go."

"Try and stop me, Mister Kilburn," she challenged with unsteady gaiety. She added wistfully;

"You've never told me that you love me, Jeff."

He flung an arm around her shoulders and laughed.

"Haven't I?" He drew her close. "You're going to hear a lot about that on this trip, Mrs. Kilburn."